Wined & Vined

Gina Hejtmanek

Trigger Warning

P lease be advised that while this book is mostly light-hearted fun, it does still talk about heavy subject matter. Your mental health is of utmost importance to me, so if any of these are difficult for you, carry on at your own risk or put it down.

Triggers include, but are not limited to, the following:

Poly Relationships

BDSM

Blood

Torture

Abduction

Parental Abandonment

Death of a Loved One

Abuse

Political Overreach

Playlist

Cross My Heart I Hope U Die- Meg Smith

The Ballad of Witches' Road (Sacred Chant Version)-
Kathryn Hahn, Sasheer Zamata, Ali Ahn, Patti LuPone,
Debra Jo Rupp, Agatha All Along Cast

Blessed Be- Spiritbox

River of Fire- In This Moment

All The Things She SAid- t.A.T.u

No Roots- Alice Merton

SANCTIFY ME- In This Moment

Pussy Is God- King Princess

LUNCH- Billie Eilish

God is a woman- Ariana Grande

The Man- Taylor Swift

Dangerous- Sleep Token

Dance in the Dark- Au/Ra

i'm yours- Isabel LaRosa

Always Been You- Jessie Murph

Pretty Little Poison- Warren Zeiders

Prologue

I have been here, waiting, for centuries. Rooted to this house, this land– destined to watch and want. I never got the chance to know love, to be touched the way some of the inhabitants of this house have been.

Although I've seen my share of affairs and abuse, I've also seen an abundance of love and adoration; hidden touches and stolen moments.

They've all made me crave to be loved more than the one before. Especially the last inhabitants. They made all the years of loneliness worth it, just to watch them dance in the living room and see the light shining in their eyes as they looked at each other.

Their love was one that would have survived lifetimes... if only it had been given enough time to bloom. A witch and a hunter, here to hide away from their reality. He adored her and she was just as infatuated. Until one day, when they were supposed to meet,he showed up before her, looking about in a feverish state, as if he, himself, was being hunted. Without taking a step inside, he placed a note on the stoop, and took off in his car so fast, the gravel bit into me as I watched him go.

I wish I could have read the letter before the woman came. I would have destroyed it before it could do the same to her. But I was limited in what I could do. So, I stayed in my place and waited for her to come.

Her face was radiant as she exited her vehicle, a skip was evident in her step as she approached the house. In her love fueled excitement, she did not notice the tire marks in the gravel, or the tiny pebbles laying in the grass near the house. Nor did she notice the letter on the stoop.

Only when her heeled shoe slipped on the paper as she took her first step inside did she register its existence. She looked down and her brows crinkled as she bent down and retrieved it. Recognizing the handwriting on the outside, she tore it open, ravenous to read what she was certain would be a letter declaring his undying love for her.

Instead, as her eyes read every word, her legs refused to hold her up and she fell hard to the cement. The howl that left her body when she was finished reading would have made even the most hardened heart shatter.

She sat there for hours, into the dark of night, before she found the strength to go inside. She wept and screamed and smashed many things before she felt well enough to face the world again. When she left, I was certain I would not see her again.

But she would come back once a month to make sure things were in order. On one of these regular visits, a crazy woman with a book that sent a burning sensation through my body stopped by, asking for help. The woman of the house told her that she had a daughter now and that this would be the last time she helped her.

They left shortly after that and the lady inhabitant has not returned for many years. The cobwebs grow thicker with each passing day. Yet the exterior remains untouched thanks to the ivy growing from my body.

I was once again left with my thoughts, watching the sun come and go, the animals traipse through the land. While I remain stationary, intrenched, alone.

My name is Hedera and I was cursed by a witch to watch over this house until it sighs its last breath.

Chapter One

Andromeda

The meeting I've been dreading is today. The lawyers will go over Aunt Merr's Last Will and Testament.

I spend the time before the meeting distracting myself from the anxiety swirling in my gut, which equates to pacing around my apartment, deep cleaning, and scrolling on my phone. When it's finally time to head to their office, I grab my stuff and pause in front of the mirror by the door to give myself a pep talk. "You can do hard things, Andromeda. Even if it feels like your whole world is falling apart around you, it is still spinning and that means you keep moving. Aunt Merr wouldn't want you to cease living because her soul has gone to the After. You can do this." I take a deep breath and head out to the meeting that will change the rest of my life.

It's probably the second worst day of my life, the first being when I watched her take her last breath. When she told me she had cancer, I figured we'd whip up a cure or call her friends and have her better in no time. We tried everything we could, but no amount of potions or spell work touched the cells attacking her body or the masses growing to unsettling proportions. She used her last breath to tell me she loved me and that she was so proud to have cultivated me into the witch I am today. Then, I watched her soul move into the After. I'd never seen anyone pass before. It was quite beautiful, if not mildly traumatizing.

The lawyer's office is nicely decorated in blues, grays, and white glass pieces. The receptionist smiles warmly at me as I walk in, feeling out of place in my bright pink blazer, tropical green wide-legged trousers, and yellow high heels. I don't typically dress up for things like this, and as I was left unattended, I got a bit carried away. Not that I care, these colors bring my heart joy and I need a serious pick-me-up today.

"Do you have an appointment?" the gorgeous red head behind the desk asks me. Her sea green eyes sparkle as she maintains eye contact.

I have to clear my throat before I can get my voice to work properly. Damn sirens. I'm already awe-struck with just five words. I'm not one to fall fast, but with the way she's looking at me and the sultry sound of her voice, I'm struggling here.

"Yes, with Jackson and Burton at 2:30." I manage to break eye contact as I fight to put up a mental block against her. When I manage to get it in place, her shoulders slump before she stands and walks down a hall behind her desk to let the lawyers know I'm here.

"Right this way," the siren says when she comes back to her desk. She holds her hand to the side, guiding me to the conference room on the left. It's one of their smaller rooms, the table big enough to sit six people comfortably. A pitcher of water sits in the middle with some disposable cups next to it, and a tray of pastries on the opposite side.

"Miss Wellwood," Mr. Burton says, holding out his hand as I approach him. He looks very prim and proper in his crisply pressed gray suit and shining black shoes.

"Mr. Burton, Mr. Jackson," I say, shaking both of their hands. "Pleasure to see you gentlemen again." I smile, but it wavers from the nerves and emotions running rampant through my mind.

"Please, have a seat. We have a lot to discuss today," Mr. Burton directs, gesturing to a chair while Mr. Jackson pours us all glasses of water, setting them in front of our places as we get situated. I drain my cup, setting it down before tucking my hands under the table to hide my cuticle picking while I wait for them to get started.

Two hours later, all documents are signed and all information is gone over. I never realized how stressful it is to be the executor of an estate. However, being her only living relative, it's the burden I must bear. I never knew her to be married, therefore there were no children to hunt down or husbands to notify. Thankfully now that everything is done, the stressful part is over. Kind of. The first order of business is finding the nerve to read the letter Aunt Merr left with the lawyers to give to me.

It burns a hole in my bag as I make my way back home. My eyes won't stop glancing at it, *needing* to see her handwriting one more time. Which is ridiculous, considering I have a handwritten cookbook she made for me with all my favorites. But this feels bigger. Crazier. The meeting with the lawyers probably doesn't help, given they informed me my childhood home had been given to Hariett's Home for Children.

I'm not sure why, but since Aunt Merr's passing, I had assumed I'd get the house I grew up in. Instead, she's left me a house I've never been to. I shouldn't be as upset as I am, as anything is better than my tiny apartment, but not getting the house in Bellville where I learned everything feels like a loss all on its own.

When I step into my tiny apartment on 5th street, I tear the envelope open so I can read her letter before the door closes behind me. My hands shake uncontrollably, so I hurry to the small kitchen and set the letter on the counter so I can finally see her parting words.

My dearest Andromeda,

I am so sorry I couldn't be there for you when you finally get married and have the live you've always dreamed of. If there was anything I could have done to stay, I would have. But, as you know, my time was up. I lived a good life. It was full of love and adventure, and most importantly, you. You brought me so much happiness and a purpose I never envisioned having for myself. Even if things weren't always rainbows and butterflies, as long as I had you, I knew everything would be right as rain.

As you know by now, I didn't leave you the house in Bellville. While I'm sure it's a shock, there are reasons for my decision— ones I cannot explain to you here. But please understand that you are the only one who can do what needs to be done. Trust in your friends to help you and seek guidance from the Goddess to steer you.

I know you're probably rolling your eyes at my mysterious ways as you always have. I wish I could explain everything to you. But Death does not allow us these favors sometimes. You will figure it all out in due time, I'm sure of it. I love you sweet girl. Remember that I am always with you in spirit. I will be right by your side watching over you.

I love you for eternity,

Aunt Merr

I crumple to the floor when I'm finished reading, her words making me sob uncontrollably. I couldn't move even if I wanted to, and coincidentally, all my will to exist has left my body. She was my best friend, my mother figure, my mentor. Everything I am is because of the unending love and trust she had in me.

And now she's just gone.

A few hours later, Kira barges through my door, calling my name. Her hair is raised and her pupils are huge as she looks around the apartment for me until she finds me in the kitchen. I'm a shivering, swollen faced mess. She pulls me into her arms and strokes my hair until I eventually find solace and fall asleep to the sound of her heartbeat. When I wake up, I'm tucked in bed, the letter laying on my nightstand. I grab it and reread it five more times before getting up and putting it in the spell work Aunt Merr got me for my 13th birthday, *Glamours and Enchantments for the Teenage Soul.* It was a gag gift more than anything, given I already knew how to do most of what was in the book, but it's sat in a prized spot on my shelf since, and is now home to many notes and letters I haven't wanted to lose over the years.

I head out to the living room to find Kira and Brent sitting on my loveseat, speaking in hushed tones. When they realize I'm finally up, they stop talking and stand to check on me. This is the extent of our friendship now. They talk in whispered words and treat me as if I'm going to explode into a million little pieces at the most inopportune time. It's exhausting.

"You guys can go. I'm good," I say before heading to the kitchen for some water. They don't respond, instead their eyes follow my every move. I don't have the heart to tell them to leave again, so I endure their concerned gazes and ignore their existence the best I can.

It's been a week since the meeting with the lawyers, and today I move into my new house. I'm dreading it like no other. This last week has been chaotic, to say the least. But, with the help of my friends, this hopefully isn't going to be so bad.

I turn into the drive of the new house, and am met by an iron gate fifteen feet high, sharp looking finials sit atop the adjoining fence every five feet. Arborvitae line the fence, making seeing into the property impossible. Though, it's already making me fall in love with this place.

Exiting my car, the cold autumn breeze bites through the holes in my purple cardigan as I push open the squeaky gate before getting back in my car and making my way up the drive, which is lined with Japanese Maple trees. I freak out as I take in all the different plants I can see from the twisting drive up to the house. There are berry bushes, what looks to be nightshade, and is that *oleander*? How is that growing right now?

When I see my new home, I stare at it in shock, double-checking my phone to ensure I have the right place.

What I thought would be a quaint little house is actually a fucking mansion. That's what Aunt Merr left me in her will. Which is still crazy to think about, considering I was certain I would get the Bellville house. But maybe this is a blessing in disguise.

Especially considering the house in Bellville is where my parents abandoned me. They couldn't handle my growing interest in being a witch, even though my mother was one too. But she turned her back on it all when she fell in love with a 'man of God'.

Originally, they wanted Aunt Merr to quell my powers; she refused. She told me it would be a crime against nature to do so. Instead of telling *them* that, though, she told them despite her best attempts, I was beyond salvation. They argued with her, screaming and yelling, before they said, "Good luck with your devil worship," and left. She cursed their names that night as I watched from the crack in her spell room door. Looking back, she probably knew I was there, but didn't say anything as she knew it was good to see someone on my side.

She held me as I cried myself to sleep for months, telling me that it wasn't my fault, that my mother had always been misguided. It didn't matter to me, though. They were supposed to love me and protect me, but instead, they left me here.

Ever so slowly, though, she pulled me out of that pit of despair and we had a better relationship than I could have ever dreamed of having with Mother.

Now my childhood home belongs to the local group home, which is the perfect use for it with the six massive bedrooms, five bathrooms, two sitting rooms, massive kitchen, and fully finished basement. Aunt Merr poured every ounce of her love into that house. Even though she's gone, her love is still felt inside, especially in the kitchen which was her sanctuary. To anyone else, the random smells of chocolate chip cookies and different spices when no one is cooking won't mean much. But, to those of us who knew Aunt Merr, they are signs that she's still there; busy even in the After. If someone looks hard enough at the walls in the kitchen, they'll see the protective spells she placed throughout, perfectly blended into the little flowers and bees she painted herself.

As I get out of my car again, this time to open the house for the movers, I look around at all the different flowers and plants in the front yard. There's black-eyed Susan's, Russian sage, all different colored asters, and yarrows dispersed along the front of the massive house. When I tear my eyes from the plants in front of the house, my attention snags on the English ivy clinging to the house. Its luscious green leaves are vibrant and full, just how I like my ivy.

I walk over to run my hand along the leaves to help soothe my aching soul. Being a green witch, plants and nature bring me the greatest joy and happiness. I run my hand along the silk leaves and something slices my finger open. I yank my hand back, hissing between my teeth before shoving my finger in my mouth as blood begins to bloom.

Great, first day at the new place and already bloodletting.

"That wasn't very nice." I look at the plant, showing it my finger as I continue my lecture. "I'm sorry I touched you without introducing myself, but *this* is unnecessary. I will not harm you and I demand the same respect from you or there will be issues with this cohabitation." I take a deep breath before continuing. "My name is Andromeda, or Andi as my friends call me. If you don't mind me saying so, you are absolutely stunning." I can't help the wave of awe that coats my words as I compliment the plant, my previous annoyance long gone as I take in the white and green of the leaves. I've never seen an English ivy plant this bountiful.

The leaves dance in the light breeze. A vision of a woman tossing her hair over her shoulder, tipping her chin in the air, plays in my head. *Insolence,* she says.

One of my abilities is seeing some plants as people. It's never been enough of a regular occurrence for me to build up, but I always enjoy it when they decide to trust me with who they are. Their faces are never clear, just a vague impression of who they are. Some are more open, while others make me work for it. This pretty girl is very open to showing me her displeasure.

I almost make it to the front door when the moving truck's brakes squeak behind me, causing me to jump. I don't know how I didn't hear the engine rumbling down the road. Kira will be pissed if she finds out I was off in La-La Land again.

Plastering a smile on my face, I turn to greet them, hoping my face isn't splotchy from my endless crying the past few weeks since Aunt Merr's death.

An older gentleman exits the vehicle and greets me with, "Where do you want all this?" He waves his hand towards the truck.

His straight-forward approach to life is a bit off-setting and it takes me a moment to mumble a response. "Um, just in the sitting room, I guess."

"Are you sure this is all you're moving in?" he asks, hiking his thumb over his shoulder as he eyes the monster of a house before us.

I duck my head, trying to hide the blush creeping over my face. "I'm sure. Thank you." My words shake, embarrassment threatening to turn me into a crying, apologizing mess.

He mumbles something under his breath and I hurry to open the door for the two moving men.

I haven't had a chance to look the place over before coming out here so I'm not sure what kind of state it's in. Adjusting my bright blue messy bun, I take the first step inside. A thick layer of dust coats every surface and spider webs decorate the corners of doorways and rooms. I sneeze three times as the dust motes tickle my nose and the smell of must and emptiness pervades. I should have come to clean before bringing my things here. Despite the immediate feeling of peace I feel, there's also an ominous feeling tickling the back of my neck. Like I'm being per-ceived by something...*other*. Freaking myself out, I hurry back outside to the movers. "Do you guys have sheets to cover that stuff up?" I ask the older man. "I forgot to request it, but I didn't know what state this place would be in." My teeth sink into my bottom lip as I clasp my hands behind my back, trying not to fidget. I hate being an inconvenience to people, especially strangers. They didn't ask for my oversight and I should have been more diligent in my duties.

He rolls his eyes and hikes his thumb over his shoulder as he bites, "Oh yea, loads of them." His sarcastic tone causes my cheeks to flush. I take the hint as I see him shaking his head and talking to his partner, overhearing words like 'entitled,' 'needy,' 'annoying.'

I guess I'm not going to get those sheets after all.

Clicking my tongue, I head to my car to unload the stuff I packed in there. Thankfully I *did* have the foresight to bring my cleaning supplies with me, along with Aunt Merr's urn, instead of with the moving company. I grab the box of homemade cleaning supplies and head inside to the kitchen. I plop the box down, raising a cloud of dust in the process.

I wave my hand in front of my face as I cough and sputter.

"Bless you," a woman whispers. Her voice sounds young and fresh, like the first spring showers of the year.

"Thank yo–" I spin around to face whoever said it, but stop short when I realize I am all alone. I thought for sure I heard someone, maybe it was a mover in the hallway? But that doesn't make sense because I already saw both of them, and I don't have enough stuff for more than two people to be moving...

Shaking my head, convinced all the grief and stress of the last few weeks is getting to me. I grab a spray bottle of thieves mix, which is clove, cinnamon, eucalyptus, and lemon oils all mixed together. Aunt Merr told me never to use store bought chemicals because the government is just trying to kill us with preservatives and chemicals not meant for human use.

This cleaning mixture holds up against all kinds of messes and hasn't let me down yet. As an all natural cleaner, it's my preferred cleaning agent. I shake it up before spritzing it all over the counters, then grab one of my millions of rags and start wiping everything down. I'm pleasantly surprised to find the kitchen to be in good structural condition. There aren't any cracks in the olive green paint and the black and gold granite countertops are smooth as can be.

Kira's voice carries in from outside, and I can't stop the smile spreading across my face as I toss my rag down, listening to her yell at the men outside for being less than careful with my belongings.

She beams at me as I walk into the foyer. Her black hair is as unruly as ever. Her hazel eyes gleam, and the sunlight glows off of her earthy brown skin so beautifully. She truly is one of the most gorgeous women I've ever met. If we hadn't been friends for so long I'm sure we'd have been lovers by now, but neither of us want to ruin what we have.

"Hey, girl!" she cries, wrapping me up in her hug. Her woodsy honey scent fills my nose, calming me; her arms are like my own personal sanctuary. "Sorry it took me so long to get here. That interview took *way* longer than they said it would." She lets me go and looks around. "Oh my Goddess. I love this place, Andi," she cries as she walks around gawking at the dirty walls. "Well, aside from the spiderwebs, that is." She shivers before turning her attention back to me. "Why haven't you brought me here before?"

A gust of wind rips through the ivy outside, sending the leaves into a frenzied dance in the sun. *What about me?* she says.

Choosing to ignore the ivy for now, I focus on Kira. "I didn't know it existed, to be honest. Aunt Merr told me a lot, but she was also a woman of many secrets." I wink at her before nodding my chin towards my car. "We need reinforcements. This place hasn't been touched in way too long." I cringe as I think of how much work we have to do. "Tell me all about the interview while we get this place clean."

"That's not the only thing that hasn't been touched in ages," Kira jokes and my cheeks flush again. "Don't worry about the cleaning, though. I pulled some strings with Brent and the boys. They'll be here in, like, twenty minutes." She throws her arm over my shoulders as we walk to my car to finish unloading it.

Brent and the boys are our good friends who run a cleaning company in Bellville. They're also all werewolves. We met Brent at a poetry slam four years ago and have been inseparable ever since. It's like he's always been with us, never missing out on a joke or a memory.

Probably because we both have a problem with over-sharing sometimes.

When I asked Brent to lead the service for Aunt Merr's funeral, he hugged me so tight I was certain my ribs were going to crack. I knew her funeral was going to be a huge turn out, given how popular she was around town, so having my best friends with me was a top priority. Brent is great with crowds of people, so I knew he was perfect for the job. Not only that, but Aunt Merr loved Brent.

"You're seriously the best." I smile up at her. She's only a couple of inches taller than me, but ever since she gained those inches she's boasted about finally not being the shortest person in the friend group. "However, we're not leaving it all up to them, so you can help me clean in the meantime." She rolls her eyes at the news, and I chuckle while we continue our way to the car.

"I know I'm the best, there's really no one else like me" Kira gloats as we round the back of my car. "Why must you do this to me?" she complains, her confidence quick to fade as she grabs the broom and mop. "What happened to smudging and banishing?" She pouts as she makes her way back into the house.

"You know just as well as I do that cleaning is part of the purifying ritual," I yell after her, glancing at the house as I wrinkle my nose. "Goddess knows this place needs it."

Shaking her head, Kira disappears inside. The movers ogle her as she walks past and I know they're mesmerized by her wild curly hair that's earned her the nickname of Medusa on more than one occasion. It's not far off considering she's a gorgon. Too bad she can't turn men to stone anymore since The Council deemed it a danger to the humans. It would have been useful a time or two in our friendship.

The Council is a group of Paranormal beings– and one human– who decide what is and isn't allowed in the paranormal community. If you go against them, you're executed, or some variant thereof if you're immortal. The rulings are unambiguous so there's absolutely no wiggle room. They know everything, so no matter how sneaky a person is, if they break the laws, there is swift justice. I shudder at the thought of the punishments they've dealt out. I'm sure there's at least a hundred vampires in the Gulf of Mexico alone, not to mention those who are staked in a casket and buried in a tomb somewhere undisclosed.

Aside from Kira's hair, her love of crop tops and short shorts don't help either. Not that it makes it okay. It's absolutely appalling, but men are, well, men.

The only time she's okay with people staring at her is if they compliment her badass owl tattoo on her stomach. I keep telling her if it helps that much she should get more, but she's so indecisive sometimes and she hasn't gone back for another one yet.

I clear my throat as I carry Aunt Merr's urn past the movers. They shake the lust from their eyes and get back to work. I'm glad I'm not the only one affected by her, though my feelings go past her looks and down into the very depths of her soul. If only I could tell her.

I set the urn on one of the counters before I start working on the windows. "So, how did the interview go?" I ask her as she starts attacking the high up cobwebs. I don't know why she chose that task as she hates spiders, but if I had to guess, I'd say it's probably out of spite.

"It went," she says, doing her best to keep her voice flat and steady. I throw a rag at her since her back is to me and she can't see my glower. She laughs before explaining. "It went the same as every other interview. They asked why I lost my last job, I tell them what happened, and they conclude the interview. At this point the only thing that's going to be available is working at Jimmy's Market in the meat department...again." She groans, resting her forehead on the wall she's standing next to.

I walk over to her and give her a tight hug. "It'll work out. It always does." I peck her on the cheek and get back to work. She pulls out her phone, turning on an early 2000's pop punk playlist to give us some good vibes while we clean, and a way to avoid any further conversation on her difficulty finding a new job.

The old man from the moving company comes in while we're deep in our tasks to let us know they're finished. I thank him and give him a tip before walking him out and making sure they leave. I know Brent and Kira wanted to help me with moving as well, but I couldn't accept it. It wasn't that I have a lot of stuff, it was just that they'd already done so much for me since Aunt Merr's death, I would have felt like I was taking advantage if I'd accepted.

When I'm finished with the windows, I start working on the glass-front cupboards. It doesn't take long, as most of the storage is in the walk-in pantry to the left of the fridge. Kira is still working on the webs, so I decide I may as well wipe the cupboards out as well, that way they're done and we can put stuff away pretty fast.

Afterwards, I check the fridge and freezer to find them surprisingly clean. I spritz them anyway and wipe them out before doing the same to the outside. The gas stove is next on my list to attack, and I'm starting to think Kira is taking her sweet ass time because she doesn't want to clean. Cobwebs do *not* take that long to get rid of.

"We've got a live one, Andi," Kira calls from the far corner of the kitchen. Her voice has a violent edge to it, so I hurry over before she kills the poor creature. Kira's shoulders are rigid and her eyes take on the incandescent glow they get when she's worked up. Her hair raises with the power flowing through her body.

I look up and see a gravid black spider staring her down, its front legs raised in a defensive stance. "Easy, girls. It's okay," I say softly, taking the broom from Kira. She keeps staring at the spider as she backs away. "There you go. Why you chose to clean the cobwebs when you hate spiders is beyond me. Back up just a little more...there. That's good." I make sure to keep a soothing voice as I play body-guard between her and the harmless spider.

When I'm pleased with where Kira is, I turn my attention back to the helpless creature and gently wiggle the broom to get her attention. "Hi, mama. How are you doing? Come on down, let's get you outside where you can find some yummy bugs. There's some beautiful ivy out there that would love to have you save it from those nasty beetles." It inches onto the broom. "Good, good. Come on, little mama." I carefully inch the broom end closer to me, holding my hand out to her when she's close enough. She wiggles her legs at me, testing me. "You don't scare me, love bug. Let's go, come on." She crawls onto my hand and hunches down into the warmth. "Good job, mama."

I take her outside, taken aback for a moment at how overgrown the backyard is. Weeds have taken over the fountain in the middle of the yard, and the grass is several feet tall. I find the perfect spot for the spider in front of the window above the sink for her to hang out, make her new home, and have her babies. She crawls off my hand and starts spinning a new web, completely unbothered by me. When she's settled, I turn back to the chaos that is my back yard, close my eyes, lift my hands, and let my magic go. I envision a green light flowing through the wild backyard, cutting the bushes and grass back to an acceptable length. Flowers bloom under the glow, providing nutrients to the pollinators scavenging for food.

I open my eyes as my magic flows through me and watch the grass shrink back, the shrubbery being shaped into different animals and shapes, the weeds falling from the statue of a fairy and gnomes. The walkways that were hidden beneath the monster of a backyard make themselves known and my heart sings as I take in my now orderly yard. I start planning where to put my herb and vegetable garden as a now calm Kira makes her way through the sliding glass door and looks at the grounds.

"Damn, girl. This is really going to be good for you, huh?" She walks over to me, tossing her arm over my shoulders.

"Yea, it really is." I rest my head on her shoulder, grateful for this small window of peace. "Listen, if you can't find a job soon, you can come stay with me. It's really not a big deal, there's plenty of room." My offer is innocent enough, but I also hope she'll take me up on it so we can maybe explore where our relationship could eventually go. She doesn't answer me, just gives me a tight smile and squeezes my shoulder before walking back inside.

I sigh as I step back and take in the ivy and the spider, thinking of ways I can help my friend without overstepping. It's the least I can do after all she's done for me lately.

Something ghosts across my ankle and I startle, glancing down. Nothing is there, but I swear a vine slithers back into place. I look back at the ivy, nodding my head. A vision of the same woman from before plays in my mind. She smirks at me.

I take the graze and the smile as a sign of forgiveness and a new start.

Chapter Two

Kira

Goddess save me. How is it that I'm in love with my best friend and she likes *spiders?* What kind of sick twisted shit is that? Ever since Kyle Heinrich put a spider down my shirt in third grade and it bit me I've been terrified of those little fuckers. Turns out, it was a purple gold jumping spider and I had to have ointment and antibiotics for weeks because they're incredibly venomous to gorgons. I paid Jenny Hothbrook fifty bucks to curse that little snot-nosed freak and I'm still not sorry about it.

I hope his erectile dysfunction is serving him well in his adult years.

My heart races as I pace around the house trying to calm my nerves from the spider encounter, but I can't shake the creepy crawly feeling. It doesn't help that I feel like I'm being watched and chills are constantly running down my spine. I'm used to being ogled, but this is different. This is inquisitive, intrusive.

Trying to outrun the sensation, I head outside to check on Andi and find her unleashing her magic on the run-away backyard. I did my best to avoid her questions of how the interview went earlier because I don't want her to be embarrassed to be my friend. I don't really have anything to offer her, just some lame jokes and okay-ish hugs. But I couldn't fend them off any longer without shouting something was going on.

So, when she offers me a place to stay if I don't find something soon...it cuts deeper than she intended. I don't want to be a mooch. I want to make my own way in this world. If only I could get this damn attitude in check.

I leave Andi to her business in the backyard and head back inside so she doesn't push the subject. However, the feeling of being watched hasn't left me a single moment, only getting worse when I'm alone, and I'm starting to go a little crazy. Pacing around some more, I try to ignore the feeling, to put it in the back of my mind and shut it out. It doesn't work. Just as I'm about to run out of the house screaming and ripping my hair out, Brent and the boys walk through the front door and the feeling lessens enough for me to be able to function.

"Kiraaaaaa," Brent squeals as he barrels into me.

"What did I tell you about being mindful of your strength, you big oaf?" I grunt as he gives me a bear hug. One of his boys, Ronnie, growls and I flip him off.

"Oh, hush. You know you love it." Brent gives me one last squeeze before letting me go and the rest of the boys pile on top of me, giving me their affectionate hellos. Which range from a polite handshakes from Toby and Scott, hugs from Ronnie and Percy, and a big ole sloppy lick up my face from Colton. I flip him off as well and he cackles before he runs off with Toby to find Andi. "How is she?" Brent asks softly, picking up a few bags he brought with him and dropped when he saw me.

"She's her usual self." I lead him to the kitchen, glancing around, my unease growing again as we get settled.

Picking up on my conflicting emotions, Percy asks, "What is it?" His worry is palpable, his musky scent growing as his heartbeat accelerates. His pupils dilate, darting around the room while he sniffs the air, looking for a threat. Percy is the pack's beta, or second in command. Sometimes he thinks he's higher in the pecking order than he actually is and tries to overstep Brent's rule, but he's quickly reminded of who the top wolf is.

"I don't know." I look from him to Brent as I choose my words carefully, so I don't sound like I've completely lost the plot. "You know how sometimes I get those weird feelings that something is watching me?" At their nods I continue, "this is one of those times. There's something *wrong* here."

"Are you sure you're not just overly worried about Andi being out here by herself? Where is her nearest neighbor? Like, five miles away? I'd be a little spooked, too, if I felt the way you do about her." He gives me a pointed look.

"Oh, shove it." I give him a vulgar gesture as he cackles at my hopeless situation. He's not wrong. Part of my unease *is* the fact that she'll be out in the wilderness all alone. While I know it's a dream come true for her, it still doesn't feel right being so far away...even if it's only fifteen minutes.

I think that's the worst part about this whole feeling, I know it's uncalled for. I know she will be just fine. I *know* it's likely just my anxiety fucking with me again. But the feeling is so prevalent and I can't shake it, no matter the exercises I try.

"Andiiiii," Brent screeches at the top of his lungs as she walks through the door behind Colton and Toby. He scoops her up in his arms and swings her around.

"Put me down, Brent. You're making me dizzy!" she protests, but her laughter gives away how much she loves it.

Brent sets her back on her feet and smiles wide at her, showing off his pearly white teeth. His sparkling blue eyes contrast his black hair that's always perfectly done, even when on the worst cleaning jobs. He's very attractive, especially for a man. Aside from his eyes and hair, his beard is a very attractive 5 o'clock shadow. He's a pretty boy through and through.

I find myself being oddly jealous of him and Andi's relationship at times. When we're out and about, people assume they're together, despite him being very obviously gay when he opens his mouth. Sometimes I find myself wishing people thought Andi and I were together instead of just two besties hanging out.

Okay, more than sometimes. Like, at least once a week, if not more...and lately? It's been more.

Agh. What is going on with me today? I've never been this overprotective or jealous of Andi and her life, no matter how much better it was than mine. But after everything that's happened the last few weeks, I can't help but feel different.

I guess that's what happens when your best friend goes through emotional turmoil and you're there comforting her every day. It feels like we've spent more time together in the last few weeks than in our entire friendship. Which is total bullshit, but the emotional vulnerability we've both shown during our time together since Merr died is something that neither of us have ever felt comfortable enough to do thanks to our past traumas. But when Merr passed, it made something click for the both of us. We aren't promised tomorrow. So, ever so slowly, we opened up more and more. Andi more so, but I've watched her for almost every moment, making sure she was safe and okay. When she wasn't, I'd comfort her and be her rock. In and amongst all of that, I found more and more things I love about her.

Like how her nose turns red when she cries, and how bright her green eyes shine. How crazy her hair is when she wakes up in the morning, and the little dances she does when she thinks no one is watching her. The way she talks to all the plants that she comes across, even if it's just a small hello, every single one gets her love and adoration. These are all things I already knew about her, but for some reason they've become even more obvious for me lately.

It's probably the suppressed emotions.

"This place is fucking amazing," Brent gushes before he turns a glare Andi's way. "Why have we never had a party here? It's the perfect place for our Samhain celebration." He crosses his arms while he waits for a response, his muscles bulging in his black v-neck.

"Yea, like that backyard is fucking nuts. I want to go roll around in it again," Colton says, his pupils dilating from his excitement as he presses his face to the sliding glass door, drool dripping from his mouth. He's the youngest member of the pack at 26 and still very much in his puppy phase. Wolves begin maturing at 30 at the earliest. Some have even been known to not mature until they're 45. Brent shakes his head at Colton.

"We aren't here to do all of that today. We have plenty of time to come back, but for now we have a job to do. Let's get a move on!" Brent dishes out assignments, sending Ronnie to grab food while we start unpacking the kitchen since it's the first cleaned room in the house.

Brent levels a playful glare at Andi when his pack disperses and I step in between them so she doesn't have to face his pretend wrath alone– it's almost as bad as his *actual* wrath. "I asked her about this place, too, but she swears she didn't know it existed." I hop up on the counter when he rolls his eyes so I can reach the top shelf as Andi hands me dishes.

Brent raises his eyebrows at Andi and she sighs before explaining. "I didn't know until the lawyers told me about it, I swear! If I did, do you think I would have been holed up in that tiny ass apartment on 5th for the last two years?

No, I would have begged and pleaded with her to let me live here instead. Especially after Garrett."

My shoulders slump and Brent whines low in his throat at the mention of that douche nozzle who is her ex, and the reason she was holed up in that tiny ass apartment to begin with. He's Brent's cousin who was integrated into Brent's original pack after his parents were brutally murdered by hunters when he was six. He's always been mean, but when he didn't get to be an alpha at maturity and Brent did, it got worse.

Talk about chihuahua syndrome. I fake a cough to cover my giggle at my own joke and Andi looks up at me with concern.

"Choked on my own spit. Sorry," I explain, giving her a sheepish smile.

She grabs a bottle of water out of one of the bags Brent brought and tosses it at me with a raised brow before putting the rest in the fridge, clearly not taking my choking excuse seriously. Oops. Then she takes one for herself and chugs half of it while keeping eye contact with me. I shift where I sit slumped over on the counter. I do not want to repeat what I just thought. While we all agree that Garret is a little bitch, it's a sore subject and better left alone.

When she realizes I'm not budging on sharing my thoughts, she turns to Brent. "Are you sure the guys are okay with cleaning this place? I really can do it on my own." Guilt colors her tone as she bites at her plump bottom lip.

He rolls his eyes as he bumps her hip with his, scooching her out of the way so he can unload the cold groceries into the fridge. "I'm one thousand percent sure that they don't mind. I promised them super bloody steaks as a reward." Andi and I wrinkle our noses at the vision of them tearing into the bloodied, uncooked steaks. "Plus," Brent interrupts the nasty vision, "they love you and care about you. You know that all of our love languages are acts of service. Why else would we have a cleaning company? They'll have this place shiny and clean in no time! Whilst we labor away, how about some wine?" He pulls crystal wine glasses from one of the bags and begins filling them.

"Really, dude?" I ask with a raised brow, my lips pursing as I judge him.

"Is it such a surprise, Miss I-drink-wine-out-of-a-coffee-mug? You know I don't spare any expenses when it comes to you bitches. We aren't going to drink *Chateau* out of one of your scummy mugs." He shudders at the atrocity. "I may be a wolf, but I'm not a fucking animal, ladies. Only in the sack." He winks and we groan, complaining about him bringing that up *again*. He cackles as he finishes pouring us drinks.

Twenty minutes later, we're done with the kitchen and have moved onto the living room. Andi already has a bit of a buzz going from the wine. Her words are slightly slurred, her green eyes are glassy, and she has more of a sway to her hips as she walks around, dusting the surfaces. She's mesmerizing, per usual.

Before I can make an ass out of myself and hit on her or kiss her, Brent startles me from my thoughts as he turns on his vacuum. When I turn to glare at him, his striking blue eyes are staring at me with his perfectly sculpted brows raised to his hairline. I roll my eyes and go back to sorting the boxes so they're easier to take upstairs.

Once the boxes are sorted, I start hauling them up the giant staircase. Andi and Brent stay downstairs, focusing on cleaning the living room, dining room, and bathroom. This place is so gorgeous. The stairs remind me of lapis lazuli with their deep blue and gold veins running through the white marble. The would-be gaudy gold banister works well with the stairs and the navy blue colored walls. Where downstairs is decorated in rich crystal shades and a sophisticated aura in mind, upstairs is where passion and wildness has been unleashed.

"Andi, you have got to see this!" I yell down at her. I would admonish the boys for not telling her earlier, but when they get their orders from Brent, they tend to hyperfocus and ignore the rest of the world. There's a reason they're the best reviewed cleaning business in the state.

Tree roots are painted on the bottoms of walls, little gnomes and fairies dance around each other in a show of lights and rainbows. Birds and squirrels run along the branches of the trees painted higher up on the walls leading to different rooms.

This place was *made* for Andi. She's going to freak out.

"Coming," she yells from the bottom of the stairs. When she reaches me, I watch her reaction to the second floor landing. Her face is already red from all the work we've been doing, and sweat makes her hair stick her her forehead, but she's still resplendent. When her pupils dilate and a little gasp leaves her parted lips, her resplendence grows significantly.

I want to be the reason that gasp leaves her lips...and more...so, so much more.

"It's gorgeous." She bends down and runs a hand over the gnomes and fairies. As her hand touches the wall, the fairie's wings flutter and the gnomes bounce in place. She yanks her hand away and nearly falls on her ass in her shock.

"Enchanted paint? How fucking sweet," I say in awe, reaching my hand to the squirrels on the upper branches. They chase each other around and around until I remove my hand. When I look back at Andi, tears are falling down her cheeks, but from the look in her eyes, they're happy. I sit down next to her on the landing, wrapping an arm around her shoulders. It doesn't take long for her to plop her head on my shoulder as we stare at the painting that was made for her.

"She always gave the best surprises, you know? It's like she knew what your soul needed and did everything she could to ensure you got it. She had a gift that was often overlooked, but one I always appreciated." She takes a deep, shuddering breath. "I miss her so much."

"I know, hon." I squeeze her shoulder and let her feel all of her emotions, cleaning long forgotten.

"Food is here," Brent calls up to us, putting an end to the moment and pulling us back to reality.

"Ronnie must have just got back." We hurry downstairs before the rest of the boys can trample us in their excitement. I grab plates from the cupboard and help Brent dish out the food as everyone settles around the big table in the dining room.

Chapter Three

Hedera

*A*nother witch. This one smells like the last one, but doesn't look much like her. Her hair is too blue and her nose is upturned. Her body is curvier.

When she touches my leaves, I can't help but take a taste so I can know what I'm working with.

The air shifts as she walks towards me, drawn in by the bright green leaves.

Maybe *she* will be my salvation. I try to quell the excitement running through my veins. I know by now that salvation is a long forgotten dream and I will rot away here for the rest of eternity.

When she runs her hand along my leaves, I focus all my thoughts on creating a thorn to slice her with. As her blood hits my system I light up. It's filled with light and reminds me of the alcove in the forest behind the house where I used to run when I was a girl.

As the blood works its way through me, a memory that is not mine overtakes me.

"Intentions mean everything, Andromeda. If you want something badly enough while casting, it is likely to come to fruition despite what you are trying to do. Remember to clear your mind and speak true to your heart," a woman with graying red hair and freckles decorating her cheeks tells a young girl with blue hair and eyes as green as fresh spring grass. The woman kisses the young girl on the top of her head, running a hand down her hair.

The young girl scrunches her nose in concentration, working to clear her mind of distraction as the older woman stands patiently behind her, a small smile playing in the corners of her mouth.

The girl begins to speak in Latin. It's choppy and slurred. She closes her eyes, concentrating as hard as she can, working to shut out the world around her as she tries her best to cast the spell the woman is teaching her.

Light flickers through the room, and the girl gasps as the energy of the spell flows through her, exiting her hands and going towards the small potted plant sitting in front of her on the old wooden table. She keeps her eyes closed, squeezing them as hard as she can, as she pushes the energy toward the pot. Her brows scrunch together creating a deep divot between them as she pushes her will to its limit.

When she opens her eyes, she cries out in glee, jumping up and down as the woman behind her laughs and claps her hands.

The dahlia that was barely a seedling has grown to full height and opened up a full bloom of a beautiful orange flower.

The memory fades as they embrace each other and I realize the woman in the vision is the last woman that lived in this house.

No wonder the girl tastes of summer.

Chapter Four

Andromeda

My screaming muscles are why I'm only slightly regretting doing so much cleaning today. Thankfully I have some salve for sore muscles in one of these boxes. It'll be a lifesaver tomorrow...or whenever I manage to find it.

Brent's pack crowds around him, trying to get as close to him as possible. I've never been so glad to not have so many people relying on me to keep me in line or safe or anything else that comes with being an alpha. I'm equally as glad that things didn't work out with Garrett so I don't have to be intimately involved with it all. It's not that I don't love my wolfie friends, I just really enjoy my alone time occasionally and having other people know my intimate thoughts and feelings doesn't really vibe with me. But when you're in a pack, everything is shared. They're all psychologically linked. When one feels pain, so do the others. The one benefit is that they know where each other are, in rough estimation, at all times.

"Thanks for staying with me tonight, guys," I say to break the silence. I don't mind the quiet, even prefer it more often than not, but I've always been an awkward host and don't know when to say something or just enjoy the peaceful silence that comes with it. "New places always creep me out."

Brent and Kira share a look before he says, "Anything for you, Andi Pandi."

I stick my tongue out at him for using the nickname he knows I hate and he chuckles in response.

"Honestly, though. I wouldn't want to stay in a strange, huge ass house by myself, especially given the mysterious circumstances surrounding it," Kira says, smiling softly at me to soften the blow.

I shiver as I stare at a vine hanging over one of the windows. The overhead light plays along the veins on its leaves and it looks as though it's waving. I blink, shaking my head to clear that wild train of thought and focus on Aunt Merr's urn on the mantle instead. I moved it there, deciding that although she loved the kitchen, it would probably be better for her to not watch over my horrific cooking skills.

Once we're all settled with the pillows and blankets Brent brought with him, Ronnie pulls out a book and starts to read to us. The cover is worn and faded, but something about it tugs at me like Gaia does when she wants me to do something and I'm being too dense to understand. After a couple of pages I can't hold it in anymore and blurt out, "Where did you find that?"

He looks at me with wide eyes and his Adam's apple bobs as he swallows hard. He's the most sheepish of the wolves in the pack, which is ironic considering when they're shifted he's one of the fiercest. "It was on a bookshelf in the master bedroom. I thought it looked cool," he stammers out. "I guess I should have asked." He whines and Brent reaches over, rubbing his shoulder before giving me one of his pointed looks.

"No, it's okay. I was just curious..." I trail off as my brows scrunch together.

Kira reaches over and smooths the space between my brows. "Hey, are you okay?" Concern shines in her hazel eyes. I could get lost in them for days on end if I could just find the courage to tell her how I feel.

"Yea, just trying to figure it all out." I shake my head, breaking eye contact with her and her hand falls away. "It's just been a long day. I need some sleep, I guess." I smile at her, but the look in her eyes tells me she doesn't believe me. I can't blame her. I've been a mess lately, and even *I've* been worried about my emotional well-being since Merr's death.

After some more reassurances from Brent and me, Ronnie continues the story about a Lord whose infidelity with a witch brought great peril to his family. A few minutes later, my eyes close and Sleep cradles me in its arms.

I dream of spiders spinning webs that make a path to nowhere, ivy tangling itself through the threads, begging me to follow it down, down, down. Answers sit at the end, but as soon as I get close, a web falls into my face, spinning me in place until I am lost once more.

I wake to the sounds of snoring and heavy breathing. My bladder screams at me to hustle before it releases its contents all over the nice plush carpet. I pick my way across the living room, ensuring I don't step on anyone, and make my way to the bathroom before heading to the kitchen for some water. A creak comes from the pantry as I chug my drink and I whip around to face it.

"Hello? Who's there?" I ask quietly, not wanting to wake anyone in the living room. No one answers. "Kira, if that's you, I swear to the Goddess I'm going to murder you. Quit fucking around and come out of there."

When she doesn't respond, my heart kicks into high gear. I set my water on the counter and tiptoe towards the pantry door. It's slightly ajar and a light breeze comes through the crack, making the door swing ever so slightly.

I take a deep breath before swinging the door all the way open, expecting to find Kira or one of the boys rummaging for snacks. I fumble around in the dark for the lightswitch and turn it on. Instead of finding Kira or one of the boys, I find a hidden door cracked open on the far wall, the breeze is stronger in here, coming from the space below. The musky scent of dampened earth permeates the air.

"What in the world?" I whisper as I slowly make my way towards it. I pause on the threshold of the hidden door, debating on going to get someone from the living room, but I decide against it when I hear rustling coming from below.

"Hello?" I call out, cursing my voice for shaking from the adrenaline coursing through my blood.

"Witch," a disembodied voice carries from below.

I gasp and take a step back. I definitely have an intruder. Is it a hunter? What do we do? I may know how to do some basic self defense moves, but none of us know how to take a hunter on. They're highly trained assassins and we're...well...us. We're fucked.

I definitely need to go wake everyone up and get us the fuck out of here. As I turn to warn them, the pantry door slams shut. I try the handle, my sweaty palm gliding off of it a few times before finding purchase, but it won't open. I take a few deep breaths to calm my nerves. Being a worked up mess is never good in a bad situation. I need a clear mind to be able to navigate this like Brent or Kira would. I try yelling for my friends, but every time I try to yell it feels like a hand squeezes my throat. Lovely.

I remind myself repeatedly that the Goddess provides what we need, always, and she will protect me.

I try to open the door one more time, and this time it works. But, as luck would have it, one of Gaia's inevitable tugs pulls me towards the stairs..

"Shit." I gather my courage, turn on my phone flashlight, and make my way down the spiral staircase behind the hidden door. Dirt walls encase the stairs on either side and the smell of dampened earth gets thicker the farther I go, calming my nerves. The stairs groan under my weight, but they hold steady the whole way down.

Halfway down the stairs, the cold dampness of the underground envelops me and I wish I had grabbed a cardigan before going on my middle of the night adventure; too late now. I breathe in deeply. As a green witch, the earth is my domain. "I am safe here," I say as a mantra, focusing on my steps.

No matter how many times I tell myself that, nothing could have prepared me for what I see when I reach the bottom of the stairs.

A young woman with blonde hair matted to her filthy face stares at me with uncertainty, her brown eyes nearly black in the low light. Sticking from her body are roots that lead to the edge of the room, a few vines hang from her body. Her skin is sunken and her bones protrude at crude angles.

Shock causes my feet to pause at the bottom of the stairs as I take in the scene before me, my hand flying to my mouth to stifle my gasp. Then Aunt Merr's voice floats through my mind, "You have all the pieces, do what needs done." The sound of her voice nearly has my knees buckling beneath me, but I find my resolve; I will not be weak in front of this creature. Taking a deep breath of the damp soil, I open my eyes and take a confident, but slow, step forward.

Chapter Five

Hedera

How did she find this place? It's been years since anyone has been down here. Vandals broke in and found me last. They came to mock me and make me feel worse than I already did. Their fists and feet did immense damage before I could gather the courage necessary to rid myself of them. I did not know I could do what I did when it happened. I thought it was due to my being on Death's door, but I have been able to control the vines on the outside of this house since that day so it couldn't have been that.

The only reasonable explanation is that when I called upon the roots holding me prisoner, I solidified my curse and this is what I will be for the rest of eternity.

I cannot even tell you why I decided to let the vandals near me to begin with. Though, I suppose one word that would make sense is hope. I had hoped they were there to save me, to rescue me from my prison. But they were not. And they suffered the consequences of their cruelty.

I do not feel guilt over their deaths. It was necessary to my survival.

The ivy almost rotted off the house that year. But I got my vengeance on them. Twisted them up and watched the life fade from their eyes. Their bodies were never found.

The woman before this one didn't know I was here. She could sense something, like this woman's friend can, but she never figured it out. She fixed this house up nice and proper. Filling the holes and painting over the graffiti left behind by good for nothing lolly-gaggers. Then her lover abandoned her and she practically stopped coming. The last time she did was when that crazy woman showed up with the book that made my skin crawl.

I shrink into myself as this witch takes in my desiccated body, the roots of the vines covering almost every inch of my skin. I know I'm a monster. Disgusting. Horrific. I don't need her to say it. I feel it every day.

"You poor thing," she says in a sigh, coming closer to me. She reaches a hand out and I shrink back, memories of those people long ago attacking my mind. A root along my spine tears and blood seeps from the wound. I hiss through my teeth. We both eye the blood dripping to the floor. "I won't hurt you."

I know she won't. I watched her with the spider earlier. I know she is a soft soul, loving and kind. But I can't stop my body's reaction to physical touch.

She bites her lip, her eyes getting a far away look before they focus on me once more. "I'll be right back." She turns and hurries up the stairs.

I watch her go, longing to follow her as much as I long for my freedom. A freedom I am certain she can provide me now that she has found me and I have felt the power radiating off of her. But it is a freedom that I cannot ask of her.

When she comes back, she's carrying a glass of water and a box of something under her other arm. She makes her way over to me slowly, so she doesn't startle me again as I stare at the box with apprehension.

"My name is Andromeda, or you can call me Andi like my friends do. What's your name?" she asks as she moves closer to me.

"Hedera." I keep a close eye on her as she inches closer.

A hiss leaves me when she gets close enough to touch me, but she doesn't stop. Instead, she keeps her eyes locked on mine and slows down, taking her time until she's right in front of me. She brings the glass of water to my mouth with a strange contraption sticking out of it.

At my confused looks she explains, "It's a straw. I figured in your condition you couldn't very well drink from a glass. You put it in your mouth and suck. It's kind of like a root in a sense." She points to the roots sticking out of my body and then smiles at me.

It's a beautiful smile that is warm and accepting of the atrocity that is my existence. It lights up my body. The way her cheeks dimple and one side raises just slightly higher than the other is adorable.

She puts the straw-thing in my mouth and I do as she says. The cold water moistens my mouth and I choke as I take too big of a drink.

"Careful. Take small sips," she says softly as she raises a hand to help with my choking. Guilt colors her face as she realizes she can't and she drops her hand.

My cheeks blush as I sputter and spit the water out. When the fit has passed, I open my mouth for the straw-thing again. She guides it in and I drink ever so slow-ly. When I've had my fill, she sets it on the dirt floor and opens the box in her other hand, offering me what looks like a biscuit.

"What is that?" My brows scrunch together as I try to figure it out.

"Crackers. You must be starving, but given how you look I don't want to give you too much." Her smile wavers and I can tell she's a little nervous about offering it to me.

After a few moments of considering whether I should eat it or not, I nod my head. She extends the cracker and I take a small nibble, learning from my episode with the water. It's like nothing I've tasted before, the buttery flavor floods my tastebuds and a small moan leaves my lips.

As I nibble the cracker, she asks, "What happened to you? How long have you been here?"

I finish chewing and take another sip of water before she sits on the dirt floor and puts her things next to her.

"A witch is what happened to me." Before I can stop myself, the truth spills from my lips. It's been so long since I've had someone speak to me and actually care about me. She looks at me as if my words don't make sense. I sigh before explaining further. "In 1887, my father fell into an affair with a Wellwood witch while my mother was on holiday in Wales. He promised the witch riches and a life very few could have envisioned back then.

"When my mother returned and found out, she hunted the woman down. When she found her, she summoned her here and beat her in front of him. My father denied having anything to do with her, though I knew it was her. She had been around a lot in the months Mother was away.

She taught me many useful bits of knowledge. How to steep tea correctly, how to identify different plants in the woods– which ones were poisonous and which ones had medicinal qualities. I knew her face well. Mother used me as proof of his infidelity.

"Before she found the witch, she came into my room and confided in me. Tears ran down her face and Mother never cried, at least not in front of me. I felt guilty and knew I had to tell her the truth or she would die of a broken heart.

"When the witch arrived at our home, my mother sent me to my rooms, but I watched from the cracked parlor door as Mother took her vengeance out on the witch. She beat her with her bare hands before heating a fire poker until it was glowing red and stabbed her and burned her over and over. I'd never been so frightened of my mother. I wanted to help the witch as she had been so kind, but I knew my interference would be punished beyond measure. I couldn't move a single muscle from where I watched. It was as if my feet had been glued to the floorboards.

"The Wellwood witch did not flinch at a single blow. She did not cry out in pain. She stared at Father with such hatred. As she bled out on our floor, she spoke the words that would be my undoing.

"'I curse your blood to witness the fall of your name. Your shame will be hers. Only when she has known the same level of depravity that runs in your veins will she be free.' Then she turned her gaze to mine, peeking through the crack in the door. She smiled sadly at me and mouthed that she was sorry. Then she chanted a few phrases in Latin until she died."

Tears run down the witch of today's face and I wish I could reach out and wipe them away. "I'm so sorry," she whispers, her words heavy with her sincere heartbreak over my tale of betrayal and violence.

"Andi?" a voice calls from above followed by mumbled words we cannot fully make out. Our heads jerk up at the sound.

"I have to go, but I'll be back, I promise. I will not forget you and we *will* get you out of here, okay?"

I stare at her in response. I learned long ago not to trust a witch. There is always a catch to the trust– always a price to pay.

Even knowing that, I want to trust her.

The mumbled words above grow louder, as if the person is moving closer to the pantry door. I look through the ivy lining the kitchen windows and find her female friend searching for her, gathering her courage to open the pantry door. The witch turns away and rushes up the stairs, the sound of the door shutting has me slumping in defeat.

I shouldn't have told her the story of what happened. But I couldn't stop myself.

But something in my gut is saying that maybe my luck is finally turning.

Chapter Six

Kira

A nightmare wakes me up from a dead sleep. It was about spiders crawling all over my body, wrapping me in their webs and pulling me down a tree-lined path. I woke up as we entered a clearing and I caught a glimpse of a blonde haired girl petting a wolf.

Groaning, I rub my eyes and look around the room to try to guage what time it is. By the moonlight shining through the window, I'd say it's at least 1 AM. I glance beside me and my chest clenches when I see Andi isn't there. I feel along her blanket, realizing it's cold. My mind starts to play tricks on me, telling me she was abducted in the middle of the night by whatever has been watching us or she went for a midnight stroll and got eaten by a rabid wolf or something insane. *Fuck, why do I feel anxious about her going to the bathroom?*

I get up and stretch my arms over my head to help allevi-ate the pain in my back from sleeping on the hard floor. It's definitely not the worst place I've slept, but it's far from the best. When I start picking my way across the living room to go hunt Andi down, I shake out my hands in an effort to calm my racing heart and expel some of my pent up energy.

"Andi?" I call out as I reach the bathroom, quiet enough that I don't wake anyone else. The bathroom door is open and the light is off. I go down several hallways, calling her name, half expecting her to jump out and scare me.

When that doesn't happen, I curse the massive house. No one should have a house this fucking big. She's going to get lost at least ten times before she figures out where everything is, if not more. Knowing Merridan, there's probably hidden tunnels and shit that lead Goddess knows where.

As I round the corner to head to the kitchen, the feeling of something watching me again sends a chill down my back. "Fucking creepy ass house," I mutter to myself.

Rolling my shoulders back to try to relieve the tension coiling there, I head down the hall to the kitchen, hoping she got the late night munchies she's prone to. It's part of why I love her so much. She's not into diet fads and doesn't care that her stomach is soft and she has curves. I find it sexy. Her hips are perfect for gripping during–

My train of thought cuts off as I walk into the kitchen and find it empty. My power rises in my veins and I feel my hair start to lift. It's not the first time my powers have awakened unwanted in this house. It's unsettling. Usually I have pretty good control over them, but something keeps calling to my base instincts and I can't put my finger on it.

Call it my generational trauma, but being a gorgon carries some stellar intuition. It's saved my ass more than once and I couldn't be more grateful to be a descendant of the great Medusa herself. It's also a blessing from the great Goddess that I got more of my looks from Medusa than her offspring. I'm not sure how it happened considering my cousin is a centaur, but you win some you lose some, I guess.

Pulling myself from my rambling thoughts, I look around the kitchen for clues that something is amiss. A glass of water sits precariously close to the edge of the counter and her scent is in the air, dull but present. I follow the trail of it to the pantry where her scent grows heavier. I assume she's hiding in there with a bag of cookies like she often does when she's stressed. Or she's sleep-eating again. I've told her so many times not to do that. She could choke and die in her sleep and no one would be the wiser. Not that she can control what she does in her subconscious state, but still. How would she like it if her obituary read that she choked to death on a Chips Ahoy! cookie in the middle of the night?

Embarrassing.

The only thing that tells me she's *not* sleep-eating is the light shining from the cracked door. She never turns on the light in her sleep, just hides in a dark corner like a goblin protecting its horde of goodies. If the light's on then she's awake and just eating her feelings, which is totally understandable given the circumstances.

"Andi, come out of there. You're creeping me out." A shiver runs down my spine again as I wait for her to respond. "I swear to the Goddess, Andromeda Wellwood. If you do not come out of there in thirty seconds I'm coming in. I don't want to invade your privacy like that, but you're not leaving me many options.

"And if you're up to some freaky shit, you could have gone to your bedroom or the bathroom. The pantry is a really weird choice, babe. But hey, no judgement or anything."

I'm painfully aware of my rambling, but I can't stop the words spilling from my mouth. I'm usually quiet and don't talk a whole lot, but when I'm extremely comfortable with someone– or incredibly nervous– the words pour out of me. Despite my nerves, I've managed to curb my powers running rampant so my hair is back to normal. One of the many things that Merridan taught us was to calm our minds, therefore calming our magic. I thought about the smell of Andi's hair when she gets out of the shower and it's still damp. Or the way the sunlight makes her freckles pop. How her hugs make the world fade away until we're just two souls dancing through the stars.

Works every time.

Just as I'm about to charge into the pantry, Andi comes out panting and looking nervous.

"What were you doing in there? Do I even want to know?" My words have a bite to them and I feel bad, but I'm tired and my head is killing me from lack of sleep, drinking so much wine, and not enough water. I'll make it up to her later.

"I thought I heard a rat," she says with such casual ease that I know she's lying. Not to mention she has a half-full glass of water and a box of crackers in her hands. Though, knowing her she was probably trying to tame the damn thing.

What gives her away, though, is the twitch in her left eye. I catch it even in my half-awake state. It's her tell-tale sign that she's lying, always has been. "I'm too tired to pry into your weirdness right now."

I turn around and head back to the living room, hoping she follows me and doesn't go back to whatever she was up to before. Between it being the middle of the night, freaking out over not knowing where she was, drinking too much wine, and my power spike, I'm wiped. Unlike her, I'm not lying.

As I begin to drift to sleep, I feel her arm wrap around me. I sigh as Sleep takes me away.

Chapter Seven

Andromeda

My shoulders sag when Kira heads out of the kitchen, and I try to come up with a reasonable story for the morning. I know she won't believe my horrible attempt at a lie. She'll bring it up in front of Brent and then I'll face the Inquisition Squad.

Sighing, I follow her back into the living room and stare at the ceiling for a while, begging Sleep to take me into its embrace once more. After ten minutes, I'm certain Kira is asleep and I throw my arm over her, needing her comfort to chase away my doubts and racing thoughts, despite lying to her. Goddess, the last few weeks have made me feel like a shitty friend. It's part of why I offered her a place to stay here. I don't want her to stress about the job situation and I owe her for everything she's done for me lately. Especially dealing with my horrible attitude.

Before I know it, the sun is shining through the windows and everyone starts stirring. I groan. My back hurts and my head is pounding. I need caffeine pronto.

As if he was summoned by my thoughts, Brent comes sweeping into the living room with Percy hot on his heels. "Good morning, you beautiful people! Who wants coffee?" They start handing out cups from Stanton Coffee, each of us getting our exact order.

Sometimes Brent's remarkable memory is jarring, but I don't complain as I close my eyes and take a sip of the life-giving bean juice. The chemicals shoot through my bloodstream and I feel ready to face the day.

That is until I open my eyes again and find Kira staring at me, her eyes glowing softly.

Shit. "Not now," I whisper.

Brent's ears pick up on my words and he sends his pack out of the room to finish whatever meager tasks are left for today, which is finish taking boxes upstairs and putting them away. We kicked ass yesterday and the whole house is somehow clean and ready to go.

Brent sits on the sofa across from me, crossing one leg over the other and taking a drink of his latte. Counselor Brent reporting for duty. His eyes bounce between Kira and me as he gives a low whistle. "You better spill, sister." He pins me with his *look*; eyebrows raised, head tilted down, lips pursed. "Kira's gonna go full power on your ass if you're not careful." He motions between the two of us before sitting back and waiting for the proverbial tea to spill. "What is it? A lover's quarrel?" He takes a noisy slurp of his coffee.

"I don't know what her deal is," I tell him. "She saw me leaving the pantry last night when I thought I heard a mouse and she doesn't believe me that that's all it is. That's not on me." I shrug my shoulders, feigning nonchalance, but my cursed voice raises a few octaves as my defensiveness takes over. I'm in serious need of grounding.

"Because it's bullshit and you know it," Kira snaps. "Not to mention, last night you called it a rat, and now it's a mouse?" The difference between a mouse and rat would be moot to anyone else, but given that I'm so in tune with all living things, it's detrimental that I fucked that up. But before I can fix my blunder, Kira barges on. "In all the years we've been friends you have never once hidden anything from me, and now that you have a big fancy house you're going to start? I didn't take you for someone who would let things like that get to your head." She glares at me and I do my best to avoid her eyes.

I try to take a deep breath and count to ten, but my temper gets the best of me. I set my coffee next to me on the floor before I unleash. "My aunt just died, Kira. It's not like I saved my meager earnings for years and bought this place outright. I inherited it from my *dead aunt*. In case you somehow missed the memo, I am *grieving*. On top of that, because I needed time to grieve, I got *fired* from my job." I throw my hands in the air. "If you don't believe me about a rat then I'm sorry, but I don't know what else to tell you." I lean back against the couch, closing my eyes so my eye twitch doesn't give me away...again. I know she caught onto it last night and that's why she's not letting this go.

I worked at Georgia's Bakery for the last six years; never missed a day of work, so to say I was shocked when she fired me for missing a week is an understatement.

I may have cursed her bread so that it never rises properly after I hung up with her the day she let me go. There's just really no way of telling why their bread mix is suddenly having issues.

Thankfully, though, along with the house, Aunt Merr left me most of her money as well– which she had a lot of. So I'll be comfortable for a while until I find something that really soothes my soul.

I hear Kira take a few deep breaths before she says, "I'm sorry, Andi. I know you're hurting and everyone grieves differently. I just thought we were closer than that. I thought you knew you could lean on us during this. You don't need to lie to me about *anything*. You should know by now that I always have your back. I mean, I've just spent the last couple of weeks with you while you work through this whole thing. Only leaving you to go to interviews so I don't have to keep relying on you guys. I just wish that was enough to prove it to you."

When I don't say anything she keeps going. "While this place *is* hella cool, something about it feels off and is sending my powers into overdrive. I feel like something is watching me all the time and it's got me on edge. So, when I woke up and you weren't here, I freaked out and went to find you. I looked all over. I thought the boogeyman had come or the hunters tracked you down." Her voice breaks and she stops talking.

"You were half awake, Kira. We all know how you are when you're sleep deprived," Brent teases, trying to ease the tension in the room.

Kira flips him off. "I know I'm not the most alert when I'm half asleep, asshole. But I also know my own mind. I *also* know that if there was a rat in here, as she claims–" she gestures to me. "— she would have gotten it and taken it outside. Conveniently, however, there was no rat. Just a very guilty looking Andromeda Lynn Wellwood." She pins me with another glare and I take that as my cue to take a drink of coffee before picking at my cuticles. Her use of my full name stings and adds to the guilt I'm feeling about lying to her.

"We were all exhausted after cleaning yesterday and I'm sure the wine didn't help any. She probably just imagined it," Brent suggests.

Kira sags in defeat. "I guess. I just– something isn't right here. You guys have to admit that much, right?" She glances between us, her eyes wide in desperation.

"Oh, definitely. But that's part of the charm and why it'll be so perfect for our Samhain party this year." Brent waggles his eyebrows at us again before his pack makes their way back into the room. "You guys are done already?"

"Yep. There's a few boxes left, but we figured Andromeda would like to put them away…" Toby's words trail off and I realize what boxes he's talking about.

Three are my spell work supplies and the other one is my personal toys.

My cheeks heat, but I do my best to save face. "I can't thank you guys enough for all the work you did," I rush out. "That would have taken me months to sort out."

"It's not a problem, Andromeda," Toby says, ducking his head.

"Andi, please. I've told you a million times already, Toby," I tease him. He blushes and heads over to Brent.

Toby and Scott are the only straight-ish guys in Brent's pack. From what Brent says, Toby has a huge crush on me. Poor guy. If I was into wolves he wouldn't be a bad choice, but my ex ruined all chances of that. I shudder at the memory of him.

We spend the next few minutes gathering up the bedding. When I try to hand it over to Brent and his pack, he explains he has way more than enough and to consider it a house warming gift. The boys help me take it all upstairs and then we meet back up in the living room, and say our farewells before they head out to their next job.

I lean against the door after I shut it and take a moment to collect myself. I look towards the living room and see Kira watching me intently.

Chapter Eight

Kira

She's not only lying to me, she's also lying to Brent who's falling for it hook, line, and sinker. *Push-over.* I stare at her as she makes excuses and pretends like everything is okay, but I see right through her. She knows I can so she avoids looking at me.

On top of her lying to me, I hate watching Toby simp over her so hard. She's too much for him and he's far too dense to realize she isn't interested. It isn't that he's an unattractive dude– and a beautiful wolf–it's that Andi's ex is a werewolf and they did not split amicably. I mean, I wouldn't expect them to when she found out he was fucking other people, not to mention his abusive tendencies. He's lucky she didn't let *me* handle the situation. Dude wouldn't be walking around thinking his shit doesn't stink anymore, that's for sure. Council be damned.

Maybe it's just that I care too much about her. Ever since we drunkenly made out with each other at one of our Samhain celebrations, I've been a goner. I just don't know how to tell her and I don't want to ruin our relationship or make things awkward if she doesn't feel the same way. I've come close so many times, but back out every time for one reason or another.

Lately it's because I feel like the world's biggest fucking loser. No job, shitty apartment that has roaches, and nothing to offer anyone. My cup is empty and I have no way to refill it unless I'm with Andi.

All I really want to do is push her against the wall and kiss her face off, tell her how beautiful and perfect she is, and solidify the feelings I know are there for the both of us. I see the way she looks at me sometimes, I just don't want to be misreading something and then have her avoid me for the rest of our lives. I also couldn't handle her rejection right now.

I sulk against the living room doorway as she chitchats with everyone since my social battery is shot and I just want some alone time.

I've never wanted to leave Andi before. In all the years we've been friends, in all the arguments we've had, I've never dreamed of leaving her side. It's usually physical torture to be away from her. But today?

Today, I want to shake her and tell her to wake the fuck up before she rips us to pieces.

I understand she's grieving so her senses are probably all fucked up, but I have a hunch that whatever is in this house is making her emotions worse. She's never ignored my warnings before, so why is she insisting everything is honky dory now?

Dread shoots through me. Maybe she's growing tired of my overbearing tendencies. Maybe I've become too much for her like I have almost everyone else in my life.

My shoulders slump further. She's always been the one person in the world that I could be myself with and not have to worry about wearing her out. She has never made me feel invalidated before last night and this morning.

Being let down by one of your people sucks, but this? This feels like she stabbed me in the heart and twisted the blade to ensure I wouldn't survive. Goddess, I sound like one of Brent's wolves. I need a fucking drink.

We say goodbye to the guys and I watch her as she leans against the front door, taking deep breaths to calm her nerves. When she's more resolved, she saunters over to me while I'm moping, and despite the whirlwind of my mind, my breath catches when she gets close.

Her aura alone is breathtaking, but mix that with the smell of her– roses and chamomile– it's heady and intoxicating.

I'm down for her so bad and it gets worse with each passing day.

"Take a walk with me? I need to ground before I lose my mind." She holds out her hand for me to take, and even though I'm still hurt that she would lie to me and disregard my feelings like she did, I link my fingers with hers and she leads us to the kitchen where we leave our shoes by the sliding glass door and head outside. The sun warms our skin and a breeze plays with the grass and small shrubs that surround a stone fountain in the middle of the huge yard. The fountain is of a fairy woman holding a vase that the water pours out of, a group of gnomes are at her feet, watching the water spill into the basin.

"I know you don't think you can trust me with whatever happened last night, and I don't know why. I would be lying if I said it didn't sting. I've never judged you or doubted you on anything. That being said, I'll leave it for now. When you're ready, you can tell me and I'll listen and support you any way I can. I love you for always." I kiss her cheek, expecting her to brush my words off. She surprises me with her response.

"I will when the time is right. Thank you for allowing me time to process it."

Finally some honesty. Though, now, my mind is racing a million miles a minute on what it could be...again. I release a heavy breath, determined to keep my word and not pester her for more information. I'm working on my patience, and Goddess is it the *worst*.

After a few laps around the backyard, I head home. I don't want to leave Andi anymore, especially now that I know she *is* hiding something. But she needs time and I have to respect that.

A few days later I'm deep cleaning my apartment when my phone rings. My eyes shoot to the screen, hoping it's Andi telling me she's ready to fill me in or one of the places I interviewed for this week.

Grace, the caller ID reads.

Just as exciting. I answer it before it can ring for a third time.

Grace is the owner of Sherman's Antiques, our favorite antique shop. Her and I have been working on a huge memorial room for Merr and the other witches of Belleville. It honors their service to our community.

"Did it come in?" I answer in lieu of a greeting.

"Always so perceptive, dear. Yes, and it is *magnificent*."

"I'll be there in fifteen." I hang up without a goodbye and haul ass to the shop.

1

Chapter Nine

Hedera

I listen to the witch, Andromeda, and her friends interact through the next day. I'm jealous I cannot be there with them. They seem fun and I haven't had fun in far too long.

Kira, her friend who almost caught us last night, is interesting. I find myself drawn to her as much as I am Andromeda. I watch her as she goes about her business. When they begin fighting over last night, I'm curious as to why Andromeda doesn't just tell her if she is so trustworthy. I don't think I would mind much if she knew. I'll have to tell Andromeda that next time she comes. Or is that too weird? I don't want her to think that I am spying on them. It's just been so long since interesting people have been in this house that my curiosity has gotten the best of me.

When the wolves leave I am filled with relief. The smell of dog starts to dissipate, and fresh air works its way through the house. They seem nice enough, but their stench is ungodly.

The ladies make their way outside and I watch closely as they hold hands and talk about their secrets. I don't know why Andromeda still won't tell her about me. It's not as if I'm something to be cherished or anything. Just a monster of a girl, stuck in this cellar.

I can tell they both love each other. But I can't understand why they don't act on those feelings. If I had a love that shined like that, I would shout it from the rooftops and everyone would know how happy I was. It reminds me of the last lady inhabitant and her lover that left. Kira better not leave Andromeda. If she does, I will hunt the ends of the earth for her and make her wish she didn't. I don't know how, but I'd find a way.

Kira kisses Andromeda on the cheek and I am overcome with both happiness and jealousy. A wave ripples through my leaves in response to my intense feelings.

I want her to kiss me. Andromeda too. I've only felt this way about one person before. Two people at once feels selfish and *dirty*. Is this normal? How do I know?

My thoughts spin in circles as I pull back my consciousness from the ladies and give them a bit of privacy.

Chapter Ten

Andromeda

After Kira leaves, I take on the task of researching Hedera's curse in the upstairs library. This room is a second sanctuary to me with its aisles of bookshelves, tall enough that there's even a rolling ladder– eek!– and a window seat with the perfect amount of daylight shining through. If that doesn't suit my fancy, there are comfortable looking arm chairs in front of a massive fireplace with a dark wooden table between them, the perfect size for a pot of tea and some cups. It's something out of a dream. However, it's going to make my task of finding a cure for Hedera incredibly difficult.

Shelves upon shelves are filled with books on witchcraft, romance, and mysteries. Thankfully the library is pretty well organized, so I don't have to really guess where the witchcraft books are– I just look next to the giant cauldron, skipping the romance and mysteries. I make a mental note to come browse them when there's not someone in dire need of my assistance.

After looking through the titles of books and determining they're all useless in my quest, I huff out a breath. A whisper pulls my attention to the aisle over, and despite the hairs raising on the back of my neck, I go investigate, certain it's just my best friend pulling a prank on me.

"Kira, I swear to the Goddess above that if you're here trying to freak me out so I'll move back to 5th I'll skin you alive," I bite out as I round the corner.

I stop short when I find no one there. Embarrassment crawls through my body and I'm glad no one is here to see the blush taking over my face. All I find in this aisle is a book hanging off the edge of an otherwise perfectly lined shelf.

I look up at the ceiling and send a quick prayer of protection and guidance to Gaia before picking up the book and opening it. The pages flip one after the other on a phantom wind, sending dust flying into my face. I sneeze and cough, waving my hand in front of me to clear the dust from the air so I can breathe again.

When the dust settles, I look back at the book and gasp as I realize I'm holding a very old diary. The date reads September 13th, 1887.

His wife has returned and I am left with nothing again. Not a thought toward what I want nor my feelings. I have been tossed aside like last year's linens. My usefulness disregarded

for the sake of a fake love, and the sanctity of a broken
marriage.
But I will have my revenge if it is the last thing I do.
I have set forth motions that shan't be undone.
Tomorrow I will be summoned to their home and I will do
the last of what needs done.
Lilith, guide my hand as I make the greatest sacrifice to date.
He shall pay for what he has broken.

The following entry was dated the next day and spoke of her growing guilt, ending the passage with the reversal of the spell she cast on the family who betrayed her.

The book falls from my hands as I finish reading, slamming shut as it hits the floor.

I have the supplies we need, but will Hedera go for it? I mean, a witch put her here...would she be willing to have more spell work cast on her?

I slump to my knees, the carpet biting into them as my skirt fluffs around me. I bow my head and pray to the Goddess again. "Goddess, please hear me. I seek your guidance, patience, and understanding. You have laid a path before me that will be difficult. I'm not sure I can succeed, but I will do my best. Please lead me on this quest and ensure I do not falter. Blessed be."

I take a deep breath before tucking the book under my arm and leaving the library. I need to read more of this diary and get a sense for the woman who was capable of such things in the name of love.

Don't get me wrong, I know love can make people do crazy things. But cursing a young woman to an eternity of *this*?

Situations such as these are why I have such a hard time confronting my feelings about Kira. I do love her, but I've seen love change people into someone they're not. I've read stories about love sending people into killing sprees or committing murder-suicides.

Love is dangerous.

I head to the master bedroom as my thoughts spin out of control. I glance around the room, calling out all the things I see and smell, trying to calm my mind. It's a trick Aunt Merr taught me when my anxiety got to be too much to handle with my breathing exercises.

The bed is a massive four-poster with white drapes tied back with blue bows that match the blue flowers someone painted on the sage green walls. The carpet is the same plush beige in the living room. It even has a wardrobe and a walk-in closet.

For once in my life I have enough room for all my clothes. I giggle as I inhale deeply, the scents of roses, lemon balm, and thieves blend work their way through my body. Once I'm calm enough, I sit in the window seat and read the journal from the beginning to get a sense of the woman who wrote it.

While I read, I realize that most witches are the same. We fear persecution for who we are and hesitate to help when we're needed sometimes because of said fear. It's stressful. Thankfully the people of Bellville are wonderful and have never once made us feel unwelcome.

In my reading, I gather that the woman– Emma– was a green witch like myself, though she dabbled in other arts as well. She had cursed a few men in the village for beating their wives and infidelity. She seems like she just wanted to help people, to belong and be accepted for what she was. But despite her best efforts, she was shunned time and again. So when Hedera's father, George, brought her into their lives and promised her safety and love, she believed him.

And it led to her death.

Fucking men.

After a few days of not doing much of anything besides visiting with Hedera and taking her food, I decide I should probably unpack my spell work boxes that have been taunting me. I take them to a bedroom at the other end of the hall. One of the many things Aunt Merr taught me is to never keep my spell work in my bedroom. It brings bad luck and can sometimes backfire if I don't finish a spell in one sitting.

There have also been reports of witches sleepwalking and doing spells and dying. So, it's best to err on the side of caution with it.

Not that I ever did spells that *could* backfire, as I mostly deal with healing and herbs, but it haunted my nightmares for months, one of the signs Gaia has sent me through my life. So I figured it would be best to listen.

She's my deity of choice, well, kind of. After I grew a dahlia seedling to a full, budding flower when I was nine, she came to me while I was playing at the park alone one day. She didn't say anything, just smiled and stroked my cheek before disappearing before my eyes. So while I didn't necessarily *choose* her, I'm glad she showed up because I wouldn't want to worship anyone else.

My anxiety had started getting bad around that time, especially around new people, but I was at complete peace in her presence. I *knew* who she was in my soul. So, I began praying to her every day. My anxiety got to manageable proportions once I accepted her as my goddess, her nudges in the right direction helping tremendously– especially once I learned to listen to them.

The bedroom I pick out for my spells is perfect with a large window on the south wall, which will give me the perfect space to meditate and seek guidance on how to help Hedera. I make plans to get a planter stand full of the different cacti and succulents that can help me with my salves and tinctures. The floor is an old burnished wood, making it easy to clean up my salt circles. The west wall is covered in built-in shelves that are big enough for all of my supplies and books. A chaise lounge sits in the corner next to it, a big work table where a cauldron, candles, and matches sit is in front of it, allowing enough room to get to the shelves.

I put everything in its place, making a list of things I need to re-up on in my phone. Once that's done, I head back to the master bedroom and flop down on the huge bed. Even though it's only 12:30 in the afternoon, I'm wiped. Since losing Aunt Merr I've needed to rest more. Maybe that was why she gave me this house when she did, she knew it would be the perfect place for me to just *be*.

Though, the seclusion kind of sucks. I like people, despite the way my brain makes me feel. They're interesting to watch.

Before my mind can travel down that depressing rabbit hole, my body relaxes into the mattress and my tense muscles release as my eyes fall shut. It's like a hug and is the most perfect thing in the world. As I relax, my mind goes back to Kira kissing my cheek the other day. It's not the first time she's done it, but this time felt different. It makes me wonder what it would feel like to have her *actually* kiss me again, like she did during that one Samhain party. Her lips grazing down my neck, her teeth nibbling the delicate skin beneath my ear.

I roll over and grab my vibrator from the top drawer of the nightstand, my body needing release. I peel off my clothes, envisioning her smooth hands trailing over my bare skin. Goosebumps follow in their path. A moan escapes my mouth as I imagine her hands trailing up the insides of my thighs and she says, "Open wide for me, little witch."

My legs part at the imagined order, knees dropping to the sides. I put the head of my vibrating wand on my clit and turn it on to a pulsing mode, knowing Kira wouldn't give me my release so easily. She'd make me *beg*.

The initial sensation is almost my undoing, but it immediately cuts off for a few seconds before buzzing in quick succession three times. Another pause. All while imaginary Kira says filthy, dirty things to me and pinches my nipples.

"You're already so wet for me, little witch. Look at how your pretty pussy *weeps* with just the faintest of touches." A long buzz follows her words and my stomach muscles clench. I pull the wand away from my needy center, not ready to come yet. Not until *she* tells me to.

"That's a good girl. I want you to beg for it. Don't hold back, now. Let me hear those pretty little moans."

I cry out at her words, the wand finding my over-sensitive bundle of nerves again. The setting has changed to a rhythm of a long buzz followed by two short ones. It drives me wild. My head tosses back and forth on my pillow as I sink my teeth into my bottom lip.

"Fuck, Kira. That's so good. Yes, just like that. Right there."

"That's right, let me hear you. Mm, you're practically gushing for me."

"More," I beg. She slaps my inner thigh.

"Ask nicely," she demands.

"More, please," I beg. "Pretty, pretty please give me more."

She shoves two fingers inside of me, pleased with my begging. I cry out at the intrusion, but then she curls her fingers just as the long buzz hits and I'm done for. I fly into oblivion, but she doesn't stop. She changes the setting to a constant buzz and turns the intensity all the way up, holding it on my clit as I writhe and try to crawl away from her.

"Stay, baby. You're going to give me one more."

"I can't," I groan as the sensations become too much.

"You can and you will. I know you can do it. Just one more, come on." She pulls the wand away from me and blows lightly on my clit, sending shivers through my body. When I'm relaxed again, she puts the wand back in place and pumps her fingers in and out of me at a vicious pace. The sound of her hand smacking against me fills the room.

I fist the comforter, needing something to keep me tethered as I'm taken on the ride of my life.

"That's it. I told you you could do it, little witch. Keep going. Cry for me, pretty girl," she says as tears leak from my eyes at the pleasure my body is going through.

She bends over me and takes my nipple into her mouth, sucking hard and gliding her teeth over the peak. It shatters my soul. I scream as fluid gushes from me. She kisses my cheek again and takes the wand away.

I open my eyes, shame flooding me. My imagination really got away from me there. I've never once fantasized about her. It feels like an invasion. Not that she'll ever know.

But still.

I go to the bathroom and clean the wand and my hands before putting it back in the nightstand drawer. I lay back down in bed, spent from my vigorous activity, and hear a slithering noise from the window.

My eyes dart to where the sound is coming from and I find the window cracked open. Strange. I don't remember opening it. I close it before laying down in the overly comfortable bed and my eyes creep shut as Sleep embraces me.

Chapter Eleven

Hedera

The nights pass in bursts of hopefulness and dread.

I want to believe this witch– that she will finally set me free from this place. But what does that look like? I know nothing of the world now. Will I even live? I've been here for so long that I don't know if I'll just shrivel up and die or if I'll actually get to have a life.

Around and around the thoughts go.

The witch has come down a few times to bring me food and water, but mostly she's been moping around the house and reading a book in her bedroom. I do not think this place is good for her, but maybe that's just all of the bad energy around here. I don't think even the best cleansing could get rid of all the dark that has been spread around this place.

One afternoon I'm awakened from a small sleep by movement above. I probe with my leaves until I find the source of the sound. The witch is in her bedroom, sprawled naked on her bed. Her skin is wet from her exertion of pleasuring herself, her damp hair fans out around her on the pillow. One of her hands fondles her breasts, the other holds something pink between her legs. I can feel it buzzing through the wall.

I know I should give her privacy.

But I am mesmerized.

My attention sharpens as her breathing quickens and she lets out a throaty moan. Heat builds in my center; something I've only experienced with one person before.

I push my vine against the window and it cracks open enough for me to slither in. The pull to touch the witch's body is inconsolable. If I feel her, maybe I can understand the draw better. My vine slithers across the floor, much like a snake as she writhes on the mattress and murmurs her friend's name, her head turning back and forth on the pillow.

Naughty witch.

I wonder what it would feel like to touch myself like her. Only the fear of my roots ripping stops me. She moves so much that there's no way for me to do what she does.

Just as my vine winds its way up the post of the bed and gets within inches of her ankle, she cries out in pleasure, startling me. I pause, not wanting to draw attention to my sneaking vine. When she gets up and heads to the wash room, I begin pulling my vine back so she doesn't catch me. I barely pull my vine through the window before she closes it, latching it tight, before collapsing back into the bed and swiftly falling into sleep.

An hour later, as my thoughts swirl around themselves, I hear Andromeda talking. I zone in on her with my vines and find her holding the same strange contraption she brought down the first night I met her. She talks into it and I wonder what it could be, what kind of magic it holds. I listen in as her friend tells her about a sale. She argues with her friend for a moment before she finally agrees and hurries to get ready, all while muttering to herself about 'no surprise sales' and 'what are they up to?'.

When she is gone, I keep watch over the house. Even though she locked the door, there are ways to enter that she does not know yet. For a while, it is the same as always. Then something foul touches my vines on the south side of the house and I rush my mind in that direction.

Three masked people covered head to toe in black, weapons glinting in the sun, stand at the south entrance to one of the many hidden passages into the house.

"It's around here somewhere," a masculine voice mutters as he probes through my leaves and vines. His touch is putrid. I've met one of these people before. Hunters. But this one feels wrong. More wrong than normal hunters do.

My heart rate triples as I think of what to do. If it was one of them I have no doubt I could take them, but three skilled hunters? There's no way.

"Are you sure this is the right place, Strauss?" a woman asks. Her eyes dart all along the property.

"Of course I am. My source is reliable. They tipped me off yesterday that a witch had just moved in and that there were other monstrosities here. I did some digging last night and found the blueprints. There should be an entrance from the 1900s right around here." Just as he says the last word, he hits the stone that opens the door.

I ripple my leaves, hoping they get the hint to stay away. The woman shivers, but the others ignore it and grab flashlights from their pockets and head inside.

"I'm going to keep watch. I'll whistle if someone comes. Don't wander too far," the masked woman informs them as she stares at my leaves. I can see the unease in her eyes.

She may be worth saving.

The other two mumble their okay's before heading into the hidden entrance, the door closes behind them, but not before I manage to slither a few vines in behind them. The pinch of the door is uncomfortable, but I push the pain aside and follow them in for a few feet before I get to work.

The woman whistles outside as Andromeda and her friend's vehicles park in the front. She doesn't know that her compatriots won't be joining her escape. They're dead. Just like those vandals who dared enter this place long ago.

They put up a good fight and I lost one of my vines in the process, but it's a small sacrifice to keep Andromeda and her friends safe from these vile beasts. I spit on the ground thinking of the vile things these hunters would do if they caught the witch and her friends.

The masked woman whistles again and curses them before running off into the trees. I wonder how she will feel once she realizes that was the last she will ever see of them.

Chapter Twelve

Kira

When I walk into Sherman's, Grace is vibrating with excitement. I haven't seen her this lively in all the time I've known her. "Come, come." She urges me with her hands. "It's more magnificent than we could have ever imagined, dear. She's going to absolutely love it." She takes my hand, pulling me behind her.

I chuckle, hurrying to keep up with her surprisingly spry steps. She pulls me to the back of the store where a giant crate sits. "Wow. That's a LOT bigger than I thought it was going to be."

"Just wait." Her voice is giddy as she lets go of my hand and goes over to the box. Her face lights up when she looks at the contents. I rush over to see, unable to wait a moment longer. Inside sits the biggest raw amethyst I have ever seen. It was Merr's favorite crystal and Andi has probably over a hundred different variations laying around her house because of it. It was a no-brainer to get one for the memorial room.

My jaw drops as I take in the beauty of the speci-
men. Excitement sends my stomach turning and chills run
through my body as its power washes over me.

"You did good, dear," Grace says as she pats my arm. I
stand in awe as she hooks the amethyst to a cherry picker
her son let us reluctantly borrow. I may or may not have
threatened to turn him to stone if he didn't help us while
Grace was making us some tea. He was much more willing
to help after that. Not that I would do that, it being illegal
and all, but the threat was all I needed.

I look at her with tears in my eyes. "I couldn't have done
it without you." I give her a smile before helping her secure
the straps around the crystal. We situate the giant amethyst
in the back room with all the other memorabilia and stand
back, admiring our work.

"She's totally gonna cry," I tell Grace, moved to tears
myself.

"I don't think so. She's a very stoic young woman." She's
baiting me; we both know that Andi is going to cry like a
baby when she sees this room. But, I would be remiss to
not offer such an easy bet.

"Wanna bet on it?" I ask, my voice lowering. We like to
wage bets against each other sometimes. It's our thing.

"Kira Marie, this is not the kind of thing you bet on," she
chastises me. I raise my brow at her and she smirks. "I've

got 20 on her not shedding a tear." She holds her hand out to me to seal the deal.

"You're so on." I slap my hand in hers and head out of the store to give Andi a call to get her over here. I should feel bad for preying on Grace with our wager, but she's done it to me before so fair is fair.

The call connects and my ears start to ring at the number of trills that come through the line. I start to think it's going to go to voicemail when Andi finally picks up.

"Yea?" she answers, her voice hoarse as if she were sleeping.

"Were you taking a nap?" It's unlike her to nap, she's always so full of energy. Her grief has really been taking it out of her on top of having to move and get settled into her new house. It's a good thing we got this surprise done for her. She needs it. It'll get her away from that house and around things that bring her good energy.

Her yawn rips through the phone before she can answer me. "I was. I'm beat today, not sure why."

"Well, get out of bed, sleepy head. Grace is doing a big pop up sale at Sherman's today and she's got some really cool shit here." The lie falls heavily from my tongue, but it's the only thing Grace and I could come up with.

"Grace never does pop up sales, Kira. To be honest, I kind of just want to hang out at home today and get more acquainted with the house, maybe make some salves for the market next week in Dell."

"Aht, aht, aht. I know she doesn't usually do pop up sales, but she did one today, so get over here. You never miss a sale. Plus, now you have that huge house to fill with all the delightful things you get from here." She stays silent for a few minutes, so I carry on. "Don't make me drive all the way there and drag you back kicking and screaming. Think of it as a little retail therapy. It's always good for your soul to be surrounded by old things."

She sighs and I know I've won. "Fine," she whines. "Give me thirty minutes."

I squeal into the phone and do a happy dance before hanging up, then rush home to freshen up before she gets here.

I only live like two blocks away so I have plenty of time to get ready. Once I tear through my closet and dresser drawers and make my bedroom look like a tornado has blown through it, I settle on a teal bralette with matching bell bottom jeans and throw on a burnt orange loose-knit crop top with bell sleeves. I tend to go for colors that contrast my skin tone the best. The crop top may not be the best idea with how chilly it is outside but ever since I got my stomach blasted with my owl tattoo last year, I've grown to love showing off my body. Even though I hate the attention, sometimes it's not *so* bad.

I throw my hair up in a messy ponytail, knowing the curls are a lost cause. I give myself a once over in the full-length mirror by my front door and realize in my rush I forgot to put on shoes.

"Goddess damn it." I run back to my room and grab my orange Vans; they're reliable and comfortable. As I head out the door, I apply some lip balm and call it good. I don't have time for much else and even if I do go all out for this, Andi would clock it the moment she saw me.

I have to play this cool and casual. I'm *so* good at that.

Sweat beads my hairline and I curse my nerves. I send a prayer to the Goddess to give me strength and resilience to get through this and not mess it up before the big reveal.

Chapter Thirteen

Andromeda

I drag myself out of my ridiculously comfortable bed and head to the walk-in closet to pick an acceptable outfit. I'm covered in dust and sweat; the last thing I want to do is show up to Sherman's smelling like I currently do. A change of clothes will have to be enough, though, because I don't have time to shower.

Leave it to Kira to tell me about a sale last minute. There's no way Grace would put on a sale with no advertising. It's so unlike her. Something is going on there. Choosing to get to the bottom of this strange situation when I get there, I focus on what to wear.

I quickly choose a green and white striped maxi skirt and match it with an olive green tank, putting on a blackberry colored cardigan to fight off the chill in the autumn air. I throw my hair into a white claw clip that's shaped like a butterfly, arranging my hair so it looks effortlessly messy—which anyone who does an effortless look knows is such a load of bullshit. I swipe on some mascara, some blush, and a nude lip tint before putting on my turquoise and gold rings and a couple of necklaces. Once I'm satisfied with the look, I head downstairs.

I think about calling down to Hedera to tell her I'll be back in a bit, but I don't want to rub my freedom in her face while she's still stuck in her own living nightmare. Maybe I can find something for her while I'm shopping. But what would a cursed woman want besides being released from said curse? I shake myself from my dark thoughts and grab my tote bag before locking up the house and heading to town.

The drive to town is beautiful, and I'm glad I'm not distracted by GPS directions so I can take in the sights. The trees that line the road will be absolutely stunning come winter. When ice and snow cover tree branches, dripping icicles down, it's one of my favorite things. I bite my lip as I realize this is my life now. This is what I get to experience every day.

If only Aunt Merr was here to see how happy I am. I send her a thank you for the life she always provided for me. She never made me feel bad about my quirks or interests, just nourished them so I grew into who I am today.

Sighing, I turn the radio up to drown out my once again depressing thoughts. I know Hedera is the cause of my negative view on life currently, and I plan to help her as soon as I can.

I pull into the parking lot of Sherman's and see a spot next to Kira's Malibu. I don't see her outside, so I assume she's already inside browsing through the jewelry. I get out of my car and lock it with the key fob, turning ideas over in my head on what could be going on.

Arms wrap around my neck and I scream. Kira cackles as my heart rate accelerates to dangerous levels.

"Goddess damn it, Kira! I almost had a heart attack. You can't sneak up on people like that!" I look over at her and see her eyes slowly losing their otherworldly glow. *That bitch.* "You used your powers on me?" I whisper-shout at her.

"That was hilarious and you know it. I saw you driving up the road, so I just blended in." She shrugs her shoulders as she gasps for breath. "It's a new thing I learned when I was trying to get Brent a few weeks ago at his house. It's fantastic." She beams at me as she hooks her arm in mine.

"It's a bloody nuisance is what it is." I give her a stern look as she drags me along into Sherman's. "Why didn't you tell me you learned something new?"

She turns towards me, all signs of jest gone from her face. "You're not the only one who can keep secrets, Andi."

Then she smiles at me and opens the door, the bell on top jingling.

My stomach twists at her jab to the secret she knows I'm keeping. I know it's not fair, but it's not like I can just blurt out, "Hey, so there's a cursed woman stuck under my house and I need to do a spell to release her, but I don't know what will happen if I do. So, in the meantime, I'm feeding and watering her like a stray pet." That would go over swell.

The smell of old books and mothballs envelops me as I step inside of my favorite store and the stress starts to leave my body.

"I thought you two would be by today. I have something special to show you, Andromeda," Grace says as the door closes behind us. Her long gray hair almost sparkles in the sunshine that peeps through the dirty windows. Even though she's at least 80, no wrinkles crease her face.

Grace is a strange woman, with mystery shrouding her like a warm cloak. Although she's a prominent store owner in Bellville now, no one really knows much about her. She showed up here one day, opened up her shop, and has been here since. Questions and concerns circulated for a few days as we don't get a lot of newcomers, but they quickly settled and life went on as if she'd been here the whole time.

She winks at Kira before grabbing my arm and pulling me towards the back. I smile at her despite being wildly uncomfortable at everything that's happening right now. I come here to relax and browse at my leisure, not be bombarded the moment I walk in. Taking a deep breath, I recenter myself. This sudden attitude of mine is not welcoming and I don't want to be off-putting to Grace when she has done me no wrong. If she is dragging me along with her, it must be something very special.

She pulls me through room after room before she stops me abruptly and puts an old scarf around my eyes. When I try to fight, she shushes me and says, "Trust me. You're going to love this." She grabs my hands and guides me along. We walk a bit farther before we enter a room that's a little bit colder and smells of nag champa and dragon's blood. She pulls the scarf from my eyes and I blink into the light that emanates from a shrine to Gaia.

All around the room are mementos of Aunt Merr and the other witches of Bellville without revealing their names, only those of us who know the history will be able to understand their significance. There's a *Book of Undying* used by Mary Clearfield to heal those not ready to pass yet; a mortar and pestle used by Clair Montgomery when she helped Dr. Reynolds cure a nasty pandemic that broke out in town; and there's Aunt Merr's recipe book that's home to her famous chocolate chip and peanut butter cookies. I was wondering where that had gone, I thought it got lost in the move somehow. Now that I know where it is, I'll be making a copy of it pronto. The original can stay here, where it will get seen and potentially used by more people.

Tears spill from my eyes as I take it all in. Candles line the shelves with little bottles of ingredients interspersed. Bundles of sage and lavender hang upside down underneath those shelves. Books upon books of spell work fill three bookshelves. Aunt Merr's favorite shawl drapes across a papasan chair, the wicker on the bottom is frayed thin, but I know without sitting in it that the chair holds steady. It's the same chair I sat in on countless days reading in the sun. Aunt Merr told me it was her mother's favorite chair and sat on our porch since before I could remember.

I turn around and hug Grace, thanking her for her dedication.

"It's really no problem, dear. I knew you would love it. Kira's been helping me make it just right. You should give her more thanks than me. She did most of the work, after all." She gives me a pointed look before pecking my cheek and heading out the door.

Kira stands in the doorway, chewing her lip. She walks over to me once Grace is gone. I throw my arms around her neck when she gets close enough. "Thank you," I whisper. Her arms wrap around me and we stand there for several minutes, taking in the love and respect poured into this room for the women who poured *their* hearts and souls out for this town.

When I finally let her go, she sits on the floor as I wipe the tears from my eyes. I follow suit and just look around at everything. New things catch my eye as I look closer; it's as if it's ever-changing. Goddess, it *could be* for all I know.

"Listen. I know I told you I'd give you time to come to me when you're ready. But I can see whatever it is is really weighing on you. Just give me a chance, Andi." Her voice wavers and I look at her to see tears swimming in her eyes. "Whatever it is you don't have to do alone. You haven't since the day we became friends. I'm always here for you."

I swallow hard, debating on what to tell her. She's right, though. She's my best friend for a reason, and that reason is her undying loyalty. "It's probably better if I show you, but I want to look for some things here first, okay?"

Kira's mouth quirks up in the corners as she nods. We stand up and go browse for some new knickknacks, our fingers interlocked.

Chapter Fourteen

Kira

T hank the Goddess she's finally going to clue me in on what's happening that's got her so worked up. But now, as we browse the store, I can't help running through the different scenarios of what it could be...*again*. A massive black mold problem? A termite infestation? Oh, Goddess, don't tell me it's *bed bugs*. I shiver as I go down another aisle, absentmindedly looking at the different jewelry displays while Andi is somewhere, finding Goddess knows what for her house.

Get it together, Kira. She needs you to have a calm mind for this; you have to be her rock right now. No matter what the problem is.

"I'm ready to go," Andi says as she turns the corner, her arms bursting with the treasures she's found. I meet her eyes over her mound of stuff, and from the gleam in them, I know this isn't all she found. I only left her for five minutes, how did she find so much in such a short amount of time?

"Do I need to call Brent for you?" I ask, exasperated. But I'm not really annoyed with her, I just like to give her a hard time. She refuses to buy a truck, but insists on buying things too big for her car sometimes.

She bites her lip and I laugh while I pull out my phone. Mouthing a 'thank you,' she heads to the front to check out.

"What's up, boo?" Brent answers on the second ring, barking and growling sounds in the background.

"Uh, are you busy?" I definitely do not want to interrupt pack issues. I head to the front with my own items.

"Nope, just running a few drills before our monthly run. We had a few...*issues* last time and I want to avoid it again, if at all possible." He shouts a few instructions before asking, "Everything okay?"

"Yea, yea. Everything is fine. I think." I clear my throat. "Can you meet us at Sherman's?"

"*Andromeda Lynn*," he curses her name. "When is she going to learn? One of these times I'm not going to be available to save her ass from her own decisions. Does she know that?"

"Yep. We've both told her a million times, but you keep showing up." I hate to put the blame on him, because he's just trying to be a good friend, but he's such a pushover.

"Oh, eat a dick, Kira," he bites, his voice has a deep growl to it from his irritation, the approaching full moon drawing out his feistiness more and more as the minutes tick down.

I should know better than to entice him so close to the full moon, which is the day after tomorrow, but I can't help myself sometimes. "No, thanks, I'll leave that to you." I make my voice come out sickly sweet. "See you soon, wolf boy." I hang up before he can say anything else.

While Andi loads her bags into her car, I hold my hand out to Grace. "Pay up, ya hag." She chuckles before giving me my well earned money.

Fifteen minutes later, Brent pulls up with his company's big moving truck and two of his boys. They all glare at me as they load up a beautiful armoire, an arm chair, and a trunk.

"What did you do to piss them off?" Andi asks as she wraps her soft arm through mine.

I flop my head to the side, resting it on my shoulder to look at her. "You know me, I like to rile them up before they go on their pack run. It adds a level of unease in my boring life," I deadpan.

"Kira," she groans. "You promised me you wouldn't do that anymore." She tries to pull her arm from mine, but I squeeze it with mine, locking it in place.

"I had my fingers crossed." I grin at her before giving her a big sloppy kiss on her cheek.

She wipes it off as she glares at me. "Maybe I shouldn't show you today. You're in one of your moods and I don't think it's a good idea to have you see this when you're in this mindset."

Guilt eats at me. The moon doesn't only affect the wolves, it also makes every other paranormal being's abilities stronger. Even humans feel its effects sometimes.

"Sorry," I say, softening my voice. "I'll behave. But it's an exciting moon this month and the energies are all fucky." I rub the back of my neck as a pang goes through it. I should make an appointment with my chiropractor. The stress I've been under lately has collected right under my skull. Not that it will help all that much considering the stress still hasn't resolved itself.

"I know what you mean." She sighs. "I'm still going to show you. Just– please swear that you'll take this seriously and help me." Her eyes fill with tears and her lower lip wobbles. Damn, this is way more serious than I anticipated it being.

"Hey, I got you. Always, remember? Moon's be damned." I pull her in for a hug, some of my stress melting away as she relaxes in my arms.

"Yo, lovebirds, truck's loaded. Let's go," Brent barks as he jumps in the driver's seat, slamming the door closed.

My cheeks burn and Andi's face is beet red as she pulls away from me to head to her car. "See you soon," she calls over her shoulder.

I shoot a glare and a vulgar gesture at Brent as he smirks at me before heading to my own car and starting the boring drive to Andi's.

When we get there, the energy feels heavier. I brush it off, blaming the full moon...again. Andi tells the boys where to put the new stuff and they get it done in a few minutes before taking off. Brent promises he'll get with us in a few days and that he'll be safe during the pack's festivities before saluting us and heading out.

Hunters have been prowling through the woods lately where his pack is sanctioned to run by the Council. Wolf hides have become popular lately, along with their canines and no one has been able to figure out who's responsible for the uptick in sales. Just one more thing to worry about lately.

Andi fidgets in the foyer, avoiding my eyes, and I fight the urge to comfort her. I don't want to come off too clingy, even though I know she needs the contact. She takes a breath before blurting out, "You're never going to believe this if you don't see it with your own two eyes, but I need you to make me a promise." She walks towards me, her hips swaying, putting me in a trance.

"Anything," I breathe.

"Don't freak out. It's...a lot." She stops right in front of me. Her pupils are wide, and a sheen of sweat beads at her eyebrows and upper lip.

"I'm, like, the chillest person ever." I pretend to flip my hair over my shoulder and we both crack up laughing at the blatant lie. I'm glad my joke helped to alleviate some of her anxiety about showing me. I may be pretty chill, but we both know I have a love for dramatics.

Once she collects herself, she says, "Wait here for a few, okay?" I nod and sit on the couch as she heads down the hall. If she brings back a super rare spider or some shit I'm going to go nuclear.

Chapter Fifteen

Andromeda

I head to the kitchen trying to build up the nerve to ask Hedera for permission to show her greatest shame. Taking a deep breath, I walk into the pantry, quickly finding the loose board on the wall that opens the hidden door. I've had a lot of practice over the last few days. When it cracks open, the smell of dampened earth works its way through my body, helping center my resolve. I grab the flashlight I put on one of the pantry shelves for my visits to Hedera and make my way down.

She smiles at me when I reach the bottom. It's one of the most stunning things I've ever seen– how she can smile when I know she's miserable and in pain. She's confided in me a bit over the last few days; mostly the roots don't bother her, but every once in a while they pull in uncomfortable ways, threatening to tear her skin open like they did the first night I found her. She says that it's the worst when it's storming out and the wind is ripping through the vines.

Poor girl.

In addition to her telling me about the roots bothering her and how they work, she's told me more stories about her time growing up and that her favorite season is spring, when everything begins blooming and coming back to life after dying off and a long, cold winter. Her favorite color is aquamarine because it reminds her of mermaids swimming in the ocean, which she hasn't seen, but longs to visit one day. During our visits, I have found more and more things I like about her. Her voice is soothing, and her matter-of-fact way of speaking is refreshing in a world where people beat around the bush, so to speak.

As wrong as it is, I have started to find her attractive as well. Which speaks volumes about me given that I'm also attracted to my best friend. Two women who are emotionally unavailable in wildly different ways. But the way Hedera smiles at me every time I come down and is genuinely interested in the things I have to say and what I do on a day to day basis is comforting. Taking care of her needs and seeing her bright smile and shining brown eyes has become a highlight of my day.

Shaking my head to clear my thoughts, I move farther into the room. "I need to ask something of you." I bite my lip as I wait for her to answer. She doesn't, instead her smile fades, but she keeps her steady gaze on me. "Well, see, I need some help to reverse your curse and my friend Kira has magic too. Since I'm a solitary witch, asking other witches isn't really something I can do, but I am confident Kira and I can get it done," I ramble. She keeps watching me. "If that's okay with you, I mean. I don't want to, like, cross any boundaries or do anything you're uncomfortable with."

"That is fine, Andromeda. Whatever you need to do to free me, I would be most appreciative of." Her words are like silk encasing my skin, sending a shiver down my spine.

"Okay, cool. I'm gonna go get her and be right back, okay?" My voice shakes, whether it's from nerves or my growing attraction to her I can't be certain. She nods her head once and I head back up to the living room to get my best friend. Before I do that, though, I head upstairs to my spell room and grab my dagger. I have to ask something of her that I never dreamed of doing, and I'll need this if she agrees.

Kira is sprawled on the couch when I find her in the living room, throwing a ball up and catching it, keeping herself entertained while she waits with me. She's so patient and trusting with me, I don't know why I ever doubted I could trust her with something like this. I clear my throat so I don't distract her and cause her to drop the ball on her face. It wouldn't be the first time. While hilarious, the black eye she got from that incident caused people to stare at her more than normal and made her really growly. So now I try to be more mindful.

She catches the ball as it comes back down and sits up on the couch.

"Are you ready?" I ask. My nerves are threatening to give me an ulcer. I make a mental note to make some peppermint tea later to help with the upset stomach and to take a nice hot bubble bath in my giant garden tub.

Kira shoots up from the couch and stalks towards me. "Goddess yes." She grins and holds her hand out for me to take.

"Before I show you I need you to make a promise to me." She looks at me with a blank look. "A witch's promise, Kira." The seriousness of what I'm asking her isn't something either of us should take lightly. A witch's promise is binding; bad things happen to the one who breaks it. Once, someone went bald. Another time, they lost their teeth. Bad luck. A house fire that killed their favorite pet. Even death.

She knows the ramifications. She's heard the stories. If she does this, she has to stand by her promise, same as I.

Kira holds out her hand for me to take. I gasp in a breath at how easily she's ready to bind herself to me. My cheeks heat as I remember my earlier fantasy about her.

I clear my throat and pull out my dagger. I slice the palm of her hand before doing the same to mine, and we link hands as I say, "I bind thee to me in a promise of loyalty and an oath of silence." She repeats the words and I continue. "Whoever breaks the bind will have trouble tenfold." We repeat the words two more times. When we're finished, a burning sensation goes through both of our hands and we hiss as it gets more intense. It becomes unbearable, but just as fast it's gone. We pull our hands apart, the cuts healed, and in their place is a silver rose with a vine wrapped around the stem.

Fitting.

"Let's do this," Kira says, bouncing on the balls of her feet.

Goddess, I love this woman and her enthusiasm for all the shit I throw at her. I take a deep breath as I set my dagger on the counter before I lead her through the pantry to the hidden door. I turn on the flashlight and grab her hand to help guide her, but also to help keep myself calm that I'm actually doing this. I love Kira to death, but sometimes she overreacts and that could be detrimental to this whole situation.

When we get to the bottom, Kira curses under her breath, "What the fuck?"

"I've been waiting for you," Hedera says as her eyes meet Kira's.

"What the fuck does that mean?" Kira bites, and I gasp. Here comes the overreaction. Though, if Hedera said that to me when I first came down I'd probably respond the same way.

"Kira, calm down," I remind her, needing her to be chill about this so she can help me break the curse.

Her eyes are bright and her hair is getting frizzy. "No," she whispers. "That was a really fucking weird thing to say and I don't like it. I feel violated."

"I did not mean to offend you, Kira, friend of Andromeda's. It's just that I knew Andromeda would bring you here. I did not know when, just that she would. Now that you're here we can be properly introduced." Hedera looks at me expectantly.

I take another deep breath before giving introductions. "Hedera, this is my best friend Kira. Kira, this is Hedera. She was cursed by a witch a long time ago to watch over this house. As you can see, her body is sustaining the ivy outside." I give her a shaky smile, hoping she chills out a bit before the promise breaks.

She takes a moment to gather herself, coming to the same realization. "Okay. This is cool. We're cool. A cursed plant woman. Awesome." She looks at me with a raised brow. "I knew it wasn't a rat." She changes the subject, her way of deflecting a situation.

I laugh, the sound reverberating off the walls. "I can't fool you, can I?" If only she would realize my feelings for her and we could move past this awkward phase of our friendship.

"So, how are we going to free her?" Kira asks.

"Well, that's not so simple. I have the spell and sup-plies..." I trail off, not wanting to say the next part out loud.

"What is it?" Hedera asks. For someone who has been stuck here for as long as she has, she's awfully perceptive. I wouldn't have expected her to pick up on there being more I wasn't saying. Being away from people for so long, I would imagine one would forget social cues. Guess not with Hedera.

"I found the witch's diary who cursed you. She wrote down how to break the curse. She *also* wrote that she's not sure what the ramifications are." I pause for a moment and lock eyes with Hedera. "There's a very real possibility that you could die." We stay silent for several minutes while we contemplate what to do.

Hedera breaks the silence. "Even if I do not get to live and experience life to its full potential, I would like to be free if you would be willing to try." Her face is completely serious as she speaks. The trust shining in her eyes has tears forming in my own.

"I've never done anything like this. It could go wrong in a number of ways." I run my hand through my hair, accidentally pulling some strands from my butterfly clip, as I think of the possibilities. "I–I–I don't want to be the reason you die. I can't fathom having that on my conscience for the rest of my life." I bite my lip as I look at my dirty Converse sneakers.

"Hey," Kira says, putting her finger under my chin and lifting my face so I meet her eyes. "Would you rather try and fail or not try at all and keep her here where she doesn't want to be?" I don't respond, so she keeps going. "You are the most capable person I know to do this spell. You're an incredibly gifted witch. Every spell you try, you succeed at first go. You don't make mistakes. You don't miss. If this is up for a vote, you lose. She wants to be free and I know you can do it." She pulls me in for a hug and I sink into her arms. Her woodsy honey scent fills my nose, calming my nerves. I'm surprised she came around so quickly to the whole idea. She was really freaking out there for a minute, but I'm glad she did. I don't know what would have happened if she hadn't.

I pull away, wiping my sweaty hands on my leggings. "Okay, let's do this." I smile at the women and try to hype myself up for what I know is going to be an exceptionally difficult spell.

Chapter Sixteen

Hedera

I should have told Andromeda about the intruders when she came down to ask my permission to introduce me to her friend, but she was nervous and I did not want to make it worse. I want to make everything good for her. Relax her. Put her mind at ease. I can see how it works over-time and makes her second-guess herself.

Now that I am getting a chance at freedom, and I'm going to be free, how could I distract her with the news? It would make things go awry and I can't have that. Maybe that makes me selfish, but I make a vow to myself to tell her once she's finished. Even if it's with my dying breath.

The thought of my greatest dream coming true has me feeling excited and giddy, despite Andromeda's warning and the secret that I'm keeping. If what Kira says is true, though, I have nothing to worry about. I can be a normal person once more and walk barefoot in the grass, explore the forest as I did in my childhood, and do all the things I never got to do because of this damned curse.

But I can't stop thinking about what the ramifications will be. I know that magic comes at a price. Will I be strong enough to pay it? Will they?

The ladies go upstairs to get the supplies needed and I keep an eye on them and the outside. It's very difficult to separate my attention like this, but it helps my thoughts from spinning in directions I cannot control.

"Are you sure you want to help with this?" Andromeda asks Kira. She bites her lip, bouncing from one foot to the other.

"Of course I am. I wouldn't have made that promise if I wasn't taking this seriously. We can do this. Just tell me what to do." Kira wraps her in her arms, and I wish I could be between them. I yearn to feel their embrace.

Maybe it is because they are going to be my saviors, or maybe it is fate, but I know these two women are mine. I have never felt anything quite as intoxicating as their presences. When they are in the house I find myself drawn to watching them instead of guarding the outside against intruders. Thankfully it has not been an issue yet.

"Okay." Andromeda takes a deep breath. "I need to tell you something."

"What is it?" Kira steps back and looks in her eyes.

Andromeda takes a deep breath, squaring her shoulders as if she's going off to fight a great war. "When this is over, if it goes well, I want–" She cuts herself off, unable to get the words out. Kira stands there patiently waiting for her to finish.

When Andromeda's cheeks redden and her words fail, Kira says, "It's okay. We can do whatever. We have all the time in the world. You don't have to tell me right now." She tucks a piece of Andromeda's blue hair behind her ear before cupping her cheek.

Andromeda's eyes light up and I watch her confidence spark to life. She leans in and kisses Kira on the lips.

I've never been more proud–or jealous– in my entire life.

Chapter Seventeen

Kira

"I want–" Andi cuts herself off, struggling to find the right words. She's done this a time or two before, and I think I know what's happening, but I don't want to push it in case I'm wrong. I tuck a strand of hair behind her ear and cup her cheek. It's a small gesture to show her I want more without pushing too hard. She likes physical contact and I like touching her, so it's a win-win.

However, I didn't expect it to lead to her kissing me, which she's doing right now. She's never been one to make the first move, but I'm not complaining. Moving my hand from her cheek, I slide it into the dense blue curls at the back of her head and pull her towards me. I've been dying for this moment for years now. Our tongues collide and we both let out breathy moans. I bite her bottom lip and her legs go weak. I hold her up by pushing her into the wall behind her and using my body as leverage.

Some sense finally breaks through my shocked brain and I break the kiss to look into her mesmerizing green eyes.

"Are you sure about this? I don't want to do something that you'll regret." My voice comes out husky from how turned on I am.

"I've never been more sure of anything in my life." She pulls me back into her and we lose ourselves for several minutes, our hands roaming each other's bodies. I can't get enough of her. I want to rip her clothes off and just lay skin to skin and talk about life. We don't even have to move past that. That would be enough for me.

I want to worship her the way she deserves to be; like the goddess she is. I would sacrifice everything for this woman. She's had a spell over me for so long now and it's finally come unleashed.

When she starts trying to take my clothes off, I step back. Her eyes widen with confusion and hurt. "Hey, no, it's not what you think," I say softly, cupping her cheek again. "I would love nothing more than to take you to your room and ruin you, Andi. But I want to take my time with you." I run my finger down her throat and along her collar bone. She shivers. "I can't do that right now. We have a curse to break, remember?" Her cheeks heat and I press a kiss to her lips to prove my point. "You have no idea how long I've waited for this," I whisper.

"I kind of figured, but I couldn't bring myself to try. I didn't want to ruin our friendship. But I couldn't keep going on like there's nothing between us. Plus, Aunt Merr always said it was best to do spells with a clear mind. With you so close to me there was no way this would go well if I didn't get it out in the open." She smiles up at me and I'm fairly certain Cupid just shot an arrow through my heart.

I help her gather all the supplies we'll need and we head back down into the cellar. Hedera grins at us with a mischievous look in her eyes when we get back underground.

"What's that look for?" I ask. She's so strange. Not in a bad way, just intriguing.

"It's about time you two confessed your feelings for one another. You have only been around a couple of times, Kira, and I could sense the tension. Now that that's finally taken care of, can we get me free?" Her question isn't one of impatience, but curiosity.

"Yes," Andi answers. "We just need to set up and then we'll get started." She smiles at Hedera.

Before we start the process, though, I ask, "How do you know what just happened?" My brows scrunch together as I stare at this strange woman.

"I can see what's happening in the house through my vines." I stand gaping at her, unable to find words. "It's how I have kept this house safe for so long. I will explain more once this is over, if that is okay with the both of you."

No wonder I've been feeling like someone was watching me. Though, now that I know who it was, I feel silly thinking it was with malice.

"That works for me," Andi says before she starts working on drawing curse breaking sigils in the dirt.

I nod my agreement and set the candles around Hedera in a big enough circle for us to walk in. When that's done, I pour salt on the outside of the candles, making sure there are no thin spots. Something of this magnitude needs all the protection. While I pour the salt, I mutter my own invocation of protection. Gorgon's aren't generally granted magical abilities, aside from our petrifying gaze and some immortality, but somewhere in my lineage someone slept with a witch and blessed my line with more abilities than normal. Which is why I can turn invisible and do some spell work.

Andi finishes her sigils and exits the circle, grabbing a bundle of sage, rosemary, and cedar. She lights it and starts swirling it around the space and each of us. The smoke is thick and the smell is potent, but that's the point. We need to have our spiritual selves cleansed of all negativity before we begin.

Hedera starts having a coughing fit as Andi lights the next bundle and starts waving it around her, this one of bergamot, nettle, and sage. I meet Andi's eyes. It's time to begin.

We enter the circle and Andi hands me a piece of paper before putting Chewing John in Hedera's mouth. It keeps falling out every time Hedera coughs from the smoke. Andi looks her in the eye and says, "Hedera, I need you to gather yourself and bite down on this while you envision the witch who cursed you while we work, okay? I know it will be difficult, but it is imperative that you maintain her face in your mind."

Hedera nods, still coughing and sputtering. Andi looks at me like I have some sort of answer for the current dilemma. I shrug my shoulders, having no guidance to give. She's the knowledgeable witch who's been doing the research. I'm just the supportive...well...friend, I guess.

Andi moves back over to me. "We will envision breaking a thick stick with our hands as we repeat this three times while moving counterclockwise." She points to the first bit. "Then we will move onto the second part, envisioning the same thick stick, repeating the other words on the paper, and moving clockwise. Stay in unison with me as much as possible." She takes a deep breath. "Are you ready?"

I nod my head and Hedera takes a shuddering breath, finally composing herself enough for Andi to put the

Chewing John in her mouth. We begin chanting right away, not wanting to waste a moment.

"*Jasius asmoxius astranada. Sanctum juvius astroxal,*" we say in perfect unison. We step to the left with every syllable, keeping a purposeful pace. I do as Andi said and envision the biggest stick my brain can conjure and focus on breaking it.

After the first word, my body starts to vibrate. I look over at Andi and see her aura glowing bright yellow. I'm sure my hair is standing on end and my eyes are glowing their incandescence. Our energy grows with each word, dancing around each other before wrapping around Hedera.

My heart races by the time we're done with the first part, but we don't pause to catch our bearings before turning and beginning the second part of the spell.

"Unbound, unrestrained, we set you free. Come what may, come what be, you are now free."

Hedera begins screaming as we start the second part, but we don't stop. We can't. We're in a trance that must be seen to the end. Our magic guides us along on our path for redemption. As the end of the spell flows past our lips, a powerful ripple goes through the room, and our magic dissipates along with the candles flames.

The spell has been completed.

Chapter Eighteen

Andromeda

Kira and I take our phones out and turn the flashlights on so we can see in the dark. We find each other first, and she wraps her arm around my shoulders as we turn as one to see if the spell worked. My legs give out when our lights illuminate Hedera. She stands where we left her. The vines are gone. Her blonde hair falls in loose waves down to her waist. Her brown eyes shine as she takes in her unmarked, unrestrained body.

Kira kneels down next to me as we watch Hedera inspect herself. She spins in a circle and jumps up and down clapping her hands. "You did it. You really truly did it. I'm free," she cries out before coming over and tackling us to the ground for a hug. Given how she held herself while restrained by the vines, I didn't expect her energetic response to being free. I half expected her to clasp her hands, bow her head, and thank us in a very posh way. I like this much more.

When her skin touches mine, it's like lightning flowing through my body. But it's not painful, it's exhilarating. She makes me feel more alive than I've ever felt. She climbs off of us, apologizing for her manners. I miss her touch already.

"Don't apologize," Kira laughs. "I'd do the same damn thing if I was trapped here for as long as you were." She looks at me. "We did it, babe. We fucking did it!" she shouts before standing up, dragging me and Hedera with her. She wraps us in her arms and the electric feeling zings through me again.

I smile as I take in the happiness and celebration, but something feels off. Something feels wrong. Kira lets go of us and I duck my head, not wanting either of them to read my expression. The last thing I want to do is ruin the mood with a mere suspicion.

"I am starving. Could I please have something to eat?" Hedera asks, snapping me out of my tumbling thoughts.

"Yes, of course." I look at Kira. "Should we order some pizza? I could whip something up, but that will take a while."

"You know I'm always down for some 'za!" She leads the way up the stairs, Hedera between us.

I glance back into the space we worked the spell, a frown marring my face. I need to seek guidance from my cards and the Goddess.

Kira and Hedera sit at the island in the kitchen, and I tell them I'll be back in a bit. Kira looks at me with her brows creased and the corners of her lips turned down. I smile at her, telling her what I would like for a pizza. I figure if I distract her quickly enough she won't question it until later when I have time to explain. She nods her head, pulls her phone out, and starts a delivery order as I head upstairs to my spell room.

Lighting my incense, I focus on my mission: find answers on what went wrong. "Goddess, please guide my hands and cards to see what is coming. I need to know what went wrong. Thank you for giving me the strength to do what must be done. So mote it be."

I grab my tarot cards from the shelf, unwrapping them from their cloth before I begin shuffling them as I sit on the ground. Four cards fall out and I set the deck aside and flip them over. The Tower, a signal of collapse for the greater good; reversed King of Swords, misuse of power and manipulation; Knight of Swords, a need to think quickly, but not irrationally or unplanned; The Lovers, the need to be completely vulnerable with those who I trust, the beginning of something soul deep. The cards loom at me from their place on the floor.

I shuffle three more times. The same cards fall every time.

"Fuck."

Given the whisperings around town about the Council's dealings as of late, things are about to get really bad. Rumors have been circulating that they've been up to some shady shit, and if it has to do with these cards, we're seriously fucked. More so than we ever could have imagined. I pick the cards up and wrap them back in their cloth and set them in their spot on the shelf. Then I head downstairs to inform Hedera and Kira of my findings.

When I walk into the hallway, a noise from my bedroom causes me to pause.

"Are you guys up here?" I yell. No one answers. "Hello?" I ask, moving towards my room. The hair at the nape of my neck raises and goosebumps raise along my body. I try to take a breath, but it stutters in my throat.

"Calm down, Andromeda. It's probably nothing. Just breathe. You're not a fish," I lecture to myself. Aunt Merr always told me the cure to hiccups was reminding yourself you're not a fish. I found it to work not only for hiccups, but panic attacks when my lungs decide to stop functioning as well.

I suck in a lungful of air as I charge into my room, only to stop short when I see a woman in a beautiful emerald dress and long brown hair standing at the foot of my bed, her hand stroking my comforter. The woman looks up at me and smiles. It takes my breath away again. "Hello, child," she says, but her lips don't form the words.

"Gaia," I state, my voice shaking with awe, my legs tremble under the weight of her stare. I blink and when I open my eyes again, I'm sitting on the window seat. I look around and pinch the underside of my arm to make sure this isn't a dream. "Ow," I yip when it hurts.

"It is I, my dear. You have called upon me many times, and I have always answered but aside from the first time I visited you, I have not made myself known." Her smile fades and her face becomes serious. "You are in grave danger. You have consulted the cards and they have warned you, but I know how they can be misconstrued and not taken to heart. I will not stand by while one of my children suffers, no matter the rules."

"Danger?" I gulp loud enough for it to bounce off the walls. "From who?"

"That I cannot tell you. I have broken enough of my covenants by coming here. I will give you this before I leave you, not everything you see is what it seems. Don't be so quick to pass judgement. There are forces at work here that

are greater than I have ever known. Be safe and be well."
She begins to fade away and I call out for her to stay, to
explain more. But she vanishes right before my eyes.

Footsteps sound in the hallway a moment before Kira
and Hedera run into my room.

"What is going on?" Kira demands. I rip my eyes from
where Gaia was standing and take in these two fierce
women. Kira's eyes glowing and hair standing on end.
Hedera hides behind her, arms covered in vines.

How do I explain what just happened without sound-
ing like I need a loony bin?

"Andi, you're scaring me. We heard yelling and the energy in the house got really weird, more weird than before.
Are you okay?" Kira walks over to me, her hair falling back
into place as she sits next to me. Hedera grabs my hand, her
vines slithering back to wherever they came from.

"You're never going to believe this..." I look both of
them in the eyes. "...but I just saw Gaia."

Chapter Nineteen

Hedera

Andromeda's voice is full of awe and wonder as she tells us the tale of her Goddess coming to visit her. I have never been one to believe in higher beings, regardless of having been made to go to church until I was cursed. It always seemed a bit fake and pompous.

"Are you sure the herbs from the spell didn't get to your head?" Kira asks, her eyebrows drawn together as she studies Andromeda's face.

Andromeda rolls her eyes and huffs. "I didn't hallucinate seeing her." Her eyes meet mine as she asks, "Where did those vines come from that were covering your arms?"

I look down at myself to find the offending pests, but nothing is there. "What vines?"

"When you guys came in here, Kira was all amped up and you had vines covering your arms. Did you guys not see it?" Her eyes bounce from me to Kira and back again.

"No, I didn't. I'm sorry." I shake my head.

"I was in front of her the whole time," Kira explains. "To be honest, I didn't even know she was behind me after I took off running." She winces.

"Try to summon them," Andromeda instructs. "Focus really hard on bringing them out." Her voice is snappy and it makes me feel like I have done something wrong. I know she does not mean to come across that way, that she is just worked up from this supposed goddess coming to visit her, but it does not change the hurt pinging through my chest.

I do as she says, despite being hurt, but nothing happens. Her shoulders slump. "Maybe I *did* hallucinate it," she says, her voice quiet.

"You just did a massive spell, Andi. It takes a toll. Maybe you just need some rest," Kira suggests, rubbing her back.

Andromeda stands and begins pacing her bedroom. I avert my eyes from the bed, knowing if I look at it I'll turn the color of a tomato. She doesn't know I saw her the other day and I intend to keep it that way.

"There isn't time to rest. You don't understand. I came up here to seek guidance and that's exactly what I got. I shuffled my cards four times and every time the same cards came out in the same exact order. The Tower. The King of Swords. The Knight of Swords. The Lovers." She lists them off as she puts up a finger for each one.

"Then, as I'm heading downstairs, I hear a noise in here. I come in and there's Gaia." She gestures to the foot of her bed. "She tells me we're in grave danger and that there are forces at work far greater than she's ever witnessed before. How are we supposed to contend with that? What are we supposed to do?" Her eyes plead with us to understand.

I walk to the foot of her bed and breathe deeply. The smell of earth and musk lingers in the air, but Andromeda has those scents, too, sometimes. I want to believe her, but it is so unlikely to happen that it is hard to wrap my mind around. Especially when I've just been freed from my prison and elation is fighting off every other emotion.

"Okay," Kira draws out. "Crazier things have happened, and she is your preferred deity. But why now? After all the times you've called out for her help and guidance, why would she choose *now* to show herself?" She begins pacing as well while her mind whirls with the possibilities.

I argue with myself on whether this is the right time to bring up the hunters I killed. On one hand, it could be crucial to what Gaia warned Andromeda about. On the other, it could be completely coincidental. What are the odds? The truth prevails as always.

"Because we're in danger, Kira." Andromeda's words come out with a bite of annoyance as she waves her arms around. "Did you not hear what she said? There's a war coming and something is coming for us."

Before the argument can get more heated, the doorbell rings, making all of us startle at the loud noise. Kira rushes down and we follow to make sure it's nothing serious. When we see it's just the pizza delivery person, some of the earlier tension falls away.

Putting our argument aside, we sit along the island in the kitchen and eat some of this pizza stuff. It is delicious and makes my mouth water from all of the flavors. Unfortunately I am only able to eat one slice as my stomach starts doing somersaults, knowing I need to tell them about the hunters from this morning. Though, waiting for tomorrow when we're all rested would probably be best.

I take a steadying breath and take a step towards them before I can convince myself to wait a moment longer. "I need to inform you of something that may be pertinent to this situation." I fold my hands in front of me and keep my face blank, my shoulders squared, and my back straight. They both look at me, their eyes devouring me. I swallow hard before telling them. "Whilst you were gone earlier there was a group of people snooping about the house. They were hunters. Two of them got into a secret passage and I disposed of them. The third ran off into the woods and I have not seen her since."

Their jaws drop, Kira's eyes begin to brighten with their unnatural glow and Andromeda's hair blows around her in a phantom wind.

"And you chose now to tell us this, why?" Kira yells. I shrink into myself, taking several steps backwards.

"I–I did not want to distract you from the spell. Andromeda was so nervous to introduce you to me and then you started speaking about freeing me. I know spell work takes immense concentration and I did not want to be the cause of something going wrong." My voice quivers as I speak. I have not felt this small and weak since my father found out I was being courted by Ronald Toneldson's sister, Rory.

That was a horrific day. Back then women and men did not see each other romantically in the light of day. It was deemed dirty, unnatural. Two women being romantically involved ended up with both of them dead and their families shunned. I had no interest in the men of our village, but the day I saw Rory Toneldson, my body did things that I did not know it was capable of doing. Just like when I saw Andromeda the other day in this bed. My eyes dart to where she laid sprawled bare, touching herself.

We thought we were being careful. Stolen kisses down by the pond, hidden touches in the market. We thought people would think we were just friends. But Mary Clearwater was jealous and told my father what she had seen one day when Rory kissed my cheek. She said it did not look becoming of young ladies of our age.

My father broke many of my belongings in his rage when he confronted me. He would not have an outcast as a daughter. I was not permitted to see Rory again. Soon her family moved from our village. Word had gotten out that she had preyed upon me. I was seen as a victim. My father threatened me into silence. It is why a part of me did not mind watching his demise. I loved my father, don't get me wrong. But he was not a good man. He disregarded his wife and daughter's feelings like we were specks of dirt on his frock.

"You should have told us about the hunters, Hedera," Andromeda lectures. "We could have always waited to do the spell. If there are hunters already coming for us, this is way more dangerous than we originally thought." Andromeda stands with her arms crossed over her chest. Her eyebrows furrowed. Kira looks angry, her face reddened with her rage.

"I–I'm sorry. You have to understand that I've waited centuries to be freed from that place. I deserved to be freed. I'd done my time and wasted away for the sake of this house and some spiteful witch." I spit the last word.

"We're not saying that you didn't need or deserve to be freed, but if all of our safety is at stake, that takes precedence. It wouldn't only end badly for you but for us, too. Do you get that?" Kira asks, beginning pacing around the kitchen. Her words cut deep. In the short time since I've been free, her and I have grown closer and her attitude at the moment makes me think she is regretting it now.

"Of course I get it!" I yell. They are not hearing my words. They are not understanding me. "Do *you* get that I have been in a living hell for centuries? Watching people live their best lives, and their worst, while I could do nothing but lay there and watch? Never getting to experience anything for myself? Do you have *any* idea how miserable that is? How excruciating it is to stand back and watch people be beaten and murdered or make love or any of the other things I've seen and not be able to experience for myself?

"So excuse me for not wanting to wait to be freed once I found out you two could perform the spell. I handled the threat, which is what I was supposed to do under the curse. Now I'm free and I thought we could figure it out together." My words rush away from me, my arms flailing as I lose my temper.

I storm out of the bedroom before either of them can respond, needing space from the two of them. My legs carry me back to my place of imprisonment. Maybe I was always meant to rot away down here, never to live, to love, to just *be*.

My thoughts storm around my mind as I sit in the dark of the cellar, thinking about what to do now. How dare they sit here and assume I meant ill on them by keeping this from them. I always meant to help them. I always meant to stay.

But maybe they don't want me to. Maybe they thought I would go. Even if this is the only home I've ever known.

Chapter Twenty

Andromeda

Hedera loses her cool on us as we try to tell her she messed up. Her words flow through her like lava from a volcano, her arms waving around like venomous snakes looking for prey. When she storms off, Kira and I look at each other, both questioning where to go from here.

On the one hand, we would be stronger with someone else on our side. But on the other hand, we don't know her and we don't know what the ramifications are of the spell; if there will be any lingering side effects or abilities. Given how she didn't even know she had vines coming from her earlier, it would be irresponsible to have someone with us who is so unpredictable. If we had more time it would be a no brainer. But that's the one thing we don't have.

Clucking her tongue, Kira sits on the foot of my bed. "She has a point. We need to do this together. You of all people should know that no one comes into our lives for no reason. There's something bigger here."

"I know, Kira." I move away from her and go check the hallway before continuing. When I see the coast is clear, I shut the door and sit next to her. She turns to face me, tucking her legs underneath her. "I get it. But we don't have time to train her. She had vines coming from her. How do we know the curse actually lifted? What if it's going to backfire? Do you really want to get attached to someone who could be ripped away in the blink of an eye? Not to mention that she kept life or death information from us for her own interest. You know I trust people too easily. Fuck, look at Garret. Even knowing my shortcomings when it comes to trusting the wrong people, this doesn't sit right with me. Shouldn't we listen to that?"

"What if I train her?" Kira offers, her eyes lighting up. "I'll take full responsibility for her. She has nowhere to go, Andi. This has been her home her whole life. She has no idea what living in today's world is like and she has no money. We can't just ship her off and forget about her. If we do that, we may as well have left her cursed in the cellar." She puts her hands together in front of her mouth and gives me puppy dog eyes. "Please reconsider. This could be really good for us."

I don't like the idea of training a newly curse-free woman with no idea that she has magical abilities. But between Kira's begging, the fact that this is the only home

Hedera's known, and my pull towards her, I can't imagine turning her away to a world she knows nothing about. Plus, the idea of being away from her causes my heart to twist painfully.

"Fine. But we have to be thorough and super careful. There's a lot at stake here and we have very little time to get it done."

Kira screeches and claps her hands before tackling me back on the bed, hugging me and kissing all over my face. "Thank you, thank you, thank you. You won't regret this." She gets up off the bed to go find Hedera leaving me laying here for a moment, processing.

The only thing I'm certain of in this situation is that both of these women mean a lot to me and if my guess is correct, we're up against hunters that are being utilized by the very foundation that's meant to protect us.

Hunters are ruthless, highly trained killers of supernatural beings. Unlike the Council, hunters only need one reason to hunt you down: having abilities. They're our world's hitmen. For the Council to be using them against us...it's unheard of.

Sighing, I get up from my bed and head downstairs to find Kira and Hedera. Maybe training for myself wouldn't be so bad either. Aunt Merr taught me a lot on how to defend myself, but I haven't practiced in a long time. Not to mention, she never imagined I'd be facing hunters while using my defensive skills. I've never really needed them either, though. Bellville is small and tight-knit. The biggest issue we've ever had is an out-of-towner robbing a few of our stores. We caught him and he spent some time in jail before going on his merry way, never to be seen again. The idea of something tragic happening to the townsfolk is enough to induce a panic attack, but I push it down and channel the emotions into being proactive.

When I get downstairs, Kira's going from room to room, shouting Hedera's name.

"What's going on?" I ask, watching her frantically search.

"I can't find her. I figured she just needed space to cool off, but she's not here." She shrugs her shoulders, trying to play at nonchalance, but the worry on her face is evident.

"She couldn't have gone far. She's here somewhere." But where? I rack my mind on the possibilities. After a few minutes, I realize I know exactly where she is. It's been her place of solace for the last few centuries. I motion for Kira to follow me and we head back into the cellar. When we get down there, we find her curled into the fetal position in a far corner of the room.

"Leave me alone," she mumbles, not looking at us. Kira and I look at each other, guilt eating at us. We never meant to make her feel so bad that she only felt safe down here. We walk over to her slowly, not wanting to startle her. She doesn't move or react to the sounds of our movements, and I take that as a good sign.

"We're sorry for upsetting you, Hedera," Kira says. She reaches a hand out to touch her, but thinks better of it and lowers it back to her side.

"We got caught off guard about the hunters. We're raised to fear them and avoid them at all costs, so to find that they've been here looking for us when I just moved in...it's bothersome. Do you understand?" I ask, keeping my voice steady and soft.

She rolls over, her brown eyes watery and tear streaks track down her cheeks. "I do understand. I have had a few run-ins with hunters here over the years. Do *you* understand that in my excitement I thought it best to not mention it? Especially after already handling it. Do you find me to be so incompetent that I cannot handle myself?" She lifts her chin, her eyes shine their defiance.

"We understand, Hedera. I swear to you," Kira says, finally reaching out to touch her. "We're sorry."

"Very sorry," I agree.

Hedera looks between the two of us, gauging our sincerity. When she is adequately assured that we didn't mean to make her feel less than us or incompetent, she nods her head once. "I'm sorry as well. I should have told you about the intruders. Things have just been happening so quickly and, well, you know the rest. Thank you for coming to find me and make amends. I've never had someone care for me so much, let alone two." She smiles at us, tears shining in her eyes anew.

We pull her in for a hug before heading back upstairs to the comfort of the living room.

The next day I lose myself in my spell room for a while. Kira spent the night last night and slept in my room with me. Our hands roamed and our mouths explored, but we didn't go any farther than that, too tired to put forth the effort. Hedera slept in the guest room downstairs. I wouldn't have minded if she slept with us as well, but I didn't want to overwhelm her.

When I head downstairs to take a break, I find Kira and Hedera rearranging the living room. "What are you guys doing?"

"Making room for training," Hedera says as she helps slide the couch towards the wall.

"We have an entire backyard. Don't you think that would be better...you know, in case things go awry? Plus, I really don't want to have to clean up blood from this carpet. It would take *forever.*"

Kira's eyes get big as they bounce from Hedera to me. "I didn't think of that. That's a better idea. Plus, the grass will help ground us so we don't get too amped up."

I nod my head as Hedera looks at all the furniture they've already moved. "Don't worry about moving things back right now. We can take care of it later." I smile at her. I want her to know she's welcome here. Being around her, even since that first day, feels right. Having her *and* Kira here? Magical. My skin buzzes when I'm in their vicinity, and I fight the urge to touch them constantly.

They're mine.

I bite my lip as I glance at my feet before looking back at them and nodding towards the backyard. "Shall we?" They nod their heads vigorously and we head out, leaving our shoes by the sliding glass door.

Chapter Twenty-One

Kira

From the moment I saw Hedera rooted to the house, I was drawn to her. Her aura is a beautiful kaleidoscope of colors: reds, greens, yellows, and purples. The colors dance around each other, swirling around and through each other, mixing and separating.

I've never seen anything like it.

Then we freed her and she became this resplendent woman. Her dress hugs her small curves perfectly. I practically salivate whenever I look at her. Being in this house with these two women is like a feast for my eyes and I'm not mad about that whatsoever. Now we're all training together? It's teenaged me's dream come true.

The ground beneath me bucks and I fall on my ass while the other two laugh hysterically. I have got to get my head in the game.

I glare at Andi, knowing she's the one responsible for that move. "Not fair!" I shout.

"Don't let your guard down. Honestly, how do you plan on being in charge of training if you don't follow rule number one?"

Brushing myself off, I get to my feet. "Yea, yea, yea. Come on, let's do this for real this time." We get into our stances again. We've been training for a while now. Leave it to Andi to notice when my mind isn't in the game. The only issue I have with this training stuff is that I don't have a lot of abilities past turning invisible and turning people to stone. I wonder if the Council will forgive me if I turn hunters to stone...

Vines slither up my legs, breaking me from my thoughts. I bend down, tearing them off of me as I focus on blending into my surroundings.

"Hey! Not fair. I can't fight you if I can't see you!" Andi shouts as she makes the ground shake again, hoping to knock me over and break my invisibility. Too bad I'm already right next to her so the shaking ground has no effect on me.

"Life's not fair, little witch," I whisper in her ear before rushing backwards as she spins around, swinging her fist. Hedera looks on, her lips tugging up, her eyes bright.

I break my invisibility and put my hands in a T shape to signal a time out. "Your turn." I gesture to Hedera.

Her eyes get big and she shakes her head. "I'm not ready. I would rather watch for a while."

"No can do, princess." I saunter over to her. "We have no idea when shit is going to hit the fan, so we need to get you prepared as fast as possible."

Her breathing accelerates. Andi and I move towards her, rubbing her shoulders as we reassure her. "It's okay. We're here to help. Just focus on what you want to do," Andi says softly. "I saw the vines, Hedera. You have some sort of ability. We just have to figure it out."

I look at Andi, and if we were in a cartoon, hearts would be popping out of my eyes. She's so caring.

"If you're sure," Hedera says, her voice barely above a whisper.

"I am. You can do this." Andi gives her a soft kiss on the cheek, the sight doing unholy things to my body.

Clearing my throat, I take Hedera's arm and lead her to where I was standing previously. I stay close, but far enough I won't be in the danger zone. "Remember to focus. You said you could see and hear through the vines on the house. Envision that in your head. Make the vines be a part of you again," I say to her.

She looks at me, worry etched on her face. "I don't want to do that. I finally got free of them." Her voice waivers and her eyes rim with silver.

"You *are* free of them. Now they're a part of *you*. You control them, not the other way around. Utilize that. Take all of that pain and loneliness and siphon it into using them to do your bidding."

Nodding, she closes her eyes and lifts her trembling hands. Andi gives her time to focus and collect herself. When the first bud appears on her arm, Andi sends a wave of her own vines towards her. But they don't stand a chance against Hedera's. Faster than we can blink, her vines have destroyed Andi's and have her hog-tied on the ground. Hedera drops her arms, panting, and rushes over to Andi to make sure she's okay.

When we get the vines off of her, she's smiling and tears of joy flow down her face. "You did it! We knew you could!" She wraps both of us in a hug and everything feels right in the world.

We spent the next few hours practicing our different skills. I found out that I can harness my magic into balls of energy and shoot them at a target. Sometimes it explodes whatever I'm aiming at, and other times it makes it float. I have no way of knowing which is going to happen. It's something I will be working on in our next training session. Once the idea of summoning an ounce of magic makes us want to cry we end our session and go take showers, falling on to any surface we can find before falling asleep.

The next day we load up on a bunch of protein and salads to help us replenish the magic that didn't come back with our rest.

"I did not think that using magic would be so exhausting," Hedera says after swallowing a mouthful of kale drizzled with oil and seasoning.

"Usually it's not," Andi explains. "Magic is a natural part of people like us, it's as easy as breathing. However, now that we're pushing it to its limits and doing things we don't normally, it takes more of a toll on our bodies."

"That makes sense," Hedera says, nodding her head. "Are you guys ready to head back out there?" She practically vibrates in her seat.

"Are you sure you're up for another round of training already?" I ask.

"Oh yes. You even said that we do not know when things are going to get dangerous, so I think it is best if we train as much as possible." She smiles at me and my heart flutters in my chest. Just like Andi, I'll give this girl whatever she wants.

"Let's go, then!" Andi says before I can manage a breath.

"We should go to Pete's for supper," I suggest, knowing no one is up for cooking tonight after exerting ourselves yet again today.

"Oo, I haven't been there in ages," Andi says, her tone giving away how excited she is to not have to cook another meal today. "I think I still have some of your outfits from when you stayed over at my old apartment. I think they might fit Hedera, too. We can all go shower and get ready. We reek of magic and desperation," Andi says.

"Shower...together?" Hedera says, her eyes wide and cheeks red. Andi and I share a look before we burst out laughing, which only serves to redden Hedera's face more.

"I mean, I'm game. It's better for us to all stay together anyway. The only person we haven't seen naked here is you, Hedera." I smile at her, but it's anything but wholesome. My teeth sink into my bottom lip as my eyes travel down her body.

"Kira, you're going to scare the poor girl off," Andi chastises.

I throw my hands in the air. I wasn't the one who suggested it, just the one who isn't too timid to go through with it. Naked women? Come on. There's no way in the Underworld that I would pass that up.

"It really is okay," Hedera says quietly. "I would like to do that if you two are okay with it." She turns her head up towards the sky as she breathes deeply through her nose. Once she's composed herself, she meets both of our eyes. "I've been alone for a long time. I miss human interaction and if I continue to live in fear and uncertainty, I'm not sure I will get to experience everything I want to...given that we have no idea how long of a life I have to live."

I rub the back of my neck as her words sink in. Andi looks over at me, her chin wobbles and her nose is turning red from Hedera's sobering words. I have to take control of this situation so we all get what we want. Andi is too submissive to do it and Hedera has no idea *what* she's doing. They both startle when I clap my hands together. "Okay, group shower it is." I look at Andi. "We'll use the upstairs shower. It's big enough for all of us." That thing is massive and has three different shower heads. It's literally made from a dream or something with how beautiful it is.

"Are you sure about this?" Andi asks, leaning in close to me so Hedera doesn't overhear. "You don't think we need to slow things down a bit?" Her eyes bounce over to the new member of our group.

"Andi, she's the one who suggested it. Plus, she makes a good point. We *don't* know how long she has. She could live forever or be dead next week. Life is fleeting and we have no way of guaranteeing anything."

Her chest rises and falls as she sighs, my eyes drawn to her large breasts. I need to be on my best behavior or I may just scare Hedera away after all. But this damn moon has my wild side ready to take over.

Chapter Twenty-Two

Hedera

I did not think I would have powers after the curse was lifted. I imagined going back to the girl I was all those years ago. Boring. Average. But it kind of makes sense, if I think about it hard enough.

When I was younger, I was drawn to the forest. Nature felt like home to me more than our house did. Mother would get so angry at me for skipping lessons to go explore. She'd lock me in my room for weeks at a time, only opening it for my tutor and to bring me meals. She said it wasn't right for a young lady to be milling about in places she didn't belong.

But my soul yearned for it.

One time whilst I was out in the forest, I came across a lone wolf. I knew wolves traveled in packs, but at the time it did not seem odd to me that this one was alone. We locked eyes and it lowered its head, showing its teeth in a smile. When I told Father about it later he said that it was snarling at me and that I needed to stay closer to home. But I knew he was wrong, and I knew I couldn't tell him the rest of what happened.

The wolf and I spent the afternoon roaming the forest until we found my favorite creek in a clearing a few miles from my house. We sat on the bank while the water burbled over the rocks and I let it soothe my bare feet. I did not wear shoes in the forest, choosing to be closer to nature without the confines of shoes to separate me from the grass and leaves. The wolf laid its head in my lap once I was settled and fell asleep. I pet its coarse fur and found a softness underneath that I was not expecting.

When it awoke, I shared some of my dried meat with it. It seemed very thankful to have the small snack. Before it meandered on its way, it licked up the side of my face and met my eyes one last time. I knew I would see it again. Our souls were connected. Then I was cursed and I never saw the wolf again. It's what kept me sane all those years, thinking about how the wolf would still be carrying on, waiting for me. Even if I know that is not the truth.

When the vines erupted from my body during our first training session, I felt like I did that day in the forest with the wolf. It was wholesome and right. This is who I was always meant to be. But it is exhausting using magic that you did not know you harbored. And smelly.

Which is why we're now heading inside to shower...together. Exhilaration sends a shiver down my spine as we walk through the yard, all holding hands. My body buzzes with energy even though I just spent it all in training.

I've never showered before, but I have seen the other inhabitants do so. However, none of them used all the features this shower has. There are jets everywhere, shooting us with water from every direction as we try to soap up our bodies.

"Kira, I know you're having a blast, but it's kind of hard to get clean when the water is just taking the soap off immediately," Andromeda complains while Kira spins in a circle, enjoying the onslaught of water.

She opens her eyes and looks at us. I am sure I look like a drowning dog because my hair won't stay out of my face no matter how many times I push it back, and the water hits me in the face when I do manage to clear it of hair, making it hard to breathe.

"Sorry," she says, grinning at us as she moves to the controls on the shower wall and turns off some of the heads. "I've never seen such a bad ass shower before. I thought there were only three shower heads. This is *way* better. I'm seriously in love with it." Her pupils are huge and, surprisingly, it is not because she has two naked women in front of her.

"It's fine," Andromeda says. I don't say much because I'm not sure what to say. My nerves are eating away at my stomach and I fight myself to be as open with my body as they are.

Sensing my mood, Kira looks over at me. Her eyes travel down my body as they so often do. She scoots over to me and asks, "Do you want me to wash your back? Andromeda can do your hair. She gives the *best* scalp massages." I nod, words escaping me. I don't want my voice to give away how nervous I am since this was my idea.

She twirls her finger, signaling me to turn my back on them. I do as she says and soon the smell of lavender blooms and her hands are massaging into the muscles of my back. The smell of roses follows as Andromeda steps in front of me a moment before her hands sink into my hair. I let out a moan at how good their hands feel on me; the tension in the room thickening with the steam.

One of Kira's hands leaves my back and then I hear them kissing. Before I can overthink it, I turn and join them. I steal Andromeda from Kira's mouth first, until she gets antsy and steals me from Andromeda. Our hands begin roaming over each other's bodies and I've never been more exhilarated in my life.

After a few moments, I'm not sure whose hands are where or whose mouths are on what. We're a tangled mess of limbs and tongues and teeth. The idea of washing is long gone from any of our minds.

"We should take this to the bed," Andromeda suggests. We untangle from each other enough to be able to walk, but entwined enough that we don't lose any of our spark.

When we get to the bed, Kira takes charge, which is fitting given her personality. "Andi lay here." She points to the spot and Andromeda lays down. "Hedera, you go here." I lay where she tells me, ever obedient. Her eyes are bright, her pupils wide, her smile stretches from ear to ear. She's in her element. She's exactly where she's always wanted to be.

As her hands travel up our thighs, we both shiver. Electricity zings through me a moment before our legs fall open simultaneously, resting on the other's. Kira's hand finds home and she pauses. "Are you sure?" she asks us. We both nod our heads, eager to have her hands on us. "If at any point it becomes too much, or you want to stop, say so." She looks at me as she says this part.

I appreciate her thoughtfulness as this is my first time ever doing anything of this sort. But I don't need her to be gentle with me. I will not break so easily. "Please touch me already." My voice shakes with my demand. I don't know where I got this brazenness from, but I like it.

Kira chuckles. "You're a dirty, eager girl. I like that." She smirks as she begins rubbing our honeypots at the same time. She begins slowly and I writhe under her touch.

Needing to do something with my body, I lean over and grab Andromeda's face. She greets me with glassy eyes and a moan. Our mouths collide, our hands grabbing for whatever we can reach. Kira's movements become faster as we lose ourselves in our lust.

Andromeda pinches one of my nipples as the wave building inside of me crescendos. I lose all sense of reality as I fall into a raging sea. Andromeda follows after me, and I'm grateful for the company. When we get our wits about us again, Kira is sitting back on her knees, a smug look on her face. "That took less than a minute. Damn, I'm good." She brushes her shoulder as if there are dust particles there.

Andromeda rolls her eyes as I giggle. My body is still floating in my bliss. I never want to lose this feeling.

Kira's eyes meet Andromeda's. "My turn." They switch spots and Kira turns to me. "Sit on my face."

My eyes go wide and my eyebrows draw together. "What does that mean?"

Kira laughs, but I know it's not malicious. "Come here. Throw your leg over me and sit on my chest to begin with." I do as she says. "Good girl. Now, scoot up until your pussy is over my mouth and then sit all the way down."

"How will you breathe?" I ask, concerned that I will accidentally suffocate her.

"Don't worry about me, princess. If I die eating your pussy, I'll die happy." She doesn't give me time to move, instead she grabs my hips and pulls me where she wants me. I barely have time to brace myself on the headboard before her tongue starts working its own magic.

I look back and see Andromeda watching. Her bottom lip is tucked between her teeth and her nipples are taught. When she sees I'm good, she bends down and begins doing what Kira asked of her. The moment her tongue meets Kira's lady parts, Kira lets out a moan that sends a delicious vibration through me. I pinch my nipples between my fingers as I begin to move my hips with Kira's movements. My head falls back as the wave begins to build anew.

"That feels so good," I moan.

Kira pushes me up a touch and says, "Your pussy tastes heavenly." Then she pulls me back to her mouth and continues to feast as my juices coat her face. Her moans come faster as Andromeda works her behind me and then I hear a new sound. This one sounds squelchy.

I look back and find that Andromeda has inserted a couple of fingers into Kira and is pumping them rapidly, her forearm muscles are tight as she works. I want to learn to do that.

Before I can voice my thoughts, Kira sucks a part of me into her mouth and nibbles on it just right. My body bursts into flames as my release finds me again, vines shooting from my arms and wrapping around the headboard. My body goes lax and I fall to the side, satiated. The vines fall away as I come down from my heightened pleasure. Moments later, Kira cries out in elation and Andromeda crawls up the bed to lay between us.

Chapter Twenty-Three

Andromeda

I f I had known that it would be this easy to get everything I wanted with Kira, I would have told her sooner. Having Hedera in the mix is even better. My heart feels full and my body feels relaxed. If only I could get my brain to follow suit.

I was worried that Hedera would be freaked out and never want to talk to us again when Kira agreed to showering together, but what we just did made all of my insecurities and worries fade away. At least we know where we stand now; together, all of us.

When we finally regain the energy we spent fooling around, we get dressed and head out to Pete's for some bomb burgers and fries. The perfect food for hangovers and to refuel our magic.

Most people say you should eat fruit and vegetables and have a clean diet, but after eating super healthy for breakfast and lunch, I feel like a nice greasy burger isn't the worst thing in the world.

Once we're all dressed and back in the same room, I ask Hedera if she's okay. "Yes," she says, her voice lacking any hesitation. "I've never been more okay in my life. That was..." Her words trail off as her face reddens.

"Amazing. Awe inspiring. The most mind-blowing orgasms of your life?" Kira suggests. Her smug smile says all it needs to.

"Is that what it's called? I have never had one before, so yes, it was," Hedera says. Her eyes meet mine as Kira and I try not to burst out laughing at her words again. "I would like you to teach me what you were doing to her earlier, if you wouldn't mind." Her words sober my want to cackle into the night, reminding me she's not as adept to the world as we are. "I'm not skilled in this and I would like to get better." Her lips turn up and my heart melts.

"Of course, yea," I agree. "It's all about the flick."

"Alright, ladies. If we want to get some food we need to leave now and we can come back to this conversation later. Otherwise, I'm going to drag you both back to that bed and we aren't going to leave it until tomorrow." Kira's voice is hoarse and serious, as if she's holding herself back from releasing the very base parts of herself. My cunt clenches in response, and if Hedera's soft gasp is any indication, hers did too. Kira chuckles to herself and stalks out of the room, my eyes captivated by the self-satisfied sway of her hips.

The car ride to Pete's is filled with giggles and jokes. For them it's because they're enjoying themselves. I am, too, but I have a nagging sensation in the back of my mind that hasn't gone away since Gaia left yesterday. I'm on edge, not even amazing orgasms able to make it fade. But I'm trying to be a good sport about it all.

Hedera is amazed at Kira's car and how fast we go down the highway. She makes it so easy to forget that she's not experienced everything we have. She asks a million questions about the car and our phones and the music playing softly on the radio.

She tells us about the music she used to listen to and sang us an old lullaby her mother used to sing to her when she was in one of her rare good moods. Her voice is hauntingly beautiful and sends shivers down my spine.

When we get to downtown Belleville, her eyes widen at all the neon lights and big store fronts. "We used to have a small market here once a week. There were only four buildings: the constable, the post, the doctor, and a tailor. All the other goods were sold by the people who lived near. Father brought me with him sometimes and would buy me special trinkets. Mother would get angry at him for spoiling me. She said that there was no need for a lady to go to the market and that buying me all the things that caught my eye would spoil me rotten.

"It never made sense to me, though, because Father was one of the few men shopping in the market. The women did most of it. They even sold the items they produced, whether it was sewing or produce or milk from their cows. Sometimes I think Mother didn't know much about the world at all and *she* was the spoiled rotten one. But Father just said 'Yes, dear. I understand.' It was a repeating cycle at least once a month." Her voice is far away as she tells us, as if she's reliving the memories.

"Your father seems like he meant well. Too bad his dick did more thinking than his brain there at the end," Kira says as she parks her car in a municipal lot.

I slap her arm. "Kira! You can't say shit like that," I chastise. What is with her today?

"It's alright. She's not wrong. He is the reason I was cursed, after all." Hedera smiles at me when I turn to look at her. There's no hurt or anger in her eyes. Only happiness.

"I really like her. She's tough as nails, as they say," Kira whispers to me. I roll my eyes before getting out of the car.

The autumn night is chilly and the leaves are falling off the trees, just in time for Halloween and Samhain next week. They crunch under our feet as we walk the block to Pete's. It's a soothing sound and reminds me of trick-or-treating as a kid with Aunt Merr.

"What are we doing for our Samhain bash this year?" I ask Kira. We're all walking arm in arm down the sidewalk. People look at us in annoyance because we refuse to part, but we're safer this way. Any of the people out here could be hunters.

Goddess, I really need to chill on the paranoia.

"Don't ask me," Kira says in an off-put tone. "Brent is the party planner of our group, you know that. If you don't ask him for ideas he'll whine like an injured dog and hold a grudge for eternity."

"He's our best friend and an alpha werewolf," I whisper to Hedera, not wanting her to be left out. Most of the people in Bellville know that supernatural beings exist, but we try to keep a low profile regardless, hence the whisper.

"I appreciate you telling me, but I already know who he and his pack are. They helped you move in and then delivered more things the other day. The house smelled like dog for a while after they left," she says in her stately tone, causing Kira and I to crack up laughing, earning us more weird looks.

Before we can explain more we arrive at Pete's. It's packed, but there's one table left. As we walk in Patty the hostess greets us with a warm smile. "Kira! Andi! It's been ages!" she yells over the cacophony of the busy restaurant and pulls us both in for a hug. She takes a step back and looks Hedera up and down with a motherly smile. "And who might this be?"

"This is Hedera. She's a cousin of one of Brent's boys," Kira lies effortlessly.

Hedera glances at her before looking back at the woman and curtsies. "How do you do?"

We look at her as if she sprouted horns, not realizing we should have gone over etiquette before leaving the house. But Patty laughs instead of making her feel awkward; she's used to Brent and his pack's shenanigans so this is nothing new for her. "Aren't you just a delight!" She turns to Kira and me. "I have a table right this way for you lovely ladies. Hopefully no one else will be joining you?"

"Nope, Brent is busy with work stuff." I wink at her so she knows what I'm talking about.

"I hope it's not too serious," she says, which is our key-word for 'I hope they're safe and don't get killed like those other wolves did.'

I grimace, but she's already turned away and headed towards a table at the back of the restaurant. "I'll let Pete know you're here. You know he loves to come say hi to you girls!" She hurries away to the kitchen.

Pete cooks all the food that comes out of his kitchen. Poor man never gets a break. We're always trying to get him to take a vacation, but he just asks who will take care of all the hungry people of Bellville.

Annie, one of the main waitresses, comes over and says, "What can I get you ladies to drink?"

Kira orders a chocolate martini, I order a strawberry daiquiri and Hedera looks at us with wide eyes.

Shit. I keep forgetting that she doesn't know how this works. I kick Kira under the table and she looks at me with a raised brow. I nod over to Hedera and I swear I see the lightbulb go off above her head.

"What was that one drink we had last month at Streakers?" she asks us. Hedera thankfully is incredibly intuitive and puts her finger to her mouth as if she's thinking really hard.

"Didn't it have, like, blackberries or something in it?" I suggest as I watch Hedera's reaction to what she could possibly like.

"No, it was sweeter than that," she says in response, her face scrunching.

"Maybe a watermelon fizz?" Kira questions and Hedera nods her head, snapping her fingers.

"That was it! It was so good." She looks at Annie and snares her eyes. "I will take a watermelon fizz, please."

Annie's eyes glaze over before she nods her head. "Sure thing. I'll get those in and be back for your orders in a few minutes." She smiles, but her eyes are clouded as she walks away. I look at Kira to see if she saw it. Given her furrowed brows I'd say she did.

"What was that?" I ask, careful to keep my tone even.

"I'm not sure what you mean. I just asked her for the drink Kira suggested. Was that not what I was supposed to do?" She wrings her hands together and begins fidgeting in her seat.

"No, it's not that, Hedera," I say calmly, reaching over to grab her hand. "You did something to her when you asked for it. Did you not see the way her eyes got cloudy and glazed over?"

She grips my hand hard. "I didn't notice anything different. Did I do something?"

"Sure looks that way," Kira chimes in. "Especially if she brings you that drink since they don't serve it here. Though, I'm sure it's not too hard to make." She shrugs before sitting forward and crosses her arms on the table. "So, we have vines and mind control. This could be interesting."

I kick her under the table again, this time she lets out a satisfying 'ow.'

Chapter Twenty-Four

Kira

Well, I'll be damned. Hedera not only has amazing control over her vines, but she can control minds, too? I think we're in pretty good hands given the circumstances...if what Gaia told Andi is true. Not that Gaia would lie to her, it's just that Andi's been under a lot of stress lately and sometimes she gets a little off when she's not her usual calm self.

A runner brings us our drinks and leaves without saying a word, including the watermelon fizz. Hedera tries her drink and her eyes light up as it hits her taste buds. "Oh, wow. That is so good," she cries out.

"I'm glad you like it." I smirk at her. I know something else she likes, too, and I can't wait to go for round two when we get back to the house. Distracting myself from my perverted thoughts, I ask, "Can you try the mind control thing on me? Since it worked to get the drink, let's see if it was a one off or something that we can actually use. Get me to do something I wouldn't normally do, like

The Chicken Dance in the middle of the dining room or something." I shrug when Andi looks at me like I'm nuts. "What?"

"We don't know what it does exactly, Kira. What if it makes you do The Chicken Dance forever? What if there are other unknown consequences?" She sighs, throwing her hands into the air. "I swear you have the self-preservation skills of a toddler sometimes."

"Do you have a better idea on how to test it? Shall we put an ad out for willing participants to be the test subjects?" When she doesn't answer I keep going with my point. "I have the best witch in town as my..." My words fail me. I'm not sure exactly what we are. We've proclaimed our feelings for each other and hooked up, but does that mean there's an *us* now?

"Your what?" Andi asks, her eyelids drooping over her eyes. Damn, she's sexy as hell. I rub the back of my neck as I try to think of words.

"She does not know what to call you anymore," Hedera explains, her voice husky as she reads my emotional conundrum. "Before yesterday you were just friends, but things have now gone beyond the thin line you two were tiptoeing before," Hedera finishes in her all-knowing tone.

How the hell does she know this?

Andi looks at me, her eyebrows raised. "Is that true?"

I clear my throat. "I mean– well–" I stutter, words failing me again. They both fluster the ever living piss out of me. It's something that's never happened to me before. I'm always suave with the ladies...and men, unfortunately.

She grabs my hand, interlocking our fingers. Sparks shoot through my body at the contact. "It's okay. I can be whatever you want me to be. Friend, lover, girlfriend. You choose and I'll wear it with honor." Her eyes radiate with her sincerity.

Before answering her, I pull her in and devour her mouth. When I pull away, I look deep into her pretty green eyes. "You're mine in any capacity that you'll allow." She looks over at Hedera and I realize I need to point out what is so obvious to me. "Both of you. Until my dying breath and beyond." Tears well in her eyes. She tries to blink them away, but it's no use. I hear Hedera sniffle from across the table and look over at her. She's as much of a mess as Andi is.

"Are you okay with this?" I ask her. I don't want either of us to pressure her into something she's not okay with.

"Yes, very much so. Since you both walked into the house I knew we would be *more*. I just did not realize how much more. But I never want to lose what we have. I feel whole, and I have never had the pleasure to feel this way before." She gives us a watery smile.

"Me either," Andi and I say simultaneously.

A moment later, Annie comes back to take our food order. The rest of dinner is spent making plans for the rest of our lives.

If only things could have stayed so peaceful.

When we're finished with supper, I pay the bill and we head back to the car. As we round the corner to head to the parking lot, a scuffling sound comes from the alley to our left. It's a dodgy alley between two dilapidating stores. I look at Andi, who paused the moment we heard the sound. Her eyes are wide, pupils blown, and her breathing is a bit erratic.

I knew something was going on with her. I knew she was putting on a front for us. She's worried. I am, too, but I've never let fear deter me from living my life.

Okay, only when it comes to her, but still.

A movement from Hedera catches my attention. I glance at her and see her vines at the ready, but hidden enough that any passerby won't see them. "Something is coming," she says and gets in the stance we showed her.

"Andi, I need you to snap out of it," I tell her with a bite to my tone. I can't have her not ready. We need her and if she stays frozen she's a liability. I shake her, but she keeps staring at the alley. "Andi, please. Snap out of it." The energy shifts and whatever was in the alley moves into the open. A shield goes around us, the gray sheen deflecting the street lights.

I turn and stand in front of Andi. No matter what I expected to see, it couldn't have been further from what's in front of us.

"Hello, ladies," Alexandria DeMarco, second in command on the Council, says from where she stares at us with her black eyes. Her blood red hair billowing in the breeze around her.

To most she looks like a young woman in her late teens or early twenties. But as a member of the Council, she's ageless, which puts her anywhere from forty to over a thousand. "I see you have a new friend, Kira. Are you going to introduce us, or shall I do that myself?"

My eyes dart to Hedera and immediately shoot back to Alexandria. I've never trusted her. She's the one who pushed for the outlaw of stoning people and even had a stint against vampires feeding for a while before it got shot down.

Hedera takes a step forward, raising her chin. "My name is Hedera. And you are?"

Goddess, I love the gall of this woman, but if she doesn't watch her tone she's going to get blasted into dust. Alexandria is a demon, a powerful one at that.

Alexandria takes a step forward and I bare my teeth at her. She smirks, but stays where she is. "I am Alexandria DeMarco, second in command on the Council of Supernatural Creatures." When Hedera doesn't immediately bow to her, she *tsks* her tongue and begins walking around us in a circle. We track her as she speaks. "I'm not sure why you don't know this, but we require all magical beings to register with us so we can keep an eye on everyone." Her eyes flare as she gets a whiff of Hedera's scent, finally getting downwind from us. She looks at me and my bones shrivel away. "Interesting." She draws the word out.

"It's a long story. We were going to take her to register tomorrow," I say through gritted teeth.

"Why wait? Someone with the power she has needs to be kept in check, dear. Or do you not trust us?" Her words are smooth like silk, but the aftertaste is harsh and cuts into my soul.

"I trust you as much as you trust me," I answer. Which is not at all.

She laughs, sending a shiver down my spine. "Now, Kira, is that any way to treat one of your leaders?"

She strikes fast, but Hedera is faster, deflecting a blast of black smoke away with one of her vines. "You will not hurt her. We have done nothing wrong," Hedera says, standing tall and powerful in all her glory.

Alexandria seethes where she stands. Hedera now has a target on her. Great.

"You insolent little bi–"

"Alexandria, what are you doing?" Alfonso Privatt asks from just outside the shield Alexandria put up.

She rolls her eyes before dropping the shield. "Nothing, your majesty. Just reminding these lovely ladies that they need to register their friend with our agency." She smiles at him, but her eyes are anything but pleasant.

"Oh, yes. Well, we have to go take care of those shifters. Come, come." He gestures to her with his hand and she shoots a look over her shoulder that promises pain and death.

"We'll be seeing each other again very soon, ladies," she says as she follows along behind Alfonso.

Chapter Twenty-Five

Hedera

Alfonso showing up was divine timing if I've ever seen it. I'm sure if Alexandria was left alone with us for any longer at least one of us would be dead. I did just stand up against a Council member, after all. Him I like. He has a grandfather-like presence to him, even if he is a bit distracted. I worry about him in the presence of that pest on the Council even though I do not know him.

"Hedera. I need you to open the car door, please," Kira says, pulling me from my thoughts. She's carrying Andromeda who has still not come back from wherever she went in her mind. The sight of Alexandria did a number on her, and I intend to get to the bottom of it.

I do as Kira asked and she lays Andromeda down in the backseat before we both get in the front. Turning to her I ask, "Do you know what is wrong with her?"

"No. I've never seen her like this before." She worries her lip. "I think I need to take her to Grace."

"Who is that?"

"A shopkeeper." At my confused look she explains further. "She owns Sherman's. She's not just a shopkeeper, she's also– well, no one really knows what she is. Her aura is constantly changing and so is her scent. But she's good. I promise," she insists when I open my mouth to object.

She drives a few blocks before parking in front of the shop she was telling me about. It's bigger than I thought it would be, and the energy is strange here. Not bad, just...different. We walk up to the building, and before we can get to the door, a gray haired woman exits as if she was expecting us. I know her. She is the woman that visited the last lady of the house before she left and didn't come back.

Before I can warn Kira about this woman and the trouble that often finds her, the woman is motioning for us to enter and Kira is doing as she says. "Come, come," she says. Kira is carrying Andromeda again and sweat flows down her face. "Oh dear, dear, dear," Grace tuts. Once we're inside, we follow the shopkeeper to a back room that has a bed and cabinetry lining the walls. "Set her down there." She points to a single bed with a quilt on top of it. She busies herself, pulling this and that from the cupboards while muttering to herself. When the energy shifts, I realize she's doing an incantation.

If she was a witch surely Andromeda would be able to tell. I wish I knew more about the supernatural community, maybe I could figure her out. But what if she doesn't want to be found out?

A burst of energy goes through the room as she finishes her incantation and I feel relaxed and happy.

"Just a little something to calm all the nerves from you two. I can't work with all that mumbo jumbo going on." She goes over to Andromeda and brushes her hair from her face. "You'll be okay, dear. Swallow this down for me." She puts a cup up to Andromeda's lips. My brain is screaming at me to stop her, but my body is relaxed and I find I cannot move a muscle. Slowly I turn my head to look at Kira whose eyes are half-hooded as she watches on.

Maybe this woman has changed in the years since I last saw her. If Kira trusts her, perhaps I can as well. With that thought, my brain finally quiets and I wait as the woman works on bringing Andromeda back to us.

At first nothing happens, then Andromeda swallows once. Followed by another and another. Her eyes fall shut and Grace sighs as she steps back. "Now we wait. It shouldn't take too long." She tinkers around the room and Kira comes and puts an arm around me. I lay my head on her shoulder, staring at Andromeda, willing her to come back to us.

"She'll be okay," Kira whispers to me before kissing the top of my head.

"How can you be so sure?" My voice cracks, and she squeezes me closer to her.

"She's Andi. She's been through a lot. It's going to take more than a little shock to take her out."

What seems like an eternity later, Andromeda gasps and sits up in the bed. "Where are we?" She looks around, her lips turned down and her brows furrowed.

"Sherman's. Grace pulled you out of...whatever that was," Kira explains as we go kneel next to her.

She looks at us with wide eyes. "How did we get here?"

"I carried you to the car and we drove. Then I carried you in. Grace gave you something to help you come back," Kira explains. "What happened?"

Andromeda rests her head in her hands and takes a few deep breaths before meeting our eyes again. "I saw my mom and then I just blanked. Everything slowed way down and then went black."

Kira's eyebrows raise to her hairline. "Your mom? Where was she? I think I would have much rather dealt with her than Alexandria DeMarco."

Andromeda bites her lip. "I had heard rumors about her getting a position with the Council...but I didn't think it was possible given that my dad wouldn't let her practice and they left me with Aunt Merr due to my magical abilities... but yea. That's my mom."

"But your last name is Wellwood," Kira states.

"Aunt Merr changed mine when I was 13 after I asked her to. I didn't want to be associated with them anymore. Not after they abandoned me. So, she gave me our ancestor's last name. She said it was powerful in its own right."

"But Alexandria is not a witch," I interrupt. They look at me like I sprouted another head. Grace stops her tinkering and listens intently as well.

"What do you mean my mom isn't a witch? I think I'd know if she wasn't." Andromeda's voice is filled with attitude. Rightfully so, given that she's getting the shock of a lifetime tonight.

"Alexandria is a demon."

Chapter Twenty-Six

Andromeda

"Alexandria is a demon," Hedera says with all the tact of a buttered noodle.

My face falls at her words. "Why would you say something like that? Do you think this is something to joke about? And even if it were, that's a shitty joke." My voice rises as I speak, by the last word I'm practically screaming. She sits there in her stoicism.

"Andi, come on. She has no reason to lie or joke about something like that. I agree with her assessment of Alexandria. You didn't see what we did. She tried to attack me with black smoke. If Hedera wasn't there I'd have been dead," Kira says, and I hate her for coming to Hedera's aid right now.

I look at Grace. "What did you give me? Why am I having this nightmare? Make me wake up." Tears stream down my face and my heart beats painfully against my ribs.

"I just gave you a tonic to help your system come back to us, dear. This is not a nightmare even though it may feel like one." She comes over to me and takes my hand in hers. Her skin is smooth and cold. "I know it's hard to process right now, but think about it, dear. Your mother was a powerful witch. She riveled her sister in terms of power and magical prowess, and we both know how powerful Merridan was. Your mother was jealous that they were comparable in everything magic. So when your father came along and promised her a family and a life of success and all of her wildest dreams, Alexandria took the opportunity and ran as far away from here as possible. Her decision was further solidified when Merridan announced her plans to stay in Bellville and carry on the family legacy.

"When you came along and weren't as easily persuaded to their vision, they sent you away. Or maybe it was the last bit of humanity left in your mother trying to protect you. I like that idea more." She smiles at me and I wonder how she knows all of this. As if reading my thoughts, she says, "Merridan shared many stories with me over the years. She was a very dear friend to me. It broke her heart when they dumped you on her doorstep. But she pulled up her witchy britches and did what needed to be done. For you."

She bends over and kisses my cheek before rising and saying, "I'll leave you for a while so you can sort this all out amongst yourselves. If you need me, just call my name and

I'll be here in a jiffy." She wiggles her shoulders and leaves the room.

I sit staring at my lap as I process everything for a while before Hedera speaks, breaking my thought process.

"I would not lie to you, Andromeda. I am sorry if I made you ever think I would. I understand we do not know each other well yet, but my word is all I have to give in this world. If I break my word then I have no reason to live anymore. But I *want* to live. I want to love you both and be something great. I just wanted you to know the truth." Her arms are crossed over her stomach and her face looks so distraught. I feel like an asshole for accusing her, but it's just so much to take in.

"I know," I say quietly. "I'm sorry. I just can't wrap my head around it."

"So, if your mom is a demon on the Council...what does that make your dad?" Kira asks the question that's been haunting me since Grace started the sordid tale of how my mom got to where she is today.

"It seems we have more in common than we originally thought," Hedera says, offering me a kind smile.

"Shitty parents?" I ask. Her and Kira nod. "Seems about right." I roll my eyes as I sigh. "Can we go home and figure this out there? I love Grace, but she meddles too much sometimes and I need some privacy."

"You bet. I'm going to let her know we're leaving," Kira says, wiping her hands together and heading towards the door. She leaves Hedera and me in the room alone.

"May I say something and have it not come off as a negative thing?" Hedera asks, wringing her hands together.

I take a deep breath, not quite ready for her tactless ways of saying things. The last half hour has been enough to make my brain want to implode. But I remind myself that she is figuring things out and needs grace and guidance. "Yea, sure."

"I believe from the information Grace has shared with us, and what I remember of my studies of Greek mythology, that your father may be a Prince of the Underworld," she rushes out in one breath, as if the information was burning a path through her and couldn't be tamed. At my blank stare she explains, "What Grace said makes it sound like your father recognized the agony your mother's soul was going through and preyed on her. He promised her all the things that she wanted and by the time she potentially realized what was happening, it was too late. His persuasion twisted her soul, therefore twisting her magic. It didn't happen all at once, but slowly over the years. The only thing I'm not sure of is if your mother knew who he was before starting their relationship or if she ever questioned what was happening before it got to the point of no return." She taps a finger against her mouth as she thinks.

I gulp. "Are you saying that my dad is a demon too?"

Her eyes are distant as she thinks about my question. "It would make the most sense. You're a witch because your mother was one. But you are powerful. More powerful than you give yourself credit for." Her thinking I'm powerful warms my heart despite the meaning behind her words. "It would make sense that it is due to a slight amount of demon magic in your blood." Her eyes focus and look at me. "If you do have demon magic, I cannot detect it. But I do not have a lot of practice detecting it and it could also be very well hidden."

I sigh again. "Great. So not only are we facing a potential war and my mom is now a demon, but I might have hidden demon magic locked away with no access to it." I give a dry laugh. "Love that for me." I roll my eyes.

"It is not that bad. I'm sure there are plenty of people in this world who have demon magic who are perfectly kind, happy people," she offers.

I wish I could believe her, but I grew up on stories about how the only things demons know how to do are destroy and fornicate. While I do like sex, I don't like destroying. It's the very opposite of what makes my heart sing.

"We will figure it out together." She grabs my hand and intertwines our fingers, that warm electricity floods through my body in response. I smile at her as Kira comes back into the room to let us know we're good to go.

Back at the house, I head to the library to find some more journals, hoping Aunt Merr left one of hers here so I can read up on my family history. After an hour of looking, I give up. If she does have a journal here she hid it well. My eyes are itchy and grainy as I trudge back to my bedroom where Hedera and Kira are cuddled up in bed watching some rom-com.

"Did you find anything?" Kira asks, sitting up slightly.

"No," I grumble.

"You'll find it when the time is right," Hedera offers. Sometimes the way she speaks makes it seem like she is so certain of things she knows nothing about. But then again, maybe she does, because she hasn't been wrong yet.

I flop onto the bed ready for sleep, but they have other ideas. "Let us make you feel better," Kira offers, her eyes alight with desire. I notice then that they're already naked and, if the smell of sex in the room is any indication, they've been fooling around without me.

"You sure do know the way to a woman's heart," I tease. I go to stand to take my clothes off, but Hedera pushes me back down.

"We are going to make you feel better, remember? Let us take care of you." She gives me a sultry smile and I can't help but give in. When she sees my resistance fade, she crashes her lips to mine. For someone who has never had sex before she met us, she's very knowledgeable on all the right moves. While she kisses me, Kira peels my clothes off, leaving kisses and soft bites as she goes.

My body is on fire from need and the electrical current that runs through us when we're touching. I need release *now*.

"I know, sweet one. Be patient," Hedera says. I must have said that bit out loud without meaning to. My cheeks flush at the boldness I've seemingly come to find.

Kira's hands trail up my legs, and I think I'm about to get some relief, but she keeps going. She pinches my nipples, making me arch my back and a moan escapes my lips.

"You go down there. I'm going to teach you all the ways our girl loves to be touched," Kira instructs Hedera.

I knew all those times I told her of my sexcapades would come in handy one day. While I thought I was speaking what I wanted into existence back then, the Goddess had other plans for my manifestations. I send her a quick thanks before focusing back on the women taking care of my needs.

Once Hedera is situated between my thighs, Kira instructs her on what to do. She licks and kisses up my thigh, biting the meaty bits with the perfect amount of pressure. When she gets to the peak of my thighs she runs her nose along my slit, inhaling. "You smell delicious," she whispers, her breath sending decadent chills through my body. "I bet you taste just as divine." She doesn't wait another moment before ravishing my clit with her tongue.

I let out a loud moan while Kira praises Hedera. "Good girl. Now I want you to take your middle finger and your ring finger and rub around down there before slowly inserting them. Got it?"

Hedera nods causing her tongue to hit new places on my clit that send me into orbit. Her fingers are clumsy at first, causing her to slow down her tongue movements, but once she pushes them into me, she finds her rhythm again.

Goddess, these women are going to be the death of me in the best way possible.

"Good, now do this motion with them while pumping in and out, you'll figure out what works and what doesn't. Andi here is a good sport and is very vocal." She winks at Hedera as she begins following Kira's instructions. While she works, Kira sucks my nipple into her mouth, roving her tongue around, timing it perfectly with Hedera's tongue on my clit.

"Oh, Goddess. Oh, fuck. Yes, yes, yes," I cry, grinding my hips on Hedera's face and sinking my hand into Kira's hair, holding her to me.

She breaks free from me and smirks. "Are you feeling good, little witch?" Her words have dark intentions hidden in them. I'd be a liar if I said it didn't excite me. I nod my head and she hums. "I need an answer. Use your words, pretty girl."

"Yes, I feel good," I cry out as Hedera hits the perfect spot inside of me.

"Good. Now I need you to come for us," she says before taking my nipple back into her mouth and suckling it like it's her own salvation.

Now that Hedera has found her flow and Kira is working magic on my tit, I'm a goner. It takes less than a minute for my body to burst apart at the seams, leaving me to pick up the pieces. When I regain my wits, Hedera is sitting back on her heels, wiping her chin, and Kira is smiling down at me.

"You're going to give Hedera here one more while I sit on your face and you pleasure me. Okay, little witch?"

I can only nod in my relaxed state. The next orgasm is sure to knock me out for the night, but is that such a bad thing? After the events of the last few days, I don't think so.

Kira gets settled above me, sitting backwards so she can watch Hedera and help guide her. She begins lowering herself as I feel and hear Hedera spit on my cunt before she rubs it around.

"You're so gorgeous," Hedera says. I would respond in kind, but Kira's pussy is planted on my mouth and I've already begun eating her like a witch starved.

Chapter Twenty-Seven

Kira

Oh the things my mind conjures up for these two women. They've awakened a beast I thought was long since sleeping. Even though we're in the middle of fucking each other senseless, I want more. I need more. I need to devour them, absorb them...

As I ride Andi's face, she reaches around and pinches my nipple hard, twisting it the way I like. "Fuck, Andi. You make my pussy feel so fucking good." My head tilts back as I lose myself in my pleasure. Hedera is doing a wonderful job pleasing our girl and I want to really immerse myself in finally feeling Andi eating me out.

It's a strange feeling sometimes, realizing that my best friend is now my lover. She's seen parts of my body I never thought she would. Tasted me. Kissed me. Loved me. The realization makes me feel exposed and raw, which would normally terrify me. Instead, I feel rejuvenated. Alive.

Andi moans underneath of me and bites on my clit as Hedera gets her closer and closer to another orgasm.

Knowing she's close, I grind harder on her face, working my pussy faster against her tongue so we can come together.

"You have no idea how long I've wanted to do this with you, little witch. I've dreamed about it, touched myself fantasizing about it. But it doesn't hold a candle to the way you feel here and now." My words come out between my panting breaths as the wave building inside of me reaches its peak.

"Do I taste good to you?" I ask, knowing she can't answer, but the slight movement of her head is all I need. "Yes, just like that. Oh, Goddess. Are you close?" Another slight movement. "Good. Come with me." A few seconds later both of our bodies are shaking with pleasure and I fall to the bed beside her, contorting my body so my head lands next to hers, panting and sweating. Hedera crawls up the bed between us and we wrap her in our arms before fading into sleep.

I wake up in the middle of the night, but can't pinpoint why. My heart races as I think of that first night in this house and Andi off on a late night adventure. I reach over and make sure the other two are in bed. When I feel their bodies and steady breathing, I take stock of my own body.

I don't have to pee. I'm not hungry. I'm not thirsty. Movement comes from the hallway and I stop breathing as I listen. Shuffling. Whispers.

Someone is in the house.

I shake the other two, thankful for the salt lamp Andi put on her bedside table, so when their drowsy eyes open and see my finger to my lips, they stay quiet. I point to the hallway and then to my ears. As they register the sounds their eyes widen with panic. We carefully get off the bed and sneak to the side of the door. I peek around the frame, but don't see anything. I turn back to the other two and whisper, "I can't see anything. Do we go out there in our birthday suits?"

One of Hedera's brows raises. "I do not have a birthday suit."

If we weren't potentially on the verge of getting murdered I'd laugh my ass off, but that's not a luxury we have at this point in time.

"She means naked," Andi informs her. Hedera's eyes widen with understanding.

"Oh! Well, we were born this way and only social constructs have made it necessary to wear clothing. I do not see any reason why we shouldn't." We pause a moment to process her words, shock making it take a bit longer than normal. This woman is something else.

"Right. Guess that's settled," I say, snapping out of it first. "On the count of three." I hold up my fingers and count up before we pop out into the hallway and sneak along the walls.

We follow the sound of movement to the library. We pause again outside the door and ready our powers. We take a collective deep breath before heading in.

"It's around here somewhere. Find it," a husky voice bites from one of the aisles.

"I'm trying. Why don't you do something aside from standing there bossing me around?" a whiny masculine voice retorts.

A thud sounds followed by a yip. "You dare question me? You are *beneath* me, scum. Find the fucking book."

The voice sounds oddly familiar, but I can't put my finger on it as we hurry down aisle after aisle, searching for the people. We stumble upon them in the spellbook section. A cloaked figure stands leering over a skinny man rummaging through the shelves.

Hedera releases her vines, entangling the intruders up in a matter of seconds. "I can't hold them for long," she pants, sweat already beading on her forehead, reflecting off the miniscule light in the room. Andi and I don't waste any time, running over to where they're writhing on the floor, fighting against their confines. Andi strengthens the vines and we hear Hedera sigh lightly behind us.

"Who are you?" I demand, my voice coming out more gruff than usual.

The robed figure laughs maniacally. "I can tell you, but I'd have to kill you, and I don't think you're quite ready for that experience yet." The familiarity of the voice jostles my mind again. It's grating on my eardrums.

Andi chants a spell under her breath. When she's finished, she says, "You are in my home and I demand that you tell us who you are."

The man who was rummaging through the books breaks. "My name is Igor Petrov. I work for Ale–" Before he can finish, the robed figure breaks free from the vines and punches him in the face, knocking him out before turning towards us with a wicked grin. Their hood covers the top half of their face, only their black painted mouth visible.

"You thought it would be that easy to find out our secrets, witch?" They say witch like it's a curse. "You thought you were powerful enough to fight against *us*?" They laugh again, leaning their head back.

Andi shoots out a ball of energy, illuminating the room enough for us to make out the person's features under their hood while they continue to laugh at a joke we don't understand. I groan as Andi gasps. Under the robe is none other than Jillian McRiven, known succubus turned hunter. We went to school together and she was the *worst*; total bully.

"Jillian, Jillian, Jillian. Goddess, what has it been? Like fifteen years since we've last seen each other? You know, if you wanted to check out Andi's badass library so badly all you had to do was call." I glance at Andi and back to the robed person, my finger tapping against my chin. "Oh, that's right. We're not friends. You don't have our numbers. Damn. What a bummer for you." I glare at her as her chest heaves with her disgruntled breathing.

"As you can see, *Kira*, I did not need an invitation. I'm not some low level scummy human who can't break and enter into magically protected places." Jillian glances at the man on the ground. "If it wasn't for this dipshit I would have been in and out in a matter of minutes." She glowers at us. "As luck would have it, however, the book we seek cannot be touched by my kind. This man is my assistant." She raises her head as if that somehow makes her important.

"Right," I draw out. "Anyway, he's knocked out and you didn't find what you're looking for, so I suppose it's time you leave before we call the authorities, yea? Unless you want us to take care of you ourselves?" I give her a wicked grin. Andi pinches the back of my arm as my hair begins to raise.

Jillian laughs again. Goddess, if she keeps it up my ears may start bleeding. "As if you lot could overtake me. I've been given certain...perks from the powers that be." She looks at her gloved hand, inspecting her hidden nails. "You couldn't hurt me even if you gave it your best shot."

Andi shoots another ball of energy while Hedera shoots more vines towards Jillian. As the girls are distracting the uppity bitch, I take the time to become invisible, hurrying around Jillian and picking up the knife that had fallen out of Igor's pocket.

I hold the blade to Jillian's throat and she pauses her movement. "Check mate, bitch." I look at Hedera. "Show me where the bodies of those *other* hunters are."

Chapter Twenty-Eight

Hedera

I hurry down the stairs to the living room, showing Kira where the other hunters broke in. Opening the door, the stench of rotting bodies rushes into the house and we all do our best not to gag.

"I got it," Andromeda says as she holds out her hands. The ground beneath the bodies opens up and they fall in before being covered again. The barren earth is quickly covered in sweet smelling flowers, working quickly to overpower the smell of rotting flesh.

"Grab a cross and a bible if you have them. It's the only thing that will hold Jillian," Kira says as she keeps a firm hold on this Jillian character.

"You piece of shit," Jillian spits. "I will *destroy* everything you love." She eyes me up and down. "I'll start with this one. I'll save you for last, Kira. It will be delectable to watch you suffer. I can taste the connection the three of you have. It's delicious." Her eyes light up red as a mist starts enveloping them.

"Fuck." Kira's skin begins bubbling where the mist touches and she barely withstands it until Andromeda comes back with the items needed. We subdue Jillian and shove her into the hidden passageway. Kira looks at us, her skin sickly pale, but bubbled. We turn towards Jillian, Andromeda ripping off her hood. Black lines cover Jillian's face, her eyes are still bright red, and chunks of her hair look as if they've been ripped out.

"I thought succubi are supposed to be attractive?" I ask. Andromeda and Kira look back at me with shock.

"They are," Andromeda explains. "Jillian used to be." She turns back to Jillian, looking in her eyes. "What happened to you?" Her voice is soft, kind.

Jillian spits at her. "Don't pretend to be concerned about what happened to me. You should be worried about what's going to happen to you once we get our hands on the *Book of the Broken*." She smiles, showing off their sharp canines. "Once we hand that book over to her highness, all of your kind will be nothing more than a memory."

At her mention of the *Book of the Broken* a memory forms.

"You have to help me, Merridan. They're after me. I messed up again. I'm so sorry," Grace says, clutching desperately to Merridan's hand. It's one of the few times Merridan has come here lately.

"Grace," Merridan sighs. *"What did I tell you last time? I can't protect you from your mistakes forever."*

Grace clutches her hands tighter, her eyes pleading for understanding. "You don't understand. I found it." At Merridan's questioning gaze she explains. "The Book of the Broken." *At mention of the book, Merridan sighs, placing a hand over her heart. "I found it at a sale. I immediately knew what it was and spent far more than I should have on it. But I couldn't let it fall into the wrong hands. You know what this book will do if the wrong people get it. Please, Merridan. I am begging you."*

Merridan begins pacing, breaking free of Grace's hold so she can think. She mutters to herself as she walks back and forth, back and forth, back and forth. When she's finished, she turns back to Grace.

"Very well. This is the final time I will assist you with such business, Grace. I have too much at stake to be swept up into your schemes all the damned time. You know I have a daughter now. If something happens to me..." Merridan closes her eyes and takes a deep breath. "She has no one. I am all she has. Don't drag me into your messes anymore."

Grace nods her head. "I know. I know. If it weren't important I wouldn't ask, you know that. Besides, if anything happens to you I will watch over her. Protect her like she is my own." Grace smiles at her while her hands twitch at her sides.

She is not the same Grace we know today. Much has changed over the years.

Merridan holds her hands out so Grace can give her the book, but Grace pauses, chewing on her bottom lip. "Are you going to hand it over or are we going to stand here all day staring at it?"

"Sorry. Sorry. It's a powerful book, Merridan. It talks. Mostly in my dreams, but it speaks to me. It promises glory and power unlike anything we've seen before." She shoves the book into Merridan's hands before she can take it and run. "Keep it safe. Keep it hidden." She turns and runs out to her Subaru, peeling out on the gravel driveway.

"No, no, no. Go back!" I shout as I come out of the memory. Andromeda and Kira stare at me, bewildered at my outbreak.

My cheeks flush. "Sorry, I–" I stop myself from explaining in front of Jillian. "I'll explain later." I smile at them to reassure them all is well. But everything is far from that and I'm sure my smile is weak.

"Are you sure?" Andromeda asks, and I nod my head. We have bigger things to worry about for now.

Kira clears her throat. "I have an idea. It's going to sound crazy, but I think it's our best shot at figuring this mess out." Andromeda groans. Apparently Kira's ideas are not a good thing.

"What is it?" I ask, eager to see what that beautiful brain of hers has come up with.

"Well, Hedera, you've shown an interesting ability to read people's minds and intentions, so... maybe you could– I don't know how else to say this– probe Jillian's mind?" Her face scrunches as she waits for the reprimand from Andromeda.

Instead, Andromeda says, "That's not such a bad idea, honestly. I had thought about it, but didn't know how to broach the subject." Kira gapes at her, but Andromeda ignores her as she bites her lip and she thinks of how to go about it. "Maybe just put your hands on her head and focus on getting into her thoughts?"

"Okay," I say, but remember something Igor had begun to say before Jillian knocked him out. "One small thing. Did either of you catch what Igor said before she broke free and knocked him out?" They share a look before returning their questioning gazes towards me again. "I believe he was going to say they were working for Alexandria." Kira curses under her breath and Andromeda audibly gulps. "If that's the case, there may be protections on their mind. I will do my best, of course. Just do not get your hopes up, okay?"

They nod and I set to work.

After hours of probing through Jillian's mind I have found very little information on why she and Igor are here looking for the *Book of the Broken*. The only information readily available is that Alexandria sent them after it with a promise of a great reward. But the reward was not shared with them. From what I've gathered from Jillian's mind, Alexandria seems the type to win her followers over with threats and promises of something grand and then not provide. She guilts them into wanting the reward instead of wanting to please her with their small missions.

I fill Kira and Andromeda in on my findings as we snuggle in bed, certain Jillian will be subdued through the night with the cross, bible, and a nice sleeping potion that Andromeda cooked up while I worked.

"I can't believe my mom is evil now," Andromeda sniffles, pulling us in closer to her. She has the middle tonight, needing to be comforted after our recent findings.

"I mean, no offense, love–but it doesn't really surprise me that much. She left you all those years ago. That's pretty shitty behavior, in my honest opinion," Kira says, trying to comfort her. Her voice is hoarse from her lack of sleep.

I mumble my agreement. "I couldn't imagine leaving someone I created due to their powers and wanting to be their authentic self. I would rather die." My eyes flutter closed and won't reopen as I listen to Andromeda get her emotions out.

Dreams of Alexandria flit across my mind through the night. In some she is head of the Council, calling to destroy everyone who ever stood against her and her cause. In others she's outcast, raising an army to overtake the supernatural world. In the last one, she was pulled towards us from the energy blast that happened after Kira and Andromeda broke the curse. The magic was like a siren call to her. She sniffed it out, craving the power that was behind the spell and whatever it unleashed.

I wake up gasping, pushing myself into a sitting position and looking around the room to get my wits about me. As much as I would like to ignore it, I cannot help knowing that the last dream was no such thing. It was a truth showing itself in the light and I must tell the others.

Andromeda blinks up at me before rubbing the sleep crusties from her eyes.

"What's going on?" she asks, her words slow as she fights off the hands of Sleep.

"I think I know why your mother was here and found us. I don't have answers about the book yet. But I know why she showed up, and it is not on behalf of the Council."

Chapter Twenty-Nine

Andromeda

Hedera's words fight off the rest of my sleepiness. I sit up fully in bed, rousing Kira in the process.

"Why are you guys awake so early?" she asks, annoyance coloring her words.

I look over at the clock. "It's almost noon, Kira. It's not *that* early. Hedera had a dream. She knows why my mom is here." I shove her shoulder as her eyes fall shut again. "Get up, lazy bones. We have work to do."

"Can we at least have coffee first?" Kira's groggy voice asks.

"Of course," Hedera says, climbing out of the large bed and heading downstairs to start the life-giving bean juice. I hope she knows how to make it. Surely she wouldn't try if she didn't.

Fifteen minutes later, I'm showered and dressed, so I head downstairs to see how Hedera is doing with the essential start to our day. The satisfying aroma of coffee meets my nose as I step off the staircase and I hurry towards it like a vampire in a frenzy hunting down humans.

Three mugs sit on the island and I see Hedera is cooking some eggs and sausage as well. "Oh, you didn't have to do that, hon. I could have cooked!"

She startles and turns towards me. Dark circles color the skin under her eyes. "It's really not a problem at all. It's been so long since I've had the pleasure of being in a kitchen, I couldn't resist. I hope it is to your liking." She smiles at me before returning to her task.

I feel bad that she looks so tired. Life has been anything but calm and relaxing since she was freed of her curse. And now we have a succubus locked up– Shit, Jillian.

"I'll be right back." I run out of the kitchen and am about to open the hidden passageway when my phone rings in my back pocket.

Pulling it out, I see Brent's name. "Hey, what's up?" My voice squeaks and I curse my inability to hide things from people.

"Hey yourself. We've got a problem. Are you busy?" His voice is gruff. Tonight is the full moon and I know that he's on edge, so I remind myself to not take his straight-forward attitude to heart.

"Uh, kind of. Is everything okay?"

"We're coming over. There's some weird shit going on around town. Stay at your house and do not leave. Do you understand me, Andromeda Lynn? Do not leave your fucking house." His words are mixed with panic and bossiness.

"I didn't plan on it, actually, so calm down. We'll be here." I remember that there's a new person in the mix right before he hangs up. "Oh, by the way, there's someone new here so, like, try to be nice. Okay?"

"Of all the days to spring this on me." He sighs. "I can't promise anything. You'd probably be better off warning her about *me.*"

"That's a good idea. I'll just do that." My nerves cause my voice to shake. I know Brent is a lot when he's not close to shifting, but on the full moon he's way worse. Only instead of in a nice happy go lucky way, it's asshole, short comments, and a moment away from violence.

Werewolves are fun.

"Uh huh. See you soon," he says and hangs up. I pop open the hidden passageway, revealing a very pissed off—and very free—Jillian. "Oh, fuck," I mutter, stumbling back, trying to shut the door.

She charges towards me, jamming her foot between the door and frame.

"Kira. Hedera," I scream at the top of my lungs a moment before Jillian wraps her arm around my throat, spinning me and pulling me into her chest.

"You thought you could subdue me, you pesky little witch? You thought you could overpower *me?* You're nothing. You're so much *less than nothing.*"

Kira and Hedera come rushing into the living room and stop short when they see the precarious situation I've gotten myself into. My eyes plead at them to help me, but I know it's useless.

"Find me the book and I'll let your sweet witch go. If you don't, I'll kill her where she stands," Jillian demands.

I give an imperceptible nod of my head. They have a whispered conversation, planning how they're going to keep an eye on us and find the Goddess damned book.

Hedera heads up the stairs to begin the search as Kira leans against the wall opposite us, ankles and arms are crossed in an air of utter relaxation. But I can see the distress in her eyes, the tension radiating through her body, and her readiness to end this succubus' life.

"Ah," Jillian purrs. "You don't trust me? Pity. It would go so much faster if the both of you searched." She heaves a sigh. "But I suppose you can't expect mice to dance all the time."

An eternity later, the front door swings open and Brent's voice carries into the room causing Jillian to stiffen and tighten her hold on me. "Werewolves," she hisses.

"You thought we were defenseless, you dumb bitch?" Kira growls. "First of all, we held you at bay on our own. They're not even here for you. They're here because they're our friends." She begins prowling around the room. "Oh, that's right. I forgot you don't know what that word means." She glares at Jillian as Brent and the boys walk into the living room. They pause as they take in the scene.

"What in the entire fuck is going on with this town?" Brent says, throwing his hands in the air. He looks me over, assessing me for injuries before meeting my eyes. "Is this the new person you were talking about? Because, I've got to say, this is not what I imagined."

"No," I choke out. "She's upstairs. This is just a minor inconvenience."

Jillian tightens her hold further on my throat, cutting off my ability to speak.

Brent sucks his teeth. "Okay," he draws out before taking a seat on the couch, his boys placing themselves methodically throughout the rest of the room. "You know, this is probably the most interesting day I've had since that one night we went to Fangs for karaoke." He smirks at me, and if my face wasn't already red from my blood being cut off from my head, I would be as red as a tomato.

Kira cackles at the memory. "Oh yea, that was a *great* night."

"Enough," Jillian screams. "Do you not care about this witch? Do you not realize that her life is in a very precarious balance that she is not on the winning side of? One move from me and she's dead." Her chest is heaving with her anger, her arm shaking around my throat.

"Oh, we care about her. But we also know that you won't do anything about it. You need the book. You don't get the book if she's dead," Kira says, crossing her arms again. Her pupils are narrowed on Jillian and I feel slightly bad for them. Being on the receiving end of Kira's anger is not somewhere I'd ever want to be. "Besides, Jillian, you were never, and never will be, scary." She examines her nails as if this is any regular day. "You're honestly a little pathetic."

Her words are harsh and while they're not far from the truth of Jillian not being scary, I don't think calling her pathetic was necessary or useful. If anything, it's being the very thing we don't like Jillian for. If I could reprimand her, I would. But Jillian's arm is too tight around my throat.

"I will end each and every one of you," Jillian seethes. In a moment of divine intervention, she loosens her hold on my throat enough for me to break out of her hold.

I spin around and punch her with everything I've got before two of Brent's boys rush in and hold her down. Smiling down at Jillian, I say, "Don't ever underestimate us again. While you may be stronger than us with your abilities, we have more numbers than you."

I walk over to Kira who's beaming at me with pride. "You're so badass. I would have pissed myself if that had been me. But you were calm as a cucumber, girl." She crashes her lips to mine and Brent ooh's and aah's behind us.

"Now *that* is a development! Percy, go get the cross thing-a-ma-jig from the back of the van. We need reinforcements."

Hedera walks down the stairs as Percy heads out to the van. She comes into the living room, her brows scrunched together. "I was not aware we were expecting visitors," she whispers to us. "I did not make enough food."

"It's okay. They're our friends and they can get their own food. As a matter of fact, I guarantee they already ate enough food to feed fifteen children today. A piece," Kira assures her, wrapping her in her other arm.

"I have missed so much," Brent whines. His eyes are the size of saucers as he looks at the three of us snuggled up to each other.

"Did you find the book?" I ask Hedera quietly. I hope she didn't. It can't go to them. It's too dangerous.

"Yes." She winks at me. She steps out of Kira's embrace and walks over to Jillian. "I have what you seek. I will warn you, though. This does not end well for you."

The boys release Jillian and she stands up, dusting herself off. Jillian snatches the book from Hedera and sneers at her. "It will end just fine for me. You're the one who needs to worry." She vanishes in a poof of red smoke.

So much for Percy going to get the cross thing-a-ma-jig.

An hour later and Brent and the boys are mostly caught up on the last few days.

"You need to ward your house, girl," Brent chides from his seat on the couch.

"I thought it was already, but apparently not. They probably faded over time since Aunt Merr didn't come here that often." I shrug before pinning him with a glare. "Spill. What's been going on in town?"

"It's a fucking circus is what's happening." He sits forward, resting his arms on the table. "There are hunters everywhere and whispers of Council members popping up in weird places. No one has seen the Council in years. But they're here now? Why? Not to mention, they've sent out a notice to all shifters that their parameters have changed for where they can shift. They have us with *bunny shifters,* Andromeda. We will tear them to ribbons." He shivers. "I don't even like rabbit meat."

Bile rises in my throat at the thought. "Why would they do something that would endanger an entire population of shifters? Why are there hunters here on the full moon?" A thought clicks in my head. "You guys cannot go to your designated shifting area."

Brent sighs, rubbing his hands over his face. "I wish it were that easy. But if we don't show up we'll get punished." Ronnie whines and comes over to rub against Brent to comfort him.

I feel so bad for Brent sometimes. Being in charge of so many people in a pack and fretting over doing something that could result in getting his whole pack punished has to be so stressful.

"You'll get punished if you kill those bunny shifters, too. Which is worse?" Kira asks from her place against the wall.

"Why don't they shift here?" Hedera asks. "They could go into the woods. It's large enough that they would be safe, but close enough that if anyone shows up they could protect us."

"That's not a bad idea." I look at Brent. "You have my permission to shift in the woods behind my house." I hold my hand out to seal the deal. It's a work around for the Council's rules. If shifters have permission from a property owner to shift on their property the Council can't do anything about it.

Brent stares at my hand for a moment, thinking over the implications. "Are you sure?" he asks, meeting my eyes.

"I wouldn't offer something I'm not sure about." I jut my hand out more and he takes it. A zing goes through our palms, this one less strong than when I did it with Kira due to the lack of blood sharing. When we pull away a wolf is imprinted on my palm and a witch's hat is on his. "I love doing that."

Since breaking the curse, mine and Kira's mark has faded. Now I have another one. I never thought I'd make so many deals with my friends in such a short time, but I'm glad they trust me enough to do it.

Chapter Thirty

Kira

Hedera and Brent get acquainted as we lounge in the living room and attempt to decompress from the insanity that our world has dissolved into. He finds her fascinating and she's eager to learn about all the supernatural beings she can.

"Damn. I knew Garret wasn't meant for you, Andi, but *two* lovers?" Percy jests. "You're almost on the same level as me." His smile is so wide I'm surprised his lips aren't cracking.

"Not even close," Andi chokes out, spit getting lodged in her throat in her haste to put him in his place. I pat her on her back to help clear it. "Two is enough for me." She smiles at me and Hedera, love radiating from her eyes. Percy hmm's before Colton steals his attention with some joke and they begin wrestling on the floor.

"Andromeda saw the lady Gaia the other day," Hedera says, beginning to list off the events of the last few days. "She sent a warning. Then we saw Alexandria downtown before Jillian broke in. Oh no. Igor is still in the passage-way. We should probably release him."

Brent's head swivels between the three of us fast enough that I'm worried he's going to get whiplash. "Who's Igor? Alexandria? Like second in command on the Council? What was she doing? I leave you alone for a few days and you guys get up to all sorts of crazy shenanigans." He shakes his head, throwing his hands in the air while his boys nod their heads, jaws dropped at all that's happened.

"Igor was hired by Jillian to find the *Book of the Broken*, which Hedera has now handed over," I say, cringing. I fill them in on the events of last night, and how there were also hunters who broke in in an attempt to kill Andi two days ago. When I confirm that Alexandria is who they think she is– and that she's Andi's mom– all the wolves in the room perk up at the implication. Andi shrinks into herself for a moment before raising her chin in defiance. There's my girl.

"We're friends with *royalty?*" Colton breathes, inching closer to her despite Percy's death grip on his arm.

"Back off. She's been through enough," I order. He growls at me, baring his teeth.

"At ease," orders Brent. The hairs on my arms raise at the menace in his tone. Colton listens, lowering his head. But his eyes don't leave me. "You have better manners than that. These are our friends, royalty or not." Brent snaps his fingers and Colton kneels next to his leg, bristling at the embarrassment.

"Well, it's not much for royalty, to be honest," Andi says, her voice barely over a whisper. I rub her back to offer her support and Hedera gives her a reassuring smile. We're not going anywhere. No matter who, or what, her mother is.

"What do you mean?" Scott asks, leaning in.

Andi clears her throat and takes a deep breath before she breaks the concerning news. "She's a demon now."

Toby's eyes widen. I'm quite enjoying putting the wolves through so much shock in one day. "How? Does that mean–"

Before he can continue, Andi rushes to explain. "Sometimes when a witch does black magic, the spell rebounds and steals their soul. Other times, they're promised great things– love, power, money– by a Prince of the Underworld and the Prince steals their soul. In this case, my father disguised himself as a simple, God-fearing man and tricked my mom into becoming what she is today." She sighs, her shoulders sinking. "That's why they sent me away. He knew that I would figure it out and try to stop him. That's what I assume happened, anyway. I've been trying to find one of Aunt Merr's journals to help put the pieces together, but I haven't found anything yet. Anyway, we're pretty sure she's trying to take over the Council and eradicate any being that opposes her rule."

"That would wipe out ninety percent of the supernatural population. Alexandria isn't well liked," Brent explains.

"We know, that's why she needs the book to bend people to her will." Andi looks at Hedera, waiting for her explanation.

Before she can, Ronnie cuts into the conversation. "But this woman handed that book over. Why would you do that?" He levels Hedera with a glare that could set the world on fire.

"I didn't," Hedera says plainly. We all gawk at her, confused, because we watched her do it. A small smile plays at her full lips. "I made her *think* it was the book. It was a small glamour, but it took forever to get it to stick. I actually gave her a very spicy romance book I found in the library." Her cheeks heat and I assume it's from remembering the short snippet she read.

A moment of silence passes before we all explode in laughter and praise for this amazingly talented woman. Once we've all settled, Brent asks the question I know he's been dying to get off his chest. "So, where did you come from? I know these two have been toeing the line of friends and lovers for a while. But I've never seen you around town before." His eyes bore into hers, daring her to lie to him. His boys still at the distrust leaking from his words, Toby the stiffest of all.

"I was cursed many years ago to watch over this house after my father betrayed one of Andromeda's ancestors. She found me on her first night here. Her and Kira broke the curse and freed me." She looks at us with nothing but adoration, like we hung the stars in the night sky.

Percy's eyebrows meet. "When was this?" His tone deadly serious.

"Thursday evening," Andi answers. A question hangs in the air.

"That explains it then," Ronnie says, looking over at Brent.

"Explains what?" I question.

"Thursday evening there was an energy blast. An hour later, the first report of hunters in town made its rounds, followed by sightings of some Council members," Scott explains, looking at the three of us, his eyes a mix of panic and awe. "Whatever you three did that day was a beacon for all the things we've ever feared finding us here."

My heart plummets. There's no way. No. Fucking. Way. I know Andi is stronger than she gives herself credit for, always thinking about the good of all instead of the good of herself, but there's no way that *we* caused a supernatural catastrophe by breaking the curse.

I shake my head back and forth, holding up my hands in front of me. "Woah, woah, woah." I give a nervous laugh. "I know you think we're badasses, but we're not *that* badass. We're not strong enough to do that."

"No, but the curse could have been. It was probably a recoil from breaking it," Brent says, guessing at things he doesn't have the first idea about.

"It's a possibility," Andi mumbles. Her eyes glaze over as she remembers what she read in the witch's journal. "She said that she wasn't sure what the repercussions would be." She looks at Hedera and me, her eyes wide, tears lining her lids. "What have we done?"

Chapter Thirty-One

Andromeda

B rent walks over to me, grabs my shoulders and puts his face close to mine. "We will be okay. You are more than capable of taking care of this, especially with all of us working together." He pulls me against his chest and hugs me tight. When he lets go, he takes a step back and clasps his hands. "You're lucky one of your best friends is excellent in times of immense stress." He smirks at me. "First order of business is redoing the wards surrounding the property. We're not just doing the house. We have to do the entire thing since there are apparently secret entrances and we don't know where they are." He continues to order us around, putting all of us to work on different things.

By late afternoon, we're all back in the living room with mixed drinks or wine to help us relax. Igor has been sent on his way, memory wiped of everything that happened last night and who we are. "What a productive day," Brent says with a self-satisfied sigh.

"How long do you think it will take them to figure out the book is fake?" I ask, fidgeting with my glass of pinot grigio.

"That entirely depends on how fast Jillian gets in contact with Alexandria. She's a busy woman and I don't see her making time for one of her underlings when she has her hands in so many different places right now," Kira says, rubbing my back. She takes a sip of her bourbon and coke, a satisfied sigh leaves her lips and makes me want to kiss her to taste it on my tongue.

"We need to be ready for when she finds out. She will come for us," Hedera says. She's the picture of calm, ready for anything. The only one in our group not drinking. I envy her ability to be so confident in her abilities and calm in this time of horror.

Seeing my unease, Toby says, "You're amazing, Andi. Quit questioning yourself. And quit worrying about hurting another living being. This is life or death. If you want to live, you're going to have to let that pure heart of yours get a little dirty."

"It goes against every fiber of my being to hurt people," I argue.

"We know," Kira says softly before biting her lip. She shares a look with Brent before meeting my eyes again, sitting up and grabbing my hand in hers. "Andi, this is probably going to get ugly. Alexandria wants to eradicate a good portion of the supernatural community. Are you willing to let her do it? Are you willing to ignore the path that's been laid at your feet?" She takes a deep breath. "No matter what happens in the coming days, know that we all love you and don't think less of you for doing what needs done, but we're going to need your help."

I know she's just being honest and telling me what I *need* to hear, but I hate it. I'm a green witch. I should be healing and growing things, not hurting them. I know this train of thought is completely illogical, because why else would we have been training? But to actually put it into practice is something else entirely. "What if I turn out like her?" I ask in a whisper, a tear sliding down my cheek.

Hedera kneels in front of me, taking my face between her soft hands. My eyes flick to her full lips before meeting her beautiful brown eyes. "You will not be like your mother, Andromeda. You are too pure and too defiant to go down that path. Hurting people who hurt you, or those you love, does not make you a bad person. It makes you a caring one. It is what I admire about you. Your spark, your heart, your sincerity." She kisses me, calming the raging in my mind as Kira scoots closer to me.

Once I'm calm enough, we start making plans for what we're going to do if shit hits the fan. When the sun sets,

Brent and the boys head outside to shift and roam the grounds. Hedera, Kira, and I camp out in the living room despite my comfortable bed calling to us upstairs. I spook at every sound in the house and howl from the boys. After three hours of being on edge, Hedera takes my hands in hers.

"May I help?" She's worried about me; they both are. I don't blame them, I haven't been the most stable person the last few days.

"How?" I ask, fighting against the lump in my throat.

"I can calm your mind and make you sleep, if you'd like."

My mind goes to filthy places even though I know that's not what she means. Her eyes dilate as she realizes what I'm thinking.

"That works, too." She smiles at me, and it's full of mischief and promise.

"This is what I like to see," Kira says as mine and Hedera's tongues swirl around each other like we've done this a million times before. She leans back on the couch, biting her lip, as she looks on. My cheeks heat at the voyeurism, but it's also incredibly sexy.

I sink my hand into Hedera's hair, pulling her closer to me as her hands slide underneath my shirt. Her soft hands glide across my belly before going up to cup my breasts. A moan escapes my mouth as she lightly pinches my nipple.

"I love it when you make those little noises," Hedera whispers against my lips.

"Aren't they lovely?" Kira asks, skimming her own stomach with her fingertips.

I look over at her for a moment before Hedera turns my head back to her. "Eyes on me, witch." The nickname sends a chill down my spine as I meet her eyes.

"Good girl." She removes my shirt, and takes a step back. "You're so gorgeous."

I try to cover my body with my arms, but Kira moves faster than I can register to hold them at my side. I've never really liked being on display; my stomach has rolls and my boobs are small for my body. But they look at me like I'm the most delicious thing they've ever seen.

Kira releases my arms to unclasp my bra. The cool air mixed with my arousal has my nipples pebbled. Kira takes one in her mouth as Hedera does the same with the other. I try to reach for them, but they each hold an arm down, refusing to let me move.

"We are going to take care of you tonight, little witch. Just lay back and relax," Kira whispers in my ear before nibbling the lobe.

"But you did that last time," I argue, feeling guilty for not being a more active participant in our sex life.

"There will be times where we need to be taken care of more as well. It is a balancing act. You are under immense stress and this helps you. Quit overthinking it and enjoy," Hedera admonishes.

Goddess this is fantastic.

Hedera begins to remove my leggings and my mind starts going about how I should have shaved while I showered earlier, I'm a bit prickly. But she doesn't mind. She rubs up and down my legs a few times before spreading them wide.

"Your nettle bed is as gorgeous as the rest of you," she compliments what I'm assuming is my vagina before she devours me. Her tongue flicks my clit as she sucks it into her mouth before running it down to my opening to taste my already flowing juices. "So tasty."

She spits on my pussy and uses her fingers to rub it viciously. Normally I wouldn't like that. I like it slow and passionate, but she does it so well, using three of her fingers to cover more area. Just like with her magic, she's a natural.

I tremble under Kira's mouth on my nipples and Hedera's hand working my cunt. My pleasure is nearing eruption, but I can't tell them to stop. I won't. Glancing over at Kira, I see she's lost her own pants at some point and is touching herself as well. That just leaves Hedera untouched tonight. I want to feel bad, but my brain refuses to focus on that.

Hedera's mouth replaces her fingers on my clit as she shoves her digits into me, working me perfectly, hitting the perfect spot as she curls her fingers. I cry out as my orgasm rips through me. My cum glistens on Hedera's fingers as she pulls them out, licking them clean, and I swear I come again watching her.

Before I can offer to pleasure her, Kira tackles her to the ground and eats her like a dessert she's been denying herself for weeks. My body is too weak to join them, so I just enjoy the show.

It's intoxicating to watch them roll around on the living room floor, both of them fighting for control. Eventually they settle on a mutual control, their groins pressed against the other's thigh as they grind, finding a perfect rhythm to meet their mutual need for release. Their words are erotic as they urge each other on.

"You like that, you dirty whore?" Kira asks Hedera. I gasp, wondering how she'll take the degradation, but to my surprise, she moans in response. Kira slaps her leg. "I asked you a question."

"Yes. It feels amazing," Hedera breathes, working herself faster against Kira. She pushes her leg up into Kira's cut, applying more pressure, making her whimper. "I love hearing your moans as much as Andromeda's. You both purr so prettily for me."

They go back and forth like this for a while before Hedera finally cries out, followed by Kira a few moments later. Slumping to the floor, they catch their breath before putting their clothes back on. I take that as my cue and do the same before we all snuggle on the floor and watch bad reality TV until our eyes can't stay open anymore.

The next morning Hedera and I are woken up by a couple of the boys barging through the front door with breakfast and coffee from the shop in town. We make sure Kira is covered up and snug on the floor before meeting them in the kitchen.

"Thanks for letting us use your property last night," Ronnie says as he holds up the goods they brought in.

"You didn't have to get us anything. It's really no problem. I'd rather you do it here than get punished for killing other shifters." I smile at him as I grab a blueberry muffin and a latte. "Where's Brent?"

"He'll be back in a little bit. There was an incident in town last night with his cousin and so he had to go check it out as he's the next of kin," Toby explains, refusing to meet my eyes.

"Garret?" I ask, my throat goes dry despite just taking a drink.

Toby nods, his face grim. "He hasn't been in a good place since you guys broke up." At the offended look on my face he rushes on. "Not that he's ever been in a good place. It's just gotten a whole lot worse. Breaking and entering, drugs, vandalism. You name it, he's doing it." He shakes his head. "Last night during his shift he apparently went downtown and attacked some people."

"He what?" I exclaim. I can't believe that Garret would do that. Well, the more I think about it, I can see it. He always did have a knack for violence. Maybe beating women he's intimate with wasn't as fun as it used to be anymore.

Goddess, I hate that man.

"That's all I know. Brent will fill us in when he gets back." He shovels his muffin into his mouth, signaling the end to the conversation.

Hedera sits next to me nibbling her own muffin. "Things have gotten very dangerous around here. I am not so sure being free is as great as I thought it would be." Her words sink deep and I must gasp because she turns to me with wide eyes. "That's not what I meant, Andromeda. Having you and Kira adore me the way you do is everything to me. But there is an outside world, too. One that I will eventually have to play a bigger part in. It scares me, if I am to be honest. There is so much hate and backstabbing and danger lurking around every corner. I didn't have to worry about that in the cellar. I just laid there and watched whoever came into the house, or the animals roaming the yard. It was easy. Peaceful."

"Well, good things aren't easy. They're a lot of work," Toby says through a mouth full of muffin, annoyance biting through his words.

"Yes, I know." She sighs. "I'm not explaining this well." She bites her lip and looks down at her muffin before meeting my eyes again. "I love you. I need you to know that. I love everything you've shown me and taught me. Your personality lights up my otherwise dull life. You are a ray of sunshine in a cloud-covered world. Even if I do not live for long, I am glad to have gotten this time with you." Her cheeks are red as she spills her heart out to me.

Confessing her love to me is shocking but not completely out of left field. Mostly because I feel the same way about her and Kira. They're my soul mates. I've known it since we all first touched each other even though it's only been a few days. But the way my body lights up every time they touch me, the way I yearn for their presence even when I want alone time– the proof is in the pudding.

No one means to me what these two do.

"I love you, too, Hedera. Truly, madly, deeply."

Our lips meet in a passionate kiss and Toby clears his throat before excusing himself from the room. I should probably feel guilty, knowing that he has a crush on me, but I remind myself that his upset is not my responsibility when I've made my feelings for him crystal clear.

A few moments later, a disheveled Kira walks in. Her wild hair is a mess and her eyes half open. "Morning," she says as she grabs the coffee with her name on it before coming and giving us both a kiss on the cheek.

"Good morning," Hedera and I say in unison. Kira's eyes bounce between the two of us, knowing something is going on, but taking a few moments to process it in her still-tired state.

"What did I miss?" Her eyes clear as the seconds pass and she downs her coffee.

"I told Andromeda that I love her and she said it back." Hedera beams as she shares the news. While she normally has a very stately way of speaking, she's giddy and excited telling Kira our news.

A nervous bit of energy zings through me as I think that Kira will be jealous, but it's short lived as she smiles. "Of course you did," she says to us. "What's not to love about you two?"

Pushing down the negative response that brims on the tip of my tongue, I blurt out, "I love you as well. I have since we were, like, 22. I was just a chicken shit and couldn't find the words." My face is burning and I look down at the countertop, unable to meet her eyes.

A moment later, she has my chin between her pointer finger and thumb, lifting my face to hers. She kisses me softly before whispering, "I know. I love you both, too, Andi." She gives me another kiss before digging into her muffin.

I'm on cloud nine and am certain that nothing can go wrong with this perfect start to a day. A clear heart, mind, and soul, good company, and coffee. What could go wrong?

Chapter Thirty-Two

Kira

After confessing our love for each other, we finished our breakfast with smiles, giggles, and just good ass vibes. It's the best start to a day I could have ever asked for. But all good things must come to an end, and with all the shit happening in town, it was only a matter of time before it came knocking on the door. Or rather, charging *through* the door.

Not even an hour later, Brent runs in, panting and looking panicked. "Jillian needs help."

We all look at him like he's lost his damn mind. Last I checked, that bitch was threatening to murder all of us. So, like, excuse me if I'm not the first person to offer my assistance.

"Please," he begs, motioning for us to go outside.

"Where is she?" Andi asks, her brows scrunched together.

"Andi, you can't be serious," I state. "Jillian literally almost murdered you the other night. You can't possibly be wanting to help her right now." The heart in this girl is seriously going to get her killed one of these days.

She looks at me, her eyes pleading for understanding. "I can't just sit back and watch if she's asking for our help. She must have given that book to Alexandria and shit hit the fan. That's *our* fault."

"Yes, but it was either that or hand over a book that would end life as we know it. I, for one, would like to see what else it has in store for me," Hedera says from where she lounges on a chaise.

Andi sighs. "I'll do this alone if I have to, but I'd rather have my back up." She eyes us.

I groan. "Fine. But I'm not fucking happy about this. She can die for all I care after the stunt she pulled holding you hostage and threatening us," I state. Hedera nods her agreement.

We go outside to Brent's van and he throws open the back doors, revealing a very bloody, very broken Jillian.

"Holy shit," I mumble. The words traitor, leech, and some derogatory slurs are etched into her skin.

Andi gasps and crawls into the van, checking out the injuries. "Who did this to you?" Her voice is watery and I know she's on the verge of crying.

"Who do you think?" Jillian's voice comes out weak as she glares at us. "I didn't have anyone else to turn to." They close their eyes. "I've made too many enemies." She opens her eyes and looks at Andi. "I know you can heal things. Please help me. I will do whatever is needed."

Andi bites her lip as rage builds inside of me. How the fuck does she think she can hold Andi hostage the other night for a life-ending book, and then show up here and ask for not only mercy but also healing?

The worst part is I know Andi is going to do it and there's nothing I can do to stop it.

Hedera opens her mouth to speak, and from the looks of it, she feels the same way that I do. So I touch her arm, making her glance at me and shake my head. Nothing we say or do will change the outcome of what is about to happen. Andi is too stubborn and too good.

"Give me a moment," Andi whispers to Jillian before exiting the van and pulling us with her until we're far enough away that Jillian won't overhear. "I have to help her. It's against everything I am not to." She meets my heated glare. "I know it doesn't make sense to you, but please trust me. If this goes to shit then you can pummel me into the dirt or whatever."

"Oh, I'll pummel you alright. Andi, this is insane. I know you already know that. I also know nothing is going to change your mind. But–" I take a deep breath to try to quiet some of the anger burning through me. "She has betrayed us time and again. Even in school. You know the saying, 'you can't change a zebra's stripes.' It's because deep down people are who they are. Just don't get too carried away with your positive thinking that it clouds your judgment. Make her swear that she won't double cross you again or something." I toss my hands into the air.

"Kira is right, Andromeda. I do not trust that succubus as far as I can throw her. I don't want you to get hurt, *any* of us to get hurt. But this path is laid before you and you must walk it the way you see fit." She kisses Andi's cheek and steps back, clasping her hands in front of her to hide their shaking.

Andi bites her lip before meeting my eyes. "I have to do this. Everything in me is yelling at me to save her." She looks at her feet, trying to hide her shame.

I grab her chin, tilting her face up to look at me. "I support you in everything you do. Until the end." I give her a brief kiss before stepping back to Hedera's side.

Andi takes a deep breath, nodding her head. She turns on her heel and tells Brent to take Jillian inside to the guest bedroom on the main floor, the same one Hedera slept in the first night she was free. We follow them in, anxious energy vibrating through everyone.

The last person I expected to ever ask for our help is Jillian. She was always an outcast in school, but when I step back and *really* think about it, I don't think it was her fault. She was bullied for her powers and pull toward sexual energy, especially in high school. With all those hormones flowing through our peers, it's no wonder she couldn't keep herself contained. After sophomore year Jillian disappeared. We all assumed she'd gone to a boarding school or was homeschooled because her whole family were odd ducks in a sea of geese.

Hedera and I stand outside the closed guest room door as Brent and Percy hold Jillian down while Andi works. Her soft chanting can be heard through the wooden door, but even if we couldn't hear her, the energy in the house would have given it away. It's heavy, but cleansing. Purposeful, but probing.

Jillian begins groaning, mixed with a few screams, as Andi works her magic. Healing is sometimes fast and done in the blink of an eye. Other times it's excruciating and takes hours. This one seems to be a mixture of both. Given that Jillian got the injuries from Alexandria, I don't think this will be an easy job. Andi will be drained afterward.

I can't help but think, what if this was the plan after all? To get Jillian here because Andi doesn't turn injured people or things away, drain her, and then attack when she's at her weakest?

I'm about to barge into the room and stop Andi when Hedera gasps. I look over and see her eyes distant as if she's in a trance. I wrap an arm around her and guide her to the living room so she can sit in case she passes out or something.

She grabs my hand, squeezing it until it tingles from lack of blood flow. But I don't complain. I simply wait.

Five minutes later, she comes back to the real world. She turns to me with tears in her eyes. "I've seen the ending," she whispers. "It is beautiful."

"What ending? What's beautiful? Sometimes you say the strangest things. It's not a bad thing, just wild. You're, like, the most out of pocket person I know. You just say shit and it doesn't matter how the other person feels, you just speak the facts," I ramble, my nervous energy getting the best of me yet again.

Hedera stares at me as I go off on my tangent, her full lips parted slightly. "I am sorry. I did not realize there were customs for speaking with friends." Her chin wobbles and I realize I just took a page right out of her book, but with less...*her*.

I rub my hand down my face. "That's not what I meant, Hedera. I'm sorry. I love it. I love *you*. Everything about you. I just ramble when I'm nervous."

"What are you nervous about?" She grabs my hand again, this time holding it gently between both of hers.

I gape at her. "Everything," I answer. "Andi healing Jillian. You saying you've seen the end and it's beautiful. How we're going to get out of any of this alive. What happens if we have to fight against our friends because they've been turned evil? Like, the entire world is falling apart right now. I do my best to be strong for you and Andi, but Goddess, my head is not okay." Tears pool in my eyes as I come to the realization.

I haven't been okay in a long time now. Even with these amazing women by my side, I hide my feelings, I compartmentalize my own problems. I avoid having to do any real work on myself. Goddess knows I have plenty to do.

"You do not have to be okay. You just have to keep trying to be better than you were the day before. Eventually it will all work out how it's supposed to, whether you do it willingly or not. I think it's best to be in control of it than to let it control you. But maybe you need that lack of control. Maybe you need to just let something take the reins for a while and just enjoy the ride."

She squeezes my hand as she gives me a warm smile. "It is okay to let go sometimes, Kira. We all have to do it."

Chapter Thirty-Three

Hedera

The end. Oh, my, it is so beautiful. But I cannot tell them what I have seen. They cannot know the outcome or it will change the course entirely, and *that* I cannot guarantee will be as wonderful as this.

But what am I going to tell them? I have kept things from them for short periods of time, sure, but to make up a completely fabricated story is not something I am accustomed to doing.

I have managed to get Kira off the topic for now, and maybe the situation with Jillian will distract them long enough so I do not have to tell them something false. Halloween is only four days away and then it will all come to fruition how it is supposed to.

Peace is coming.

Five hours later, Andromeda comes out of the guest room. She has sweat through her sweater, her blue hair sticks to the sides of her face and forehead, and she has dark circles under her eyes.

She walks over to Kira and I on the couch and collapses atop us, her head in Kira's lap and her legs in mine. Her eyes close as she mumbles, "Jillian is okay now. But I need food and sleep. Not necessarily in that order."

Brent comes into the room, his eyebrows bunched together as he takes us in.

"Did everything go okay?" Kira asks him.

Brent looks at Kira as he says, "Yea, everything went smooth. Jillian was pretty fucked up, but Andi is a rock star and got it done." His eyes keep pinging back to Andromeda and I know something is amiss.

"What happened?" I ask. I cannot read his mind. His thoughts are too sporadic and they do not make much sense to me. It's the same with his pack mates as well. It must be the werewolf in them. That's a problem I will figure out another time.

He glances at me before looking back at a snoring Andromeda. He sighs before sitting on the loveseat across from us, his arms braced on the tops of his thighs. "I'm not entirely sure. I've seen healing magic done before. I've *been* healed before several times. But that– what she did– was otherworldly." His eyes go unfocused as he remembers. "There was this green light interspersed with silver threads dancing around Jillian's body, mending her, stopping the bleeding. Then the blackness came."

I shiver at his mention of the blackness. I think it is the same blackness I came across in Jillian's mind.

"It poured out of Jillian onto the bed. It seemed as though it was searching for something, but it wasn't interested in any of us. Part of it raised up off the bed and looked around the room before it laid back down. At that point Andi's magic had sensed it and in a burst of green and silver it was gone."

I raise an eyebrow at him. That sounds like a good thing to me, but I am not very knowledgeable on the workings of magic yet. "Doesn't that mean Andromeda's magic worked?" I question him.

"I mean, technically, yes." He shuts his eyes, scoffing. "Honestly, it's probably just the effects of the full moon last night fucking with me." He pauses a moment, collecting his thoughts. "It just seems like that wasn't the end of whatever the blackness is. I mean, yea, it's gone, but it's not *gone* gone. It's still here. I can sense it just on the edge of my psyche."

"Dude, you need some sleep," Kira jests, unable to take the gravity of this situation to heart.

Brent glares at her. "Fuck you, Kira. I know what I saw and I know how I feel. You weren't in that room. You didn't see the shit we did. Percy can back me up. He saw it. He felt it. He still feels something isn't right." He looks around the room. "This is going to sound crazy, but I need you to hear me out, okay?"

Kira and I nod, eager to hear what he has to say.

"I don't think the wards matter. I think that if Alexandria wanted in here, she'd just walk through," he rushes out.

"I think you are correct," I say quietly. I had known this since they put them up. The wards are strong enough. They're just not the right ones. I am not sure there *are* right ones. Alexandria is not a demon by birth, but by corruption. That kind of evil energy has something that regular evil does not.

Need.

It needs to feed on the loathing and hurt of others. It needs agony to sustain itself. It is why Alexandria wants the *Book of the Broken*. She will become untouchable with that much power at her fingertips.

Alfonso cannot submit to her. The entirety of the supernatural world depends on it.

"What are you guys talking about? Wards work on everything," Kira states in a way that makes it seem like our brains are malfunctioning. I explain my thought process to her, and her shoulders slump. "So we're fucked, is what you're saying," she mumbles.

"No. We just have to be very careful," I reassure her before returning my attention to Brent. "I think it would be best if you stayed here until this whole mess is sorted. This house is too big for the three of us to be on guard constantly."

"Sure. I'll send a couple of the guys to grab our stuff. No one does anything unattended."

Kira raises her eyebrows and Brent rolls his eyes in response. "Not like that, you pervert. If the guys or me are on duty and you guys need to shower we'll stay outside the bathroom door. There's only two ways in, the door and the window. I imagine you can handle the window, yes?" he asks with a fake coyness that even I understand.

Kira glares at him, giving him a vulgar hand gesture. "We've got it, dick."

He blows her a kiss and I wonder how they are friends when they speak to each other in such violent and sexual ways. I find it fascinating more than anything. Before I was cursed there were expectations and rules to follow when fraternizing with the opposing sex. We had to keep a certain distance apart. A kiss on the hand as a greeting or farewell was allowed, but hand holding, hugging, a kiss on the cheek– even more so the mouth– was not allowed until marriage.

Not that it mattered what happened in the hidden parts of town where nobody saw anything. Those were the places the "vermin" hung out, or so Mother would tell me. She forbade me from ever going there. However, Rory would drag me along with her when we would meet at the market. We would spy on the couples who would go there to have some privacy from prying eyes.

We saw things we had never seen before. Hands going places that they were not permitted to be. Mouths doing unimaginable things.

This is the place Mary found us one day before telling my father that we were doing unlady-like things. She was not wrong, but it also was not what she made it seem to be.

It was not that I did not find Rory attractive. It was that I knew my parents would punish me severely for ever even having the thought. Much like Father did when he found out we were courting each other, if you could even call it that.

Not that any of that stopped the thoughts of Rory running through my mind on the cold winter nights.

If we hadn't been outed by Mary, I fear it would have been a matter of time before we were one of the 'vermin'. Oh, how Mother and Father would have loved that.

Once Andromeda woke up from her nap, Brent informed us that the cops had to kill Garret during his rampage. They tried tranquilizers and stun guns, but he was so out of control that nothing worked. They tried for over an hour to get him to stop, but he just kept going.

Surprisingly, none of them are upset at the loss. Garret caused a lot of hurt in his life. His death is a small favor in the grand scheme of things, according to Brent and Andromeda.

But I can see the hurt in his eyes and smell the grief on his body. Despite their disagreements, Brent cared about Garret in his own way. Having to identify his body had to have taken a toll.

Three days have passed and there has not been the faintest whisper of Alexandria's whereabouts or what she's up to. Though, yesterday there were a few twinges along the wards, like someone– or something– was trying to break through. The boys did not find anything when they went to investigate, and it put us all on edge. We have used our nervous energy to focus on training our abilities and working together to fight against anything she could possibly throw at us.

Tomorrow is Halloween, where it all goes down. I have managed to escape explaining the vision I saw the other night by the skin of my teeth. Several times Kira has asked about it, but before I could come up with a response one of the werewolves would say or do something outrageous and take the attention off of me.

Jillian is fully recovered, but has not once left the guest room. It has a bathroom attached to it and Andromeda delivers all of her meals, and spends a lot of time in there. I wish I knew what was going on, but I've been working on not prying into her and Kira's thoughts when they do not want it, and something about the way Andromeda is acting tells me that is the last thing she wants right now.

Which only makes me want to pry more.

"Are you sure it's a good idea to have our Samhain bash with everything going on?" Kira asks Brent and Andromeda who are busy planning their annual party. We are all sitting on the kitchen floor carving pumpkins. It is disgusting and stinky and difficult, but I am having a great time watching everyone's creations come to life, so to speak.

"No, but who would we be if we didn't?" Andromeda says before looking at Kira with big eyes and a pouty mouth. "It's my favorite holiday. We *have* to celebrate. Please," she begs, pulling on Kira's arm, covering it in pumpkin guts. Kira smiles at her and I know before she says it that she is going to give in. Her soft spot for us grows every day.

Andromeda and I have been conspiring on ways to make Kira feel better since her and I's heart to heart the other day. Once I informed her of the reason for Kira's need to control everything her eyes lit up and her mouth parted slightly. She said she'd had no idea. How she's so intuitive and in touch with Gaia and *didn't* see it is confusing to me, but I will not judge her oversight.

"Fine," Kira concedes. "But we're going to keep it *small*. Okay?"

Andromeda does a dance where she sits. The house is already decorated. We spent the entire first day we were on 'house arrest,' as they call it, setting everything up. There are fake spiderwebs hung on the walls with creepy hairy fake spiders hanging on them. Andromeda makes them move and wiggle with a point of her finger. No matter how many times Kira asks her to stop, she just laughs and does it again, usually when Kira is walking by them.

Skeletons sit on the chairs in the living room that don't get used, fake pumpkins and witch's hats are set on every available surface. Ghosts hang from the ceiling, and much like the spiders, Andromeda enjoys using her magic to move them, making them drop onto some of the were-wolves while she giggles like a maniac in the corner, her eyes dancing with delight.

I can tell from the reactions of her friends that this is not new behavior. She relishes in it. Apparently, she does pranks and different tricks every year to see which ones are the best. She has not come up with a new one this year, much to everyone's surprise. They are all waiting with bat-ed breath for a vampire to break through the floorboards or a ghoul to fall from a closet. These are all things I've heard them whispering or thinking about.

Personally, I cannot wait to see what she decides to do.

Chapter Thirty-Four

Andromeda

Having Kira finally agree to our annual party is a relief unlike any I've ever felt. I need to let loose and have some fun. We send out texts to all of our friends letting them know to be here tomorrow night and to invite all of *their* friends.

Jillian sits across from me, her legs crossed as she carves a pumpkin into a scene of a haunted forest. The artistic skill Jillian possesses is astonishing. It makes me feel inadequate with my smiling jack-o-lantern whose lines aren't even remotely straight which makes its face crooked and wobbly. She's all healed and blending in with everyone better than anticipated. There are still some hiccups with how she lived her life before and how she was treated previously, but that was to be expected.

Brent had his boys do some shopping while they were in town grabbing their stuff the other day. They brought back some clothes for Jillian and Hedera, and even stopped by Kira's place and grabbed her some as well. We figured it would be kind of gross having them wear the same thing for days on end and we hadn't had time to go shopping for Hedera yet.

We spend the rest of All Hallows' Eve drinking spiked apple cider, carving pumpkins, and gorging ourselves on Halloween treats and candies. By the time the sun sets we're all feeling very tipsy and our worries of war and impending doom are long forgotten. Brent plays a club playlist from his phone, the music booming out of the Bluetooth speakers he and the boys set up. I sit on the couch, smiling at all my friends dancing and having a great time. Even if our party turns out to be just this, I'd be happy.

I look over at Kira as she bends over, wobbling from side to side. She's the drunkest out of all of us which is only slightly disappointing because Hedera and I had plans for her later. But we can wait to take care of our sexy little gorgon. She picks up one of the skeletons from a chair and wraps its arms around her neck so it dangles behind her. She sways herself and the inanimate skelly boy to the beat of the music. Giggling, I nudge Brent who's sitting next to me. When he gives me his attention, I tip my chin towards Kira and his smile turns mischievous. I twirl my finger in a circle and the skeleton tightens its arms around

Kira, its legs growing until they reach the ground. It spins Kira around and dips her before kissing her cheek.

She screams and tries to scramble away from the horrifying creature, but he holds tight. "Someone fucking help me!" she screams at us, true fear in her eyes until she sees us all cracking up. Her face falls and anger sparks in her eyes. "Andromeda Lynn. Call off your fucking skeleton or I swear to the Goddess..."

Hedera walks up behind her, setting her to rights and removing the skeleton's arms from around her before it turns back to plastic. "Or what, little gorgon?" she asks, her voice low.

Okaaayy, guess we're doing this tonight as planned. Goddess, I love my life.

"Alright, boys, that is the sign for us to go to our rooms and mind our own business," Percy says from where he stands next to Hedera and Kira who have begun making out in front of everyone. Some of them salivate at Hedera's tone and make out session with Kira, while some of them gag at the thought of a vagina. Brent and his lovers share a room while Toby and Scott sleep in the room right next door. It's how they live in their house as well. It saves them from being subjected to all the butt stuff.

Jillian's face is flushed at the sexual tension radiating in the room. "I think I, too, shall call it a night. Thank you guys, for everything." Her eyes well with tears as she expresses her gratitude for us being so welcoming. I give her a quick hug before everyone heads to their rooms.

Her gratitude makes my heart swell. It wasn't easy letting her stay here at first. My friends and I got into a fight when Jillian came out of her room perfectly healed and ravenous. Kira stood in front of her, one hand on her hip and a scowl on her beautiful face. She pointed at the door and told Jillian to kick rocks. Everyone but me was very hesitant to let Jillian stay after that. But since it's my house, my say goes.

"Stop it, Kira. Jillian is staying," I say, stepping between them.

Kira looks at me, hurt contorting her face. "What do you mean she's staying? Did your healing bit make you lose your memory or something?"

I roll my eyes at her. "You know that doesn't happen." I glance over at Jillian before returning my attention to Kira. "She has dangerous enemies out there and no friends. We cannot let her go home. For fuck sake, she's been staying with Alexandria for months now, preparing to overtake the entire supernatural community. Anyone who knows or has an inkling of an idea that she's been involved in that will have a target on Jillian's back. She's safer here with us. If we all work together we have a better chance. There is no one who knows Alexandria's capabilities or thought processes better than Jillian. She is our best bet of winning this thing." My eyes beg her to understand what I'm saying, to hear that I believe in everything I just said.

If Jillian leaves this house alone, she will die.

Everyone else mumbles their agreement. Kira stays silent for several minutes, staring Jillian down. She finally meets my eyes as she says, "It's your house, Andi. If you think you can trust her, then we'll play it your way." She returns her attention to Jillian. "But if you even think about betraying us or leading us astray, I will be the one to kill you. I will make you wish you were never born. These people," she motions to the room full of our closest friends and me, "are everything to me. I don't play lightly with that. Do you understand?"

Although I disagree with how she's handling it, I can't deny that it's hot as hell that she's so protective.

"I agree. Would you like to make a formal agreement? I am more than willing to lay my life on the line to stay here. It is the least I can do since Andromeda healed me from a certain death."

They clasped hands and a burst of aquamarine light shined between them as they made their pact.

Now, a few days have passed, and things have calmed down. Kira even speaks to Jillian like a normal person. It's nice. Peaceful.

Everyone heads to their rooms as Kira, Hedera, and I linger in the living room. We don't want to seem too eager to get our hands on each other, but the tension is practically visible. If it wasn't for us all having to stay here for our safety, we three would be at each other like animals in heat all hours of the day.

But not all things can be butterflies and rainbows, so we make do with what we're given.

Once everyone is in their rooms, Hedera pulls out the big bow she had wrapped in her hair this morning, unraveling it before tying it over Kira's eyes.

"What are you doing? I swear to the Goddess, if you two are pulling another dumb fucking prank on me, I'm going to turn to the dark side. It'll be the beginning of my villain origin story." She's rambling and it's adorable. Hedera and I smirk at each other as we let her talk. The fewer responses she gets the more she rambles. "I'm not fucking around, guys. I don't like not being able to see. Where are you taking me?" she asks as Hedera begins to lead her to our destination. We had a feeling she'd be extra vocal tonight and we want to savor the sounds for ourselves, not sharing them with our guests.

Plus, it's kind of rude to fuck your girlfriend into oblivion with your other girlfriend when you have friends staying with you.

There's a carriage house a few yards from the house hidden behind a copse of trees. A nice room is upstairs, used for the coachmen of days past. Hedera and I laid blankets and pillows down while Brent had Kira busy whipping up some cider earlier, bossing her around and pissing her off.

When we step into the cold night air, Kira shivers. "Where are we going? Please tell me. You guys are really freaking me out."

"Be a good girl and trust us. You *do* trust us, right, Kira?" Hedera asks her as we make our way down the pathway.

"Yes, I trust you." Her voice comes out breathy and I know she's a goner for Hedera's control. Hell, it's not even directed at me and I'm having to fight to keep my legs beneath me. I've been curious about how she's got such a filthy mouth for someone who was raised to be prim and proper. But I suppose after all the years of her watching over the house she saw some things and learned.

"Good. Now, we're going to go up some stairs, okay? I will help you the whole way up. Are you ready?" Hedera asks, her voice stern. Kira nods her head and we begin the ascent.

I open the door and am still amazed at how beautiful we made the place in the little time we had. There are string lights glowing softly along the walls and blankets and pillows are piled on the floor to provide us a comfortable spot to play. We lit some candles as well, to help light the area and give it a romantic feeling. It's very cozy. Too bad we're not going to be enjoying it like that for very long.

I step to the side so Hedera can lead Kira in. When I shut the door behind them, Kira's chest is rising and falling rapidly, her heart beat visible in her throat. Hedera removes the bow from Kira's eyes and she gasps before turning to face us.

"What is this?" Her eyes bounce between the two of us. She swallows hard when she's met with our hungry gazes.

"We're going to take care of *you* tonight," I say, walking towards her. I run my hand down her arm and she shivers. "You take such good care of us in every aspect. It's our turn now." I kiss her as I remove her shirt and bra, needing them gone before the next step in our plan. I do my best to ignore her hardened nipples that are begging to be sucked.

Hedera sends her vines toward Kira, who eyes them warily, but she stands still as they wind their way up her legs. They entwine her hands, pulling them together behind her. Once she's bound I guide her to the nest on the floor. Her body is on fire.

"So needy," I whisper in her ear before nibbling it. She moans in response. We've barely touched her and she's already worked up more than I've ever seen her. Her pupils are wide and her lips are swollen and kissable. Unable to contain myself a moment longer, I crash my mouth to hers, cupping her breasts as I devour her mouth. Hedera works on her pants as I get my fill.

Kira breaks contact with me and looks down at what Hedera is doing to her body. Hedera's vines have now tied her legs so they lie far apart, giving us ample access. She plops her head back down, closing her eyes and taking a deep breath.

"Are you doing okay?" I ask from where I lay next to her, running my finger along the outline of the owl on her stomach. "Is it too much?"

She shakes her head, but doesn't say anything.

Hedera slaps her inner thigh and Kira's head shoots up to glare at her. "Use your words, darling. That is the only way this continues. Do you understand?"

"Y–yes," Kira breathes out as she lays her head back down, her body shaking from the adrenaline soaring through her body.

"Good. Answer Andromeda's question so we can either end this or begin." She rubs the spot on Kira's thigh that she slapped, soothing the sting.

"Yes, I'm good. This is– this is perfect. Thank you," she says quietly.

I smile at her before bending my head to take her nipple into my mouth. She hisses in a breath through her teeth at the sensation. Hedera moves up to her head and reties the scarf around her eyes.

"I want you to *feel* everything we're about to do to you, darling. No peeking. If it gets to be too much say 'barnacle' and we will stop and release you. Tell me you understand."

While we were planning, I filled Hedera in on the use of safe words and their purposes. Unsurprisingly, she caught on quickly and we moved on to everything else we needed for our plan.

"I understand," Kira mumbles.

Hedera nods her head at me and heads to get the bag of goodies in the closet by the front door. She unzips it and dumps the contents on the floor, causing a loud clatter that makes Kira jump and her breathing pick up.

"What was that?" she asks, her head moving back and forth trying to find the cause of the ruckus.

"You'll find out soon enough, love," I tell her as Hedera hands me my first tool, a Wartenberg wheel. It has five rows of spikes that spin as you run it over someone's skin. I make sure not to put too much pressure on it because this one is sharp and will draw blood if I'm not careful.

We'll get to that bit later.

I run the wheel over the meaty parts of her breasts before gently trailing it down to her stomach where I add a bit more pressure. She moans and bites her lip as she begins rolling her hips.

Hedera grabs a black dildo and a vibrator from the pile and joins me in my ministrations. She sets the toys to the side before she rubs up and down Kira's legs with some lotion I didn't see her grab, digging deep into her muscles.

"That feels so good," Kira moans as she begins to relax. Hedera and I grin at each other, knowing what is about to happen to this poor woman.

After Kira is nice and relaxed from the leg massage, Hedera turns on the vibrator and puts it to Kira's clit. She jumps at the sudden sensation, but begins moving her hips in earnest as her body realizes what's happening.

"Yes, Goddess, yes." Her head tips back on the pillow and she pants from the pleasure.

I take the Wartenberg wheel down to her thigh and put enough pressure to draw little droplets of blood. She cries out, but not in pain. Hedera removes the vibrator as I keep going down her leg with the wheel, going back to the light traces of her skin.

"Goddess damn you two. I was about to come," Kira whines.

"Oh, you poor, poor thing," I tease.

Hedera grabs the dildo and rubs it up and down her cunt, getting it nice and wet before slowly inserting it. Kira tries to pull her legs up to get a better angle, but the vines keep her in place. I send some of my magic to them to strengthen them, knowing how strong she is.

As Hedera begins working Kira's pussy with the dildo, she puts the vibrator back to her clit and I suck Kira's big toe into my mouth as I trace her foot with the wheel, making sure to miss the ticklish bits as best as I can.

"Fuck," Kira cries out. The noises she makes are animalistic as her body climbs higher and higher. When Hedera turns off the vibrator and stops moving the dildo, I release Kira's toe.

I grab the nipple clamps from the pile of goodies as Kira curses us again. "I'm going to get you bitches back so ha–" Her words cut off as I attach the nipple clamps to her hardened buds.

"You can try. But you and I both know you're out of your depth here, love. Enjoy it," I demand.

"Then let me come!" she cries.

"In due time." Hedera's words are punctuated as she starts the vibrator again.

Now that she's properly worked up, restrained, and clamped, I can begin my favorite part. The wax play. I grab one of the candles we had lit, thankful that Kira didn't notice what kind they were, and begin dotting her skin with the hot wax. Her body tenses every time a bead touches her sensitive skin.

"I want you to beg us to come, darling. Make us feel bad for you. Make us pity you. Only then will we allow you to do so," Hedera instructs as I paint my masterpiece on Kira's skin. The white wax contrasting with her darker complexion beautifully.

"Please let me come. I've been so nice to you guys. I don't deserve this torture. I thought you loved me."

She definitely needs to work on her begging.

Hedera slaps her inner thigh again and takes the vibrator from her clit. "That was not begging. I did not tell you to guilt trip us. *Beg us,*" she demands, pulling the dildo from Kira's dripping pussy.

Kira groans and thrashes where she lays. I'm glad I strengthened the vines because she definitely would have broken free in her tantrum and we would have been in for it.

"Please. I'm begging you. I'm going to explode if you don't let me come. I *need* you. Please. Pretty, pretty please. I'm being so good for you. You're making me feel *so* good. Please let me come for you."

She's lying about being good. She wouldn't have gotten the last slap to her thigh if she was. But the rest was good enough for me. Hedera looks at me and I shrug. She's in control here, I'm just here for moral support and back up.

"I suppose we could maybe allow that," Hedera says before setting the vibrator back on her clit and turning it all the way up. She moves over and nods her head for me to come help. I remove the dildo from her pussy before sinking my fingers into Kira's soaked cunt and fuck her the way I know she loves, getting that perfect spot.

Seconds. That's all it takes for her to scream at the top of her lungs as fluid gushes from her perfect pussy, soaking my hand.

"Look," Hedera commands as she removes the bow from Kira's eyes, knowing what I'm about to do. Kira listens and I bend my head and lick up her juices.

"So delicious," I moan as I meet her eyes.

Her head falls back onto the pillow and her eyes shut in exhausted bliss.

Chapter Thirty-Five

Kira

T hose evil little vixens. They've been conspiring against me behind my back. I can't say that I hate it, because that would be a lie. I fucking *love* it. I'm not sure what I did to get so lucky to find this kind of love with not only one person, but two. But, Goddess, I think I've died and gone to the good place.

They leave me tied up as they take turns pleasuring each other, demanding I watch them. Andi makes Hedera get on her hands and knees and eats her from behind like she's a starved woman. Hedera's arms can barely keep her held up as Andi works her magic. How Andi ever dated a man is beyond me. That mouth was *made* for eating pussy. She's insightful and knows all the right moves.

When Hedera holds her climax back on purpose, Andi growls before spitting on her asshole and pressing her thumb in as she continues working her pussy with her tongue. A few minutes later and Hedera is crumpling to the floor as her orgasm overtakes her.

Andi smiles, proud of herself. "That'll teach you to hold back on me again." She goes to lay down between us, but Hedera– who is somehow not exhausted yet– tackles her and has her tied up just like me in seconds.

Hedera looks at me with a wicked smile. "Shall I fuck her like I did you or should I use this interesting contraption?" She holds up a strap on and the laugh that leaves me is diabolical.

"You should use that, but you should let me go first. I want *more*."

"You dirty girl," Hedera says before the vines slither away from my body, going to Andi's and double restraining her.

"Hey! This isn't fair!" she cries, pulling at the vines. She could easily make them fall away, but she doesn't. That tells us all we need to know.

"Life isn't fair, princess," I say before giving her a quick kiss and straddling her face. "Now have your dessert." I sit on her face as Hedera puts the strap on and positions herself to fuck Andi's dripping wet pussy.

Hours later, we're laying tangled up with each other, panting and sweaty. I don't know how many times we went round and round again, trying to outdo the other with the most kinky shit we could think of, but I do know that it was the most mind blowing night of my life.

"That was lovely," Hedera says, her eyelids drooping.

"Agreed," Andi mumbles as Sleep comes for her.

I can't say anything because Sleep has me by the hand, dragging me into Dreamland.

The next morning we're woken up by yelling outside. It takes us a few minutes to realize it's our names being yelled by Brent and his boys. I think Jillian is out there, too, but I can't be certain.

"What time is it?" Andi asks, rubbing the sleep from her eyes.

"No idea. But it must be decently late if they're looking for us in such a tizzy. I don't even know where my phone is."

"It is past noon," Hedera says, looking out a window.

"How do you know?"

"The position of the sun." She stands and gets her clothes on, throwing her hair into a messy ponytail. "When it is your only friend for years, you learn its comings and goings. Plus, it is how I would tell when it was time to go home when I was a young girl. If I was late for supper, Mother would discipline me and I did not like that."

I give her a blank stare for a moment. "It's too early for all of that, babe." She shrugs her shoulders and waits for us to get our clothes on. We take the walk of shame back towards the house, but don't make it ten feet before Brent is loping towards us.

"Where have you been? We've been looking for you for *hours*. You can't disappear on us like that. Especially not right now." He crosses his arms and taps his foot against the leaf littered lawn.

"We were in the guest house," Andi explains, ducking her head so he can't see her flushed cheeks.

"You don't have to be embarrassed by being caught," Brent says. "I can smell the sex on you. I know what you were doing." He throws his hands in the air. "Just tell us where you're going next time. We thought you got abducted or something." Now that Papa Wolf has gotten his lecturing out of the way, he scoops us all up into a hug, relief washing through him.

"Why are you so worried?" I ask when he releases us and I can breathe again. Dude seriously needs to remember how to control his own strength.

"Because they did raids last night in town. It's all over the news. Alexandria has asked the public for help in looking for something. I'm guessing it's the book. But she won't say what it is, instead she's instructing people to go to a discrete location and receive instructions." He won't meet our eyes and it sends alarm bells through my mind.

"Who?" I demand.

He shakes his head. "Let's go back to the house."

"No, Brent. Who was it?" I demand again.

He's trying not to tell us until we're in the house because it's going to be devastating. Which means it's only one person. I brace myself for his words, but it doesn't help the blow.

"Grace," Toby says when Brent presses his lips together. He reaches out and rubs Andi's arm as he breaks the news. "They tore Sherman's apart and took everything magical. She's being held at the Prison for Magical Beings."

Andi's legs give out and I barely catch her in time.

The Prison for Magical Beings is a cutthroat prison where only the worst of the worst go. They torture their prisoners to the brink of their death and then bring them back just to do it again and again until the person goes crazy and tells them anything they want to hear. Activist groups have been trying to get it shut down for a century now, but all of their efforts fall on deaf ears.

"Why would they take her there if she did nothing wrong, though?" I ask, my brows furrowing.

"Alexandria has control of that prison," Jillian speaks up, ducking her head as if she's expecting a blow to the head or reprimand. "It's where we would take people she wanted to question or people who spoke out against her."

"We have to get her out," Andi says, finding her legs again. She stands, raising her chin and stares Brent dead in his eyes. "Today."

"Girl. I love you, but there is no way in the Underworld we can break in there in a day, find Grace, and get her out. Plus, it's probably a trap. They know how close you were to her. They know everything," Brent informs her, patting her arm, trying to console her.

She tears away from us. "I'm going to get her out of there. One way or another. You guys can either help me or stay here and hide forever. It's time this ends." She stalks off towards the house as we all stare after her.

Apparently last night woke up the badass in her. Not that she wasn't a badass before, but she was always so cautious and mindful of the rules and laws we have to follow. Not anymore, I guess.

"Are we going to allow her to go there on her own?" Hedera asks, watching her go.

"You don't understand," Percy says. "That place is worse than anything your mind could conjure up. They have vampires walking the halls and reapers hidden about ready to devour or infect you. Walking in there uninvited is asking Death to take you before your time."

"My question still stands," Hedera says, staring him down.

I sigh, rubbing my face. "We're going with her. She'll be killed before she even steps foot through the door if she goes alone."

Brent curses under his breath, his face a mask of rage and resignation. "Sometimes I really hate you guys."

"Love you too, big guy." I slap his shoulder before heading after my girl to start planning our march toward Death.

Chapter Thirty-Six

Andromeda

Instead of heading inside, I take a lap around the back-yard to try to calm down. Once I realize it's a lost cause, I head inside and stop short when I see Jillian leaning against the kitchen island waiting for me. "I know how to get in without detection."

I roll my eyes. "Of course you do. Tell me everything."

"The others are in the living room waiting for us. They won't let you go in there alone." At my questioning look, she explains. "I was Alexandria's favorite for a long time. She would send me on errands to retrieve things, whether it was an item or information recovered from the Prison." She shrugs before turning and heading toward the living room.

When we walk into the living room everyone's eyes fall on us, all conversation stopping as they take in the deter-mined look on my face. I settle in between Kira and Hedera as we listen to Jillian's plan. It's tricky. It's dangerous. But in my heart of hearts, I know it's the path that we must follow.

"I'm going to go meditate for a while and pray for protection. We leave in twenty minutes," I say before heading upstairs. I may be putting on a brave face for them, but in reality, I'm panicking. I've never broken into anything before. Not even when a group of kids in my grade broke into the abandoned hospital on O'Malley because they'd heard it was haunted. They made me keep a look out, but I ran away when the first vehicle drove by.

It turned out to be Miss Robertson on her way to the vet clinic. Thankfully, they didn't get caught and nothing bad happened. But they never let me live it down either.

I've always been a rule follower. A genuinely good person who just wants to bring love and light to the world. I know that this path I'm on will change that. I will probably have to hurt people and beings in order to accomplish what needs to be done. I will lose a part of myself and be one step closer to following in my mother's footsteps. And I don't want that.

I settle myself in my spell room after lighting the nag champa and cleansing myself. "Gaia, please guide my feet as I embark on this path you have laid before me. Make sure my heart is true and wrap me and my friends in your protection. If anyone falls, please accompany them to the

After. They need a kind god to guide them. Thank you. Blessed be."

I take some deep breaths, letting the incense settle in my lungs to calm me. I envision a green and purple bubble enveloping myself and everyone downstairs.

A soft caress runs down my cheek and I lean into it. The smell of turned earth and musk tickles my nose and I know Gaia has heard my prayer. I stay in this place of peace for as long as possible before her presence disappears, telling me it's time to move. Standing, I look around my spell room, rubbing my hands on my leggings.

A voice in the back of my mind tells me to check the library before leaving. Why, I can't be for certain, but as always, I listen. I stand in the middle of the room, spinning in a small circle to see what it could be. After several minutes of doing this, I get dizzy, so I sit on the floor and breathe for a moment. I don't have long before we need to go, but a few minutes won't hurt.

I run my hand along the rug beneath me and feel a bump underneath. "What in the world?" I stand up and peel back the rug to reveal a small hidden door. I try to pull it open, but it doesn't budge. Sitting back down, I huff out a breath. Of course I would find something that catches my attention right before I march into certain death and I can't open it.

"*Blood*," a phantom voice whispers. It sounds vaguely like Aunt Merr's voice and causes tears to prick my eyes. I've missed hearing her voice.

I stand up and walk over to the spell section, remembering seeing a sewing needle laying next to the cauldron the other day. I pick it up and return to the door. Taking a deep breath, I prick my finger before I can think better of it. I don't know if this needle is sanitary, but I don't have time to find something else that would work. Bending down, I wipe my bleeding finger on the lock on the door and wait. A moment later it pops open. I heave the surprisingly heavy door open to reveal several different sigils and protective wards drawn on the walls of the small area and the door itself.

Inside is a black cloth wrapped around something. When I pick it up, the cloth falls away and a book is revealed. Whispers begin to wind around in my mind as I hold the book in my hands. "*Unimaginable power. Sacrifice. Kill. Death. Power.*" The words tumble through my mind in a whirlwind, repeating themselves, growing louder and louder.

An invisible force pries my hands apart and the book falls back to the ground with a deafening boom and the voices stop.

"Thank you," I whisper to Gaia for what I assume is her assistance in releasing me from the book's pull. I rush downstairs to tell everyone my findings. When I get to the living room, panting and barely able to speak, they all look at me with concern.

"What is going on?" Kira asks, coming over to me and helping me to the couch.

"I found it."

"Found what?" Brent asks, crouching in front of me.

"The *Book of the Broken.* It's up there. In the library. Don't touch it. It's evil," I pant out.

Jillian, Hedera, and Toby go upstairs to investigate as the rest of us stay downstairs, far away from the book. When they come back, Hedera is carrying it with a hungry looking Jillian right behind her. Toby is several steps behind, a sick look on his face.

"That's it, isn't it?" I ask Jillian. She barely glances at me before gluing her eyes back to the bundle in Hedera's arms.

"Yes. This is what Alexandria has been looking for." Her words are bland, but her eyes tell a different story.

"Why are you holding that thing, Hedera?" Kira asks, backing away from the power coming off the book.

"I am the only one who would touch it. It really is not that bad. It is just a book to me." She shrugs as she sits on a chair.

Interesting.

We all converse over what to do with the book. Historically speaking, we can't burn it as it is incombustible. We can't leave it here unprotected. Now that we've opened the hiding place it was in, the sigils and protective spells are ruined, so we can't just put it back either.

"What if we take it with us?" Hedera suggests.

"Are you insane?" I ask. "There's a very real possibility we will be imprisoned, at best. They'll confiscate it and then it will for sure get to Alexandria." She glares at me, holding the book closer to her chest. Apparently she isn't as immune to the book's call as she claims.

"She has a point, though," Kira says. My head snaps towards her and she holds her hands up in the air. "Listen, we can't leave it here, and we're all going with you to the prison. We have no one else to hold onto it. We *have* to take it with us."

Sighing, I drop my head into my hands. "Fine. But that means we have to be even more careful than we're already planning to be." Everyone nods and we rework our plans to ensure that we'll be as safe as possible so we're not found out.

Once everything is planned, the others head outside to get into their vehicles and I take a moment to look around the foyer before heading out. "This is it, Aunt

Merr. Everything you've taught me, everything that's laid before me comes to a head today. I wish you were here to help. I know we would for sure succeed if we had your help. I miss you." A single tear runs down my cheek and I wipe it off.

When I feel at peace with what we're about to do, I head outside to join the others. "Let's do this."

The ride to the meet up point is uneventful aside from seeing groups of the Council's mercenaries patrolling the streets downtown. We don't recognize any of our friends in the people who are milling about. I pray that they're hiding out in their homes and not held prisoner like Grace.

When we get to the agreed upon spot and step out of our respective vehicles, a chill runs down my spine. "No matter what happens, just remember I love you guys," I tell my friends, fighting back my tears. I look at Kira and Hedera. "Don't let me fall too far from grace. I don't want to end up like *her*."

They wrap me in their arms and whisper their promises and love.

"If you're finished with your mushy gushy bullshit, we need to get a move on," Jillian snarks, inspecting her fingernails where she stands next to a tree.

We let each other go and follow Jillian as she leads us through a wooded area to a supposedly hidden entrance. I find it hard to believe that the people of this prison don't know about it, but Jillian swears it's hidden well and is used to smuggle things in and out. Unfortunately, we have no option but to trust her and the scar is still intact from the deal she made with Kira, so I take it as a sign that she isn't trying to hand us over.

A few minutes into our hike through the thick trees, a branch snaps in the distance.

"Percy and Ronnie go check it out. Make it fast," Brent instructs. The men shed their clothes and shift in the blink of an eye before they tear through the forest on eerily quiet feet.

"Well, well, well, what do we have here, Mikel?" a voice asks behind us. I spin around and find two hooded men stalking us, holding very sharp knives.

"Alexandria will be pleased to have some new toys. Oh, but one of them isn't new, are they?" The one on the left looks Jillian up and down, a smirk visible underneath their low-hanging hood.

"Mikel, how unpleasant to see you. I'm assuming your butt-buddy there is Erich since you guys have been attached at the dick since you started working for Alexandria." Jillian crosses her arms, completely unaffected at the obvious hunters standing in front of us. Their cloaks give them away, along with the nasty looking knives that I'm sure have spell work etched into the blades. Some hunters prefer a more subtle approach to their attire, but hunters like these two make it their entire personality and dress the part.

"You sniveling little cunt," Erich says, taking a step forward before Mikel holds out an arm, catching him in the chest.

"Chill, Erich. She's going to get what's coming for her."

Erich deflates, pouting. "Fine, but what about the others? Can we at least gank *them*?"

Mikel looks at him, considering the possibility of them versus us. "I suppose we could have a little fun. But first–" He lifts his arm, rolling his cloak up to reveal a triangular tattoo with swirls and crude lines cutting through it. He slices his finger on his blade and runs it along the tattoo, which glows red before the blood fades away. "A little back up call in case things take a turn."

Jillian rolls her eyes. "Of course you need back up, you washed up, good for nothing moron." Then she releases a blast of red smoke towards the two men. "RUN."

We don't think twice before turning on our heels and getting out of there. We have bigger fish to fry than to deal with an entire group of hunters.

Thirty minutes later, we arrive at the secret entrance. Percy and Ronnie met back up with us ten minutes ago, covered in blood and gore. They took out three hunters on their own and Ronnie only has a small cut on his bicep from the altercation.

I reach out and heal him while Kira hands them both bottles of water to remove the blood enough that they aren't dripping it everywhere. The hope is that the three hunters have been around enough that the vamps won't track down their scent before we get to Grace's cell.

"Kira, your blood, please," Jillian asks. Kira holds her hand out to her. The scent of copper fills the air as Jillian slices Kira's palm, rubbing the blood on a brown stone. It is not a natural brown stone as I thought at first glance, it's actually covered in dried blood. How many times has this entrance been used?

A low rumble sounds from the stone wall in front of us as a door wide enough for one person to go through opens. A dark corridor looms in front of us. Another shiver runs through me. I am so not ready for this.

Brent goes in first, followed by his pack, Jillian, Hedera, Kira, and finally me. I glance behind me as the door starts rumbling shut and see the two hunters from early, and a few of their buddies, ten feet away. Panic wells in my chest. They're going to get in here before this cursedly slow door shuts all the way.

"Guys," I whisper, but they don't hear me above our shuffling feet and the rumbling of the door. "Guys, we have a problem." My voice will not go above a whisper no matter how much I try, so I tug on Kira's arm, but she just reaches behind me and takes my hand, focusing on the corridor in front of us so she doesn't trip over the rocks.

Six feet.

We're all going to die. Not like there's any room in here for us to maneuver anyway. They'll kill me first and then the rest of our friends, one by one.

Four Feet.

I'm not ready to die. I don't want my friends to die either.

Two Feet.

Finally the door closes with a low whooshing sound. My shoulders slump in relief.

One threat down. Another million to go. I shake off my nerves in the dark corridor. I cannot be off of my game for this. Putting the hunters behind us, figuratively and literally, I center myself. We can do this. We can get Grace out and go home. Everything will be totally fine.

For a moment we are totally blind before a lantern is lit at the front of the line. It's still dark in here, but the light makes it less suffocating. We begin inching our way down the corridor. Jillian said we will go about a thousand feet until we get to the exit. I count down the minutes, focusing on the passing numbers to keep my heart rate down so I don't release pheromones in the air, making the vamps' jobs way easier in locating us.

A few minutes later, the corridor widens a bit and the shuffling of feet quiets as we reach the exit. "Now comes the hard part," Jillian sing-songs. I'm not sure how they're so calm and having fun with this, but I'm kind of jealous. And angry. They pull something from their pocket and press it to the door. An eternity seems to pass before they signal that it's time to take our first steps into the prison. A single whistle signals the beginning of the end.

We file out into the hallway and are all surprised at the opulence of the place. The floor is a thick red carpet that helps in our mission, muting our footsteps. Paintings and tapestries hang from the walls. Some of beautiful sunsets or ocean views, and some of grotesque scenes of torture and death. The walls that are visible are white quartzite, making breaking through them next to impossible without the proper tools. It's truly the perfect prison.

Jillian says something to Brent and he nods before waving his goodbye to us and leading his pack down one corridor while Jillian leads us down another. This was part of the plan I despised the most, no matter how much it makes sense. We have no idea where Grace is being kept and having such a large group meandering about a locked down place is asking to get caught.

Once Brent and his boys get to the fifth corridor on the left, they'll break apart into two groups of three. Jillian showed me how to do a kind of communication spell on everyone while they were telling us how to get in and out, hopefully unscathed. A small freckle sits on all of our hands. It will burn if someone is in danger and grow cold when they find Grace. It's not ideal, but it's the most inconspicuous way we could come up with.

Jillian drew each group a map so they wouldn't get lost. As hesitant as I am to trust her, I'm glad we have someone from the other side on our team or else this would be hopeless.

We take our first turn down a corridor and I nearly jump out of my skin as a werewolf charges towards the door of its cell, saliva dripping from its jowls. I hold my breath to hold in the scream begging to be released. I only breathe again after a buzzing sound causes the werewolf to whine, backing up and shaking its head.

Jillian is staring at the werewolf when I rip my eyes from the poor thing. Hatred shines in the orbs. I nudge her with my arm and nod my head for us to keep going. She shakes her head to clear her thoughts and keeps moving.

It's of utmost importance for us to stay quiet as talking in the cells is not allowed. If there is talking, the higher ups release a gas that puts the prisoners to sleep. Thankfully, most of them seem to be sleeping already or so far gone in their heads that they don't even notice infiltrators.

We take some more turns before we get to a set of stairs that leads to the lower levels. Boots sound from below, moving towards us. We look to Jillian to see what she wants us to do. It's not like we can just disappear.

Jillian looks at Kira and swirls her pointer finger. Kira opens her mouth to protest, but Jillian sharply shakes her head and twirls her finger again, confidence shining in her eyes.

Jillian leads us to a far corner of the corridor and Kira grabs mine and Hedera's hands. We take the hint and grab Jillian's as Kira closes her eyes and her brow furrows in concentration. A tingling sensation washes over me, but I don't know if it did anything because I can still see all of us plain as day. This could be catastrophically bad.

The guard walks up the stairs and enters the corridor, looking left and right. His eyes linger on us for a few moments, but then he releases a belch and heads in the opposite direction.

My shoulders slump. This is way too close for comfort. Speaking of comfort, my house sounds like a really cool place to be right now. I want to leave. Grace can figure it out on her own, right? She's a powerful...whatever she is. I chew on my lip until I taste copper.

Eyes wide, the other three look at me and my now bleeding lip. I suck it into my mouth and hold it there, hoping it didn't trigger any of the vamps. You'd think with all of their prey so readily available to them they wouldn't care about some random person's blood.

Unfortunately for us, a single bell sounds through the hall. Jillian's head falls to her chest before she looks at me with death shining in her eyes.

I fucked up. I always fuck up. Why did I think I could do this?

Jillian holds up two fingers, signaling for us to move faster than is comfortable, but necessary to finish what needs to be done. We keep contact with each other, hoping our invisibility lasts until we find Grace, but I'm not confident it will. Plus, now that the vamps have my scent, they'll be able to sniff me out easier. I should be left behind. I'd rather my friends come back and save me than lose out on this opportunity to save Grace.

But they won't go for that. Not like I can suggest it anyway.

We rush down the stairs and I cringe at how loud our footsteps are on the stone steps. Why couldn't they carpet these too?

At the bottom of the steps, we turn right and hurry down another hallway. A rush of air passes us and we see a blur of black.

Vampire.

I take deep breaths to calm my heart, but it's no use. No amount of calming breaths or incense or *anything* could keep me calm right now. I've endangered everyone I care about because of my damn anxiety.

The door we need to go through is up ahead and we're so close to our destination I can taste it. But as we're about to walk through, it slams shut and someone chuckles behind us.

"You thought you were so sneaky. But we can smell you, *witch.*"

Chapter Thirty-Seven

Hedera

We all twist, making sure to keep contact so they can't see us. Not that it will do much good. We start to inch around the man and I focus on him, trying to persuade his mind that we are not here, that we are not now right in front of him. But his sense of smell is too strong. He lashes out faster than I can see and grabs Andromeda by the neck, pulling her towards him and breaking our connection. He smiles wide, showing his fangs until he sees the rest of us standing around her.

The idea of putting my hand on the book that's hidden inside my shirt and harnessing its power blares through my mind, and I do everything I can to ignore it. I'm not opposed to harnessing the power, but I won't do it for a lowly vampire when we have a demon to potentially fight.

I lied to them earlier when I said that it was just another book to me. It whispers promises of greatness and peace to me. All I have to do is answer yes. If I had told them the truth, there would have been no way they would let me hold onto it. But the thought of letting it go is torture.

"Well, well. What do we have here?" He sets her back down and she sucks in lungfuls of air.

Jillian steps forward, leaning against the vampire. "I was just doing what Alexandria asked of me."

He chuckles. "What was that, succubus? Bringing her a snack?"

"You know, the usual. Gain their trust, get them here, sacrifice them for her. Just another Friday afternoon."

This bitch. Vines extend from my arms, ready to snap her neck like I've done to so many before her. But before I can, she shoves a syringe into the vamp's neck and he drops like a ton of bricks.

"I really thought you were serious there for a sec," Kira says as she wipes perspiration from her forehead.

Jillian looks between us for a moment before rolling her eyes. "I made a promise. I don't break them." Her eyes meet Andromeda's. "Your mother gave me purpose at one time, but I realized after failing my last task that she is a dangerously vindictive woman and I will have no part in that. I gave her *years* of my life and she threw me away like I meant nothing. You saving me after everything I had done and said told me more about your character than I was willing to think about when Igor and I broke into your home. I have given you guys my loyalty and I will die before that is broken."

"You are an excellent liar," I admire.

She turns on her heel and heads back towards the door. We need to hurry before another vampire finds us.

Another bell sounds, this one lower than the first.

"They've stopped looking for you," Jillian says to Andromeda. "They must have found another prisoner bleeding. Probably some bloke who's bashing their head against the wall again."

The image makes my stomach turn. I have been held prisoner for a long time, but I was never subjected to the torture and cruelty that these people endure on a daily basis, and even I wanted to die sometimes. But to have your mind broken over and over again. I cannot imagine how that must make these people feel.

Jillian pauses in front of a door with a big dial on it. "She's probably in here. Let's hope they haven't changed the code since I was exiled." She begins turning the giant contraption, her muscles bunching and releasing with every turn.

"Can we help?" Kira asks, bouncing on her feet and looking around the open area we're standing in. She's been more quiet than usual and I will have to reward her later for not babbling like a lunatic with how nervous I know she is.

"No," Jillian grunts out. "It has sensors on it, anyone unauthorized for entry will set an alarm off and we will be surrounded in a matter of seconds. This is my mission, I must bear it alone."

Five minutes later, the huge door swings inwards, revealing another darkly lit hallway. Jillian stands to the side, letting us enter. Movement at the end of the corridor causes us to pause and reach for each other's hands again. But we soon realize it is part of Brent's pack.

They see us and freeze as well before heading towards us. "What the hell, Jillian? Why are we here with you?" Toby asks, chest heaving with his anger. Percy and Colton stand behind him, eyeing Jillian warily.

Before Jillian can answer, Brent, Ronnie, and Scott round the opposite corner.

We all look at Jillian, whose eyes are wide as she shakes her head back and forth. "No, no, nononononono." She grabs Kira's hands, making Kira and me tense up. "I swear I didn't know this was going to happen. Please believe me. She–she must have figured out you would come for the woman and set a trap. Please. I never would have brought you here if I knew she was going to do this."

Jillian falls to her knees as Kira looks at her in confusion. "What are you talking about Jillian?"

Before she can answer, a laugh that makes my blood run cold reverberates down the hallway. "It's about time you show up. I've been waiting."

We turn and see Alexandria standing at the end where Brent and his guys had just come from. Blackness surrounds her and she seems to float on it as she moves towards us.

"What a good little dog," she says to Jillian, who is doing their best to hide behind Kira, her body shaking and eyes wide with terror. "Come. I have a treat for you." She curls her fingers and Jillian slides across the floor, her fingers trying to find a hold in the smooth floor. We try to reach for her, but it's no use. Alexandria just pulls her past us.

As Jillian gets closer to Alexandria, she's lifted into the air by black bands. "You little bitch. You thought you could double cross *me* and get away with it? Did you really think I wouldn't know?" Alexandria laughs again. "The plans I have for you, you little freak, are unlike any you've ever seen. You'll beg for your death. And if I'm feeling generous I may just give it to you." She slams Jillian against the stone wall, her head bouncing off a piece jutting out. Her head slumps to her chest as blood oozes from the wound. She falls to the ground and doesn't move again.

"Hello, mother," Andromeda says, stepping forward, ignoring our injured friend so she can face our shared enemy.

Chapter Thirty-Eight

Kira

"Hello, Mother." Andi steps towards Alexandria and my heart falls to my stomach. I try to reach for her, but my arms don't move. I glance down at my arms and see that I'm bound by black bands.

Anger courses through my veins.

"Andromeda, dear. How nice it is to see you again. I see my sister raised you well. Where is she, by the way? I want to give her my thanks." Her smile is wicked and if I could get free of these bounds, I'd knock her pearly white teeth out of her head.

"She's dead," Andi says softly, her heartbreak still fresh.

"Oh. How sad." Alexandria's voice is sarcastic, lacking any of the empathy a mother should have for her daughter losing someone she loved.

Andi scoffs. "Don't act surprised. I called and told you. You didn't show up." Her shoulders rise and fall in a shrug. "Not that it's surprising seeing as you dumped me on her doorstep and never checked in again. Thanks for that, by the way. I had a much better life with her than I could have *ever* had with you." She looks her mother up and down with nothing but disgust etched on her face, her grief forgotten for the moment.

I'm so damn proud of her.

Alexandria's face contorts with rage. "You insolent little–"

"I would watch what you say next," Hedera says quietly. Her head is bowed and she looks up at Alexandria from beneath her lashes. The energy coming off of her is wild, more potent than any of the times we've trained.

"Or what? Are you going to magically tear free from your confines and kill *me?* You're not even close to strong enough to go against me, little girl. I have more power in my pinky than you do in that entire puny body." Alexandria laughs at the thought.

"Why don't you release me and we will see just how true that is."

Alexandria stares at her for a minute, considering the idea. Then she remembers our run-in the other night and thinks twice. "I don't think that will be happening today. See, I have everything I need, my daughter, this succubus, and the access I need to the book. There is nothing you or your friends can do to stop what's about to happen.

"You are looking at the next head of the Council. No one will be able to overthrow me once I claim my rightful spot, and you and everyone like you will be my *slaves.*"

As she goes on her dumb little tangent, Hedera works her wrists free of the black restraints with her vines. She sends them under the sea of black covering our feet and slithers them up our backs, releasing us as well.

"I am no one's slave," I say as I unleash my petrifying power on her. She grabs Colton with a black tendril and throws him in the way of my gaze, leaving me no time to stop, to prevent him from falling to the curse.

"No," I cry, falling to my knees as Alexandria shrills in laughter again. It's cut short by four vines encircling her neck as Hedera slowly walks towards her. Brent and his boys get behind Alexandria while her attention is on the girl we never would have guessed would be this powerful. The boys shift while Hedera, Andi, and Alexandria talk.

"You will not be the next head of the Council. We will rise up and overthrow you before you even get *close* to taking that seat," Andi says, stalking closer to her mother.

"Your plan is flawed in more ways than one if you think there are not those here that know what you plan to do," Hedera says. "In addition to underestimating us."

She unleashes a bundle of vines straight for Alexandria's red face, who bats them away with a wave of her hand.

Andi sends a blast of purple light towards her, but it's met with a wall of black and she's flung backwards towards the wall.

Scott leaps over her head and tears into her neck, black blood spilling to the floor. He spits and coughs when he lands, doing his best to get the acidic blood out of his mouth.

I need to move. I need to act, but I took out one of our own. I didn't mean to, but it reminds me of the time when I was a kid and accidentally petrified one of my best friends. I stayed home from school for months after that, too afraid to look another person in the face. My parents sent me to therapy for years to get over the accident. They would constantly tell me it wasn't my fault. I started to believe them. I got more comfortable.

Then I was attacked while out with friends and did it again. They shunned me for it. I wasn't their perfect daughter. I was reckless and a danger to their livelihoods. I grew up in foster care after that. Home after home. Family after family until I aged out and made my own way in the world.

Alexandria sends Scott flying into the wall behind him. A sharp whine leaves his throat before he lays still on the floor.

It cannot end like this. We cannot all be taken out by this power-hungry monster.

I rise to my feet, taking a stumbling step and meet Brent's eyes as he prepares his own attack. We have to work together to get her down. We talked this out. We planned. We can do this.

What was the secret word again? Come on, Kira. *Think.*

"Cornucopia," Hedera calls out and I remember.

We get into our positions, Andi and I chanting as we begin our spell. Hedera summons a wall of vines. She puts her hand in her pocket to check on the book while Brent and his remaining men surround Alexandria.

"You fools think you can take me down, but you're wrong. *Nothing* in this world can take me down. *Nothing,*" she yells as she begins blasting Hedera's ivy wall and the wolves in front of her with black balls that act like acid. The wolves jump out of the way in time, and Hedera puts new vines in place of the ones that fall to Alexandria's attack.

Brent roars, signaling go time.

Hedera tears down her wall of ivy, sending it tunneling towards Alexandria who blasts it with a sea of black. Brent and the remaining three of his wolves go for Alexandria's throat, two of them sinking their teeth into it, another biting her face, and another getting her upper arm.

Andi and I finish our chant, holding our hands out towards her. A wave of blue and gold surrounds her and she screams as the soul that was once hers wars with what she's now become. While we work the spell, we're shown the true nature of Alexandria and how she fell from grace.

Alexandria was a good woman once, if not always a bit jealous. She was kind and thoughtful, but always wanted more out of life. She needed to be validated by those around her for every small deed she did. It made her feel important, loved.

At first, her parents were proud of her for volunteering and baking for families in need. But when her mother found her journal while cleaning her room one day, they realized that at some point her acts of service had changed from a place of love to a place of selfish need.

Coincidentally, it was around the time that Alexandria met Nathaniel, Andi's father. They told her that he wasn't good for her, but she ignored them as all young girls do. Her selfish tendencies grew as the years passed. They thought she would get better once she announced she was pregnant with Andi, but it got worse.

Every time Andi met a milestone, Alexandria made it about herself in one way or another. Getting sympathy for how hard she worked to make Andi be such a good girl and meet said milestones.

When Andi started coming into her powers and Alexandria realized she was a natural, she tried to shut them down. Her and Nathaniel told her that it was unnatural for her to have the powers she did, even though she's always been a green witch and drawn to nature.

Andi's pureness was a bane to her parent's plans. It hurt them when she healed things around her without meaning to. So, they sent her away. She would not get in the way of ruling the supernatural world for them.

But they were wrong. Because here we stand, fighting against Alexandria's vision for the future.

When our spell is done and the blinding light fades, Alexandria is crumpled on the ground, black smoke covering most of her body.

Brent and his boys stand back, panting, blood dripping from their mouths. Whether it is theirs or hers I'm not sure due to the amount of it there is. For all I know it's a mixture.

A sniffle comes from Alexandria's form. "I just wanted to make a difference in the world," she cries. "I wanted to be good once." She raises her head and stares at us. Her eyes are the same green color as Andi's. A sardonic laugh escapes her. "But all roads to the Underworld are paved with good intentions."

Her eyes darken again as she sits up, wiping blood from the corner of her mouth.

Chapter Thirty-Nine

Andromeda

"**M**om, you can stop this. You can come back with us and we can work through everything. Please," I beg as I walk towards her, holding out my hand for her to take. The proverbial olive branch. It's my last ditch effort at getting through to her. If this doesn't work, we're going to have to kill my mother. I knew it would come to this. Her or us. But I don't want to have to do that. Seeing her eyes clear from the corruption has given me more hope than I could have ever imagined. She's still in there. I know it.

She smiles at me, but it lacks warmth. She gains her feet and raises her chin. "What makes you think I want *anything* to do with *you*?" Alexandria raises her arms above her head and begins chanting. I run through all the spells I know, but come up empty on what she's trying to accomplish. The ground begins to tremble under our feet as her voice booms through the enclosed space.

"Look out," Hedera yells, backing away from Alexandria. She holds her hands out and we all rush behind her. But before Percy can get past her, he's sucked into the abyss that opens behind my mother. Brent howls his pain as his mate falls to his death. Then he lowers his head to the ground and bares his teeth along with his remaining wolves.

"Did you think I was going to allow you to gang up on me and not call in reinforcements? *Tsk, tsk.* My friends want to play, too," she taunts as black masses rise from the abyss behind her. She smiles before the horde of demons she summoned are unleashed upon us. "By the way, Andromeda dear, your mother sends her regards." Her words are the slice of a well sharpened knife.

My mom was right there. I saw her, I heard her. Why won't she fight against the control of the demonic powers?

"Mom, please. Please come back to me. We can fix this," I beg over the roaring noise of the demons coming up from the Underworld and barrelling through the halls looking for their first victims.

Alexandria gives me a cruel smile before snaring Toby with a black tendril and snapping his neck. Something inside of me breaks at the sight of him dying. I begin rendering things in two, sending blast after blast of energy towards our enemies. I have no *care* that these are living creatures. The only things I care about are making sure my remaining friends and I get out of here alive. We'll rebuild after that. But we *will* get out of here.

"I'm tapped out," Kira calls to my left. She's panting and her skin is soaked with sweat.

"Same," I answer. I don't have a kernel of power left within me.

"I have enough for one last move. But I cannot guarantee that it will work," Hedera says, sparing us a quick look.

I see her intentions in that look and I cry out, "No, you can't! We need you!"

She answers with her soft smile. "There's always the other side, little witch."

Before Kira and I can stop her, she takes a step forward and unleashes her full power. The room fills with vines that have sharpened thorns and leaves that look sharp enough to slice through flesh and bone.

When I'm certain she's spent, she puts her hand back in her pocket and doesn't bring it back out. The vines get thicker and she makes a movement with her free hand. A thick rope of ivy makes itself into a spear with a thorn tip.

A black substance drips off the end of it. Hedera screams all of her rage and pain as she hurls the spear towards Alexandria, holding her hand out to guide it home. When it hits Alexandria in the chest, a bright burst of white light tears through the room and we're blinded.

Screams of agony and anger flit through the air as the smells of copper and sulfur clog my nose. I'm not sure who the screams are coming from or if it's from both of them. When the vines fade away, the only things left are blood and two crumpled bodies. Hedera and my mother.

Instinct tells me to go to Hedera and heal her, save her before it's too late. But a hand guides me, urging me to finish our mission *now.*

I hold my hand out to Kira and she entwines her fingers with mine as we begin the spell that will incinerate my mother's dead body. "I loved you even when you didn't deserve to be loved. You gave me life and I will always regard you with respect due to that, but you did me a great service by sending me to your sister's. She was a better mother than you could have ever been. She taught me everything I know. Even how to be strong when your entire world is falling apart around you. So, thank you for giving me a chance at a life you couldn't provide for me. Because we both know I would have fallen a long time ago if it wasn't for Merr."

I watch as my mother burns to ash.

We wait around long enough to ensure her body is completely turned to ash before limping our way out of the maze of prison cells. Hedera and I walk hand in hand while Brent carries Jillian on his back as Scott, who regained consciousness as we burned my mom's body, helps Kira walk. She got a gnarly cut to her calf that makes it impossible for her to put weight on it without it gushing blood, and potentially a broken arm. Ronnie drags Colton behind him. We'll unpetrify him once we're home and our magic is replenished.

I make a mental note to ask Hedera what exactly happened with my mom as soon as we get somewhere safe. I've never seen her do that move before, and with her holding onto the book, it has me worried about her.

When we finally make it to the main floor, we stop short. Alfonso and a couple other Council members are walking down the hall. They look at us and back at each other before focusing their attention on us.

"Who are you and what are you doing here?" Draven Kavanna, head vampire and third in line to lead our people, asks.

"Where is Alexandria?" Alfonso asks Draven completely unbothered by us coming up the stairs.

"She was in charge of interrogating the new inmates. Last I saw she was in the south containment hall," Draven answers, anger lilting his tone. He's obviously annoyed that Alfonso is not one bit worried that there are intruders in their super safe, super secure prison.

"Alexandria is dead," Hedera says matter-of-factly, holding her head high.

Their bodies go stiff at the news. "What do you mean she's *dead?* How did she die? Certainly not you lot," Alfonso interrogates us. If it were anyone else, the assumption would be offensive. But he's been alive for a very *very* long time and there have been whispers through our community that he's finally losing his mind after all these centuries.

"It most certainly was us," Kira growls, sweat making her hair stick to her face. Her skin has a sickly sheen to it and I wish I had more magic so I could heal her enough to get her home comfortably.

I cringe at her admission. Killing a Council member is punishable by death, no matter that we had damn good reason to do so. We're so fucked.

Alfonso stands there gaping like a fish out of water and Draven's eyes darken as his fangs descend. "Who do you think you are killing one of *us?*" Draven bellows, the veins on his face popping out in his rage. We need to be very careful with what we say next, a vampire on a spree from anger is almost as bad as a starved one.

Hedera raises her head impossibly higher and I wish we had told her that they prefer people to be meek and vulnerable, despite how powerful they may be. "She was going to send us to the Underworld. She opened a portal and some of our friends *died.*"

At the mention of Percy and Toby Brent whines in the back of his throat, lowering his head as tears well in my own eyes.

Quinn Hodera, succubus and the newest member of the Council pipes in. I almost didn't notice her there with how powerful Alfonso and Draven are. "Well, do you even have permission to be here? I've never seen you here and I've been here for months getting things ready." She seems like a total know-it-all, but one that doesn't know how to keep their mouth shut.

My suspicions are confirmed when Draven shoots her an evil look and she rolls her eyes.

"Yes, we had permission," Jillian lies, finally regaining consciousness at the perfect time.

I groan internally.

"From who?" Draven asks, pinning her with a glare.

"The very woman who we unfortunately had to kill," they explain, patting Brent's shoulder so he will put them down. "Alexandria sent me this earlier today." Jillian holds out her phone, showing a text thread between her and a random number.

All three of the members read it over before turning away from us and having a whispered conversation. My mind reels with the implications as I glance down at Kira's palm. Her scar is still there, but if Alexandria gave us permission to be here...

"Very well. But it is still a crime to kill a Council member, so with the power vested in me, I put you all under arrest," Draven says, his voice smooth as silk.

Goddess damn it.

Chapter Forty

"Are you fucking kidding me?" I yell at them. "We just saved the entirety of the supernatural community from someone who wanted to kill us and you're arresting us based on some bullshit law that doesn't even make sense?" If my leg wasn't fucked and my arm in excruciating pain, I'd kick their asses and *really* deserve to be put under lock and key. The hairs on my arms raise and I'm sure my hair is going crazy with the amount of anger coursing through my body despite not having an ounce of power left.

"Oh, don't be dramatic," Quinn lectures, rolling her eyes. "Alexandria may have been ambitious, but she had her heart in the right place. We all know Alfonso is on his way out, she has big shoes to fill."

"She had her heart in the right place when?" Andi asks, hurt and anger contorting her beautiful face. "When she abandoned me on my aunt's doorstep? When she sold her soul and became a fucking *demon*? Explain it to me like

I'm dumb, because I am clearly missing when she thought of *anyone* but herself."

"The Council prides itself on having representation on all supernatural entities, you know that, Andromeda," Draven drawls. Her name on his lips causes my skin to crawl. "Do you not think that demons deserve representation as well?"

Andi scoffs, throwing her hands in the air. "How are you guys so blinded by what's been happening under your noses? Are you aware that she was looking for the *Book of the Broken?*" At their shocked expressions, she nods and continues. "Yea, her heart was certainly in the right place with that, wasn't it?"

"Well, that book shouldn't be out in the wild for anyone to stumble upon. It should be protected in our private library like all the other dangerous books are," Quinn explains, folding her hands in front of her stomach.

"While I agree with you that it shouldn't be out freely for just anyone to get a hold of, I can assure you it is more protected where it is than it would be with you guys," Andi says, taking care to calm her voice. "If you don't believe that she was out of control and on a power trip, then let us show you the portal she opened. That should be testament enough. Because we all know that *no one* who has good intentions would open a portal to the Underworld that would allow demons and other monsters loose upon the world."

Quinn and Draven share a look before agreeing to Andi's plan. I really do not want to go back down there, but I want to leave her and Hedera with these two even less.

"Fine," Draven yields. "Show us this so-called 'portal' and let's be done with this once and for all." He gestures for us to lead the way.

"I will stay here with Alfonso and those of us who are wounded if that would be okay," Hedera says. Her eyes have a hardness to them and I know she's going to pull some crazy shit while we're gone. I just hope she's successful and doesn't get herself killed.

"If you must. Can we go now?" Draven asks, annoyed that we're taking valuable time out of his busy schedule.

Brent carries me on his back as he and Andi lead the way back to where we fought Alexandria. He knew better than to leave me behind despite my injuries. On the way I pray to the Goddess that the portal is still open and didn't magically close when she died. There was too much going on and I was in too much pain to pay attention to anything that was happening aside from Andi standing over her mother and watching her burn.

It was beautifully tragic. Her mother put so much doubt and self-hatred in her mind. Merr did her best to fight it and worked miracles to get Andi the small amount of confidence she does have. But I see her struggle with it to this day. I hope being the one to send Alexandria to the afterlife was therapeutic to her in one way or another.

Chapter Forty-One

Andromeda

The sound reaches us before we get to the room. Screams, howls, and shouts of alarm ring through the halls surrounding where everything went down. An alarm is ringing, but the sound from the chaos drowns it out.

Draven disappears first, taking off with his vampire speed to investigate what's happening. Quinn cuts in front of us, scanning the area. If we get ambushed we're royally screwed. We're all tapped out on magic and the Council aren't likely to protect us if danger comes looking. It will be a bloodbath, and not one we cause.

Draven reappears a moment later, his face more pale than normal. "It is true. There is a massive portal opened up ahead and there are—things that I have never seen running in the halls, *devouring* the prisoners." He swallows hard. "I've never seen anything so gruesome. This place is a lost cause, we must get back to Alfonso and get all of the workers out of here at once."

"What about the prisoners?" I ask, baffled that he wouldn't mention them.

"It would take too long to release them. They're criminals and deserve what is coming to them, anyway." He lifts his head, certain of his decision.

"They're people. Sure, they may have committed crimes, but if the demons and monsters are bad as you say they are then they deserve better than that!" I try to get through to him, but it's no use.

"We don't have the time!" he yells, spit flying from his mouth. His eyes are black again, but from the look on his face it's from terror this time instead of anger.

"We have a friend here who isn't a criminal. She was rounded up last night or this morning for interrogation. Where is she?"

"Are your ears broken? There's no–" Draven begins, but I cut him off.

"I know there's no time!" I scream. "But if I die saving at least one person, it'll be a good enough death for me. Where. Is. She." My spine is straight, shoulders back, and I stare right into Draven's black eyes, daring him to refuse me.

He looks behind him before looking back at us, shaking his head. "You're insane. All of you. She's in block seven. May the Goddess bless your souls." He takes his keycard out of his pocket and hands it to Brent before scooping Quinn up and rushing out of the building. I hope he goes to grab Alfonso, old dude won't make it very far if he doesn't.

We head back to our friends, needing Jillian's insight on where to go. When we reach them, my heart breaks. Alfonso is sitting next to Hedera against one of the walls and they're talking in hushed tones.

Draven left him to fend for himself. What a fucking dick.

Hedera looks up and smiles at us before Alfonso does the same and gets to his feet, coming over to us. He takes my hands in his. "You sweet girl. Thank you for ridding us of that vile woman." He wraps me in a hug and I stand there in shock for a moment before hugging him back.

"Alexandria had put a spell on him. His mind knew it was there and was constantly fighting against it, that's why he seemed like he was losing his marbles," Hedera says as she stands up, dusting off her skirt. "I got rid of the blackness overtaking his mind with the little magic I had left. He's good as new now." She beams at us and I smile back, unable to stop it even though death is fast approaching.

Though, I suppose dying wouldn't be so bad if I had these people around me.

"Where are Draven and Quinn?" Jillian asks from where she sits against another wall. Her gruff voice startles me. I figured we'd have to bring her back to consciousness when we got back. I give her a small smile, hoping it shows her that I'm happy she's awake again.

"They saw the portal and booked it out of here," Brent says, setting Kira down. She sucks in a breath through her teeth as pain shoots up her leg and arm. Dark circles are under his eyes and he looks like he's aged ten years in the time we've been down here.

"We need to get to block seven," I say to Jillian, crouching in front of her. "Where is it?"

Jillian points to the way we've come and I swallow hard. Somehow I knew that was going to be her answer.

Chapter Forty-Two

Hedera

"You can't be serious," Jillian says, struggling to stand. "You can't go in there. You'll die."

"We can't leave Grace to be eaten or tortured or whatever the hell these things do. I couldn't live with myself if I just left her there to die," Andromeda says, her arms waving around in the air.

"No one is worth risking you going in there!" Jillian shouts. In her time with us, she's grown close to our group. I am very proud of how Kira and Andromeda have let her in. Even myself. Jillian was just a misguided person trying to find her place in the world. Alexandria preyed upon that and once she turned on Jilliian, she saw who Alexandria truly was and made a vow to herself to never go back. It had to have been incredibly difficult for her, considering it was the only place she ever felt she mattered. I can see it on her face sometimes, the uncertainty in what to do. I feel it, too, sometimes when Kira, Andromeda, Brent and his boys start joking and laughing about things that I do not understand. They do their best to include me, but there is something about their friendship that is so solid and strong that, even with the best intentions, it leaves me out.

It is okay, though, because everything will be right soon. There will be no more invisible lines and blurred relationships. Everything will be as it should.

"You don't get it, Jillian," Scott says followed by a heavy sigh. "Grace has been around for our entire lives. She's like a grandmother to us. I know you don't know what having a normal family feels like, and that's totally cool, but to us family is everything. If we die saving her, or even if we die before getting to her, then so be it. At least we tried. But to do nothing, to not *try* would be morally wrong."

Jillian rolls her eyes. "Morality is dead now. Why won't you just save yourselves? She's probably already dead anyway."

"Don't say that," Andromeda bites. "You don't know. You can leave if you want, but we're going back in there."

Kira puts her hand on Andromeda's arm to get her to calm down before she scoots over to where Jillian leans against the wall, using it as a crutch. "You have kept your word and helped us take down Alexandria. I release you from our promise." She takes Jiliian's hand in hers and a bright light shines. When it fades, they both look down at their hands and Jillian's head shoots up to meet Kira's eyes.

"Why did you do that?" Jillian asks, seething.

"Because you earned it. You helped us. Now you can go and live your life. Thank you for everything you've done. We wouldn't have gotten this far without you."

Jillian pauses for a moment, unsure what to do before throwing her arms around Kira, pulling her in for a crushing hug, putting even Brent's hugs to shame. When Jillian releases her, they both step back and wipe the tears from their eyes.

"I'll come with you. No one has ever made me feel the way you guys have. I–" Jillian closes her eyes and takes a deep breath before opening them again. "I know what you mean about family now. If you'd have me I'd be more than happy to go on this next adventure with you all." She looks at each of us, bloodied, bruised, and bone tired. We surround Jillian and officially welcome her into our chaotic circle with a group hug.

"Okay, enough with the mushy bullshit. Are we going to go save Grace or what?" Kira asks, breaking herself free from the hug.

Andromeda makes sure to meet each of our eyes. "Until the end."

We all nod and repeat her promise. "Until the end."

"If I may," Alfonso says from where he's been watching our interaction. We all startle when he speaks, having forgotten he was watching us. "A parting gift." He smiles at us before raising his hands and bestowing said gift upon us with a blinding purple light. When the light disappears, we're shocked to find all of our injuries healed.

Though it's too bad he couldn't have restored our magic too.

We tell him thank you before he meanders off to wherever he's going.

When we pass the corridor where we fought Alexandria everything is deathly silent. It sends a shiver down my spine.

"This way," Jillian whispers at the front of our group. We hurry down the halls, desperate to find Grace. The silence eats away at our nerves. "Just a few more hallways."

A sniffing sound followed by a hiss causes us to freeze, doing our best not to run into the person in front of us.

"What is that?" Ronnie says, his voice shaking. Kira elbows him in the ribs and he lets out a grunt as the air whooshes out of him. Feet scuttle towards us, creeping ever closer, and despite knowing that the end is coming, my heart races painfully in my chest.

"Run," Jillian orders when the scuttling sound pauses for a moment. "Take the second right and we'll be there," she tells us in case we get separated.

We all take off sprinting down the hall and I wish we had had more time to practice running. I have not run in such a long time that after a few feet my lungs and legs are burning. Or maybe it is the strange mist hanging in the air. It must be one of the precautions the Council has in place for instances of an uprising.

Ronnie and Scott are close behind me as we cross the first hallway, Ronnie is the last in our group as he pulls Colton along with him. A rush of air sends my hair flying in front of my face and I glance back. I almost stumble over my feet as I take in the horror that is behind me. Ronnie and Colton are held between the two massive pincers of a centipede type of monster. Ronnie's screams are cut off as the beast squeezes and both of their bodies are sliced in two, blood splatters the walls and ground beneath them. The only good thing that has come so far is that Colton was not conscious to witness his own death.

I turn my head and vomit on the ground as I urge my feet to move faster. Brent howls up ahead, feeling his pack mates depart. Out of all of us, he's suffered the most today. I don't know how he's still going, I would have given up by now. But maybe that is what true strength looks like. Mine is just a façade.

It feels quite liberating to admit that to myself.

The scuttling resumes behind me, quickly gaining on my slower pace.

"Go, go, go," Scott and I scream as we leap forward, barely escaping the pincer that was aimed right for us.

Brent grabs us, yanking us down the next hallway as the monster crashes into the wall, causing it to crack. I meet Scott's eyes and we nod at each other before rushing to our destination.

"She could be in any of these cells," Jillian says through her panting breaths, leaning her head against the cool stone wall as she motions down the hall.

Thirty cells loom in front of us, taunting us with their secrets.

"Grace," Andromeda begins shouting, not caring about the monsters lurking about.

Chapter Forty-Three

Andromeda

"Grace," I yell. I pause, hoping I'll hear her voice call out to me, but am met with silence. I step up to the first cell on my right and look in the dingy window. A woman lays on a cot, her face contorted into terror, frozen. Her body does not move as I pound on the window.

My heart freezes in my chest. "We're too late," I whisper.

Kira wraps her arm around me a millisecond before my legs give out. Tears stream down my face as I turn into her arms. "We're too late," I tell her.

"Sh, sh, sh. You don't know that. Maybe she died before anything could get to her. We don't know exactly what they do here, remember? There could still be a chance. Come on, we can't give up yet." She kisses the top of my head and sets me on my feet. The others are looking in each cell window, searching for our friend. We get to the last cell and come up empty-handed.

"Where the fuck is she?" I yell, pulling at my hair. We have to get out of here and soon before the entirety of the Underworld is unleashed upon this place, but I can't give up. I scramble to Jillian and grab her shoulders, shaking them. "Where else could she be?"

"I don't know, Andromeda. I swear. If Draven said she was here then that's where she should be!"

A sound catches my ear at the other end of the hallway. My head whips around and the breath whooshes from my lungs as I see Grace being held at clawpoint by none other than a-supposed-to-be-dead Garret.

"Looking for someone, Andi?" His smile is cruel as he digs his razor sharp claw in deep enough to draw blood. Howling and groans sound from behind him at the smell of fresh blood and I know we have mere minutes before those creatures descend upon us for their next meal.

"Garret?" Brent asks, walking towards him, his brows furrowed. "I identified your body. You're dead." He shakes his head as Garret laughs at him.

"Poor sweet cousin. Did you think I would pass up the opportunity to come back when that portal opened? When word got out that you and your bitchy friends were the cause of it opening I just *had* to come see what all the fuss was about. Imagine my surprise when I caught Draven by surprise with a gwendyl fang and he started spilling all your secrets to me in hopes that he would get to live." His smile is sharp as he takes in our collective shock.

A gwendyl is a demon in the Underworld, known for hunting down and eating vampires who cross over. Their venom is a vampire's biggest weakness.

"I just couldn't help myself but to snatch this lovely woman up and wait it out until you got here."

"Just leave me," Grace gasps out before Garret tightens his hold on her.

"Shut the fuck up. No one gave you permission to speak, bitch." He takes a deep breath before returning his attention back to us. "I'll make you a deal. Andi, you come with me and I'll let all your friends go. They can live happily ever after and you can get what you deserve for breaking my heart."

"Not a chance, dickwad," Kira says, her hair rising and falling. I know she would turn him to stone right now if she could, but with no magic in her body it's useless.

Garret throws his head back and cackles. "A bit short on mojo there, are you, Kira? Pity. Guess you won't be saving anyone today." He takes a step towards us as the noises from the demons and monsters grow closer. "Just hand over Andi and I'll let this old bitch go. It's really quite simple."

"Not a chance. How about you come fight me like a real wolf and we can settle this once and for all," Brent growls at him. Scott moves into position to offer back up. Alfonso may have healed our injuries, but there's no way that either of them have enough energy to shift and fight Garret who seems to thrive on chaos.

"Brent, no," I whisper to him. He ignores me, keeping constant eye contact with his cousin.

"Oh, cousin. You know that won't end well for you. See, I may have lost the challenge against you back in the day, but I've since gotten some– upgrades." Garret quirks a brow as he smirks before shoving Grace away from him and shifting.

Tendrils of shadows glide off his massive form. He used to be a beautiful wolf with a white coat that was accented by black and grey swirls along his sides. But now he's hideous. Chunks of his hide are missing, revealing sinew and muscle. One of his eyes is white while the other is black as a starless night. The stench that comes off of him is nauseating, but from the sound of the monsters charging down the surrounding hallways, it's intoxicating to them. A beacon of fresh meat.

Brent takes one second to look away and give us all a loving look before his own shift overtakes his body. His wolf form is much smaller than Garret's now and we all know he's not going to win. Scott follows suit and is dwarfed by them both. Even against Colton he was the smallest of the pack, but he was also the stealthiest.

Garret charges first, running straight for Brent who dodges out of the way. But one of the tendrils slices through his side. Instead of turning back to Brent, Garret keeps going towards me. Jillian pushes me out of the way and I watch in horror as he tears their body in two. Kira jumps out of the way of one of the tendrils, barely escaping getting scraped.

Scott charges towards him to try to save us, but Garret is too fast.

Turning away from the carnage that's about to ensue, Kira, Hedera, and I link arms and rush towards Grace who's sprawled out on the floor.

"Come on, we have to go," I say to her, letting go of Kira's arm so I can bend down and help Grace up. "Hurry. We don't have much time."

"Just leave me, dear. I have lived long enough and I won't make it out of here anyway. At least without me you can maybe escape." She pats my cheek, pure love shining in her eyes. "Thank you for being so selfless and for being such a bright part of my life. Your aunt was so proud of you."

"What? No, you have to come with us. We can make it. Please," I beg her, tears welling in my eyes from her acceptance of death and the gruesome sounds coming from the wolf fight behind us.

"Dear girl, I was never meant to leave this place. They've been poisoning the air in the cells since I got here. Now that it's under attack, they've released it in the halls as well. Even if I make it out, it's only a matter of time before I succumb. At least here I can try to fight some of these monstrosities off to give you time."

I finally notice the light mist in the air. "How did we miss that?"

She coughs a few times, her face paling. "I don't have much time left. Go. I'll be right behind you." She smiles at me, tears flowing down her face.

My heart shatters and then disintegrates as I hear Brent whine in pain behind us over the growls and barks of Garret as he taunts my best friend and his remaining pack mate.

They can handle it, Andi. This is what they do. This is how their lives play out. It will be okay, I tell myself as I make my feet move one in front of the other.

Hedera, Kira, and I link arms again and take off down the halls. Our pace is much slower now that the poison has worked its way into our system. It's as if knowing makes it worse, working faster against our bodies. Our path is clear until we get to the corridor that holds the secret passage we came in.

Three demons block the way, grinning ear to ear at us as drool drips from their fangs and hisses on the soft carpet. "Mm, tasty," one of them says in a deep, rumbling voice. It takes a step forward and we turn and run another way.

"There's only one other way I know out of here. Jillian told us while you were with Draven and Quinn," Hedera says, pulling us along with her. She looks the worst out of all of us. Her cheeks are sunken and her skin is deathly pale. Using the book took a toll on her and I plan on giving her a lecture once we make it out of here.

We go to turn down another hall and see it packed with reapers. My ankle pangs with pain as we turn faster than should be possible to escape that miserable death.

This wasn't supposed to go down like this. I knew there was a risk in breaking in, but it was *nothing* like this. These are my worst nightmares coming to life. All of my loved ones are dying one by one and I can't do a damned thing about it.

By the second set of stairs we're moving at a slow walk. Our legs won't go any faster. Our lungs won't breathe in enough air.

A growl sounds behind us and we glance back, hoping it's Brent and Scott letting us know they're there. But in his place is Garret's decaying form. My heart drops to my stomach as his stench reaches my nose. He lowers his head and bares his teeth at us before charging.

We try to run, to get away from certain death, but he's too fast in his demonic form. I try to reach for Hedera and Kira, but my body won't move fast enough. The last thing I remember is a scream ripping from my throat as his tendrils slice through my skin.

Chapter Forty-Four

Kira

The last thing I remember is Garret hunting us down after he killed Brent and Scott. He gutted us like fish with his tendrils. I watched my girls bleed out as I laid there in agonizing pain before I succumbed to my own blood loss. Garret half shifted after we were incapacitated and stood there watching over us, a look of pure glee on his face as he chuckled and sniffed the air. Before I lost consciousness, I watched him unzip his pants and piss on Andi's dead body.

I prayed for the Goddess to take me then, relieve me from this tortured existence. I'd seen enough. I'd done *enough*. If she wouldn't take me, I prayed that she would give me my powers back and heal me, so I could kill this sick son of a bitch once and for all.

But unlike Andi, the Goddess has never answered my prayers and I laid there for several minutes while I watched him defile her corpse some more.

I open my eyes, surprised that I can open them at all. I blink into the bright light, thinking maybe the Goddess finally answered my prayers and I can get vengeance for my loved ones. The bright light is simply because the prison must have crumbled down around us and the sun is beating down on me. But once my eyes adjust, I gasp.

"It's about time you woke up, sleepy head," Andi's voice says softly from beside me. My head whips to the side fast enough to give me whiplash, only there's no pain. She's resplendent in a light green dress, her hair falling in her signature blue waves.

"We were worried you were going to sleep forever," Hedera says, peeking around her shoulder.

"Where are we?" I ask, confused.

"Home," Andi says, standing up and reaching for my hand. I let her pull me up and see that we're in a field of wildflowers. In the distance is a house almost identical to Andi's, but the ivy that clung to her house is missing and her backyard wasn't overrun with these flowers.

"We died," Hedera explains. "Goddess Gaia walked us here and promised she'd bring you when you were ready. We've been waiting." She smiles at me before throwing her arms around me and squeezing me. "I missed you." She kisses my cheek before stepping back.

Thoughts tumble through my mind. How am I here? How did I deserve to be brought here? Is Garret still alive? What happened to Grace? The most prevalent question breaks through. "What about Brent and his pack?"

"They're running in the forest. Gaia brought them too. She said she usually doesn't mess with werewolves, but because we were so brave and trusted her plan she would make an exception," Andi says as she points to a line of trees that are full and green. In the distance a howl rings out and a flock of birds takes flight.

"So, this is it, huh? This is how it ends?" I pin Hedera with a look that lets her know I didn't forget what she said.

"This is how it begins," she breathes, taking my hand and pulling me along behind her.

Faster than what seems possible, we're inside Andi's Afterlife house and I'm sprawled in a soft, plush bed.

"Let us make it better for you," Andi offers, slipping her dress from her shoulders and Hedera does the same. The sunlight bathes them in its warm light as I take in their curves and perfect breasts. I stare at these beautiful women I call mine and thank Gaia for allowing me to spend the rest of eternity loving them.

My two lovers crawl onto the bed and strip me of my shorts and tube top before kissing every inch of my body, quickly working the shock and confusion from my body.

Hours later, we're laying wrapped together as Andi explains what happened after we died.

"Gaia and the other gods and goddesses were summoned by Alfonso to help seal the portal. They battled the demons and monsters that broke through, including Garret. It took them days to defeat them all and some of the gods didn't make it back.

"During the battle, the prison fell. A lot of the people being held prisoner were already dead, but the rest unfortunately perished in the fallout." She wipes a tear from her eye. "I haven't seen Grace yet. I'm not sure if it's because she didn't worship Gaia or if she made it out and is still alive. Gaia won't tell me no matter how much I beg." I reach up and wipe away another tear falling down her face.

"What about the *Book of the Broken?* It was in Hedera's pocket when...everything happened." I still can't admit that we died. We had a whole life ahead of us. Not that this is bad, it's just not what I imagined our lives to look like.

"I gave it to Alfonso," Hedera says, brushing my hair from my face. "He is pure at heart and plans to make things different after they rebuild. He will keep it safe."

Andi smiles, confirming what Hedera said. "Why did it take you so long to come to us?" she asks softly.

I shift on the bed, nerves eating at me. "I was trying to bargain with the Goddess, make her give me my powers back so I could take Garret out." I swallow hard before continuing. "I watched you two die. I thought that was it. Then I watched what he did to you." The words are difficult to get out, but I need to get it off my chest so I can move on. "Pure rage tore through my body and I begged and pleaded and compromised with her until I finally passed." I look away from them, ashamed at how I feel. "She's never been my biggest fan. Not like you, little witch." I smile at her, and though it feels a bit forced, it helps heal something in me.

"She likes you more than you know," Andi assures me. "Otherwise she wouldn't have brought you here to her sanctuary." Then she gasps and her eyes light up despite the tears forming. "I almost forgot to tell you! Aunt Merr is here. She's down the hill at the town's orphanage. She watches over the lost children until their loved ones can join them here or another family takes them in because their parents went somewhere else."

My doubts and frustration seep away at the news. "We have to go see her!" I sit up in bed, but they pull me back to them.

"We have all the time in the universe. Let us enjoy you for a while longer," Hedera says.

I'm not sure how long it was before I woke up here, but from the way they can't keep their hands to themselves I'm beginning to think it was weeks or months. Shit, maybe it was *years*. I know time works differently in the After, I just don't know how different it is and I'm too afraid to ask.

Nightmares plague me through the night. I do my best to keep myself calm when I wake up, reaching over and feeling my girls sleep soundly helps ground me. I keep a hand on each of them to keep the nightmares away until morning comes. The next morning we have coffee like any other day and get dressed in light clothing before heading down the hill. The weather is perfect here, a soft breeze blowing through the grass and trees, but not touching our skin.

Despite the perfect bliss of this place, nerves eat at my stomach, which is annoying because I figured that those would disappear after I died, but no dice. I also don't know why I'm nervous to see Merr again. She was always so welcoming to me. But the thought that keeps running through my mind is what if she doesn't approve of our unique relationship? It's not like we're a conventional couple. Not that I want that. I've never been happier than with these two, but I know how other people think and it's less than enthusiastic with anything outside the norm.

Andi and Hedera pull me along cobbled streets, past a fountain and different shops and houses. It's like a normal little village. I love it. We pause outside of a big four-story building, the sign reads 'Gaia's Home for Waiting Souls.'

"Are you ready?" Andi asks, linking her fingers with mine.

I take a deep breath. "Are you sure she's going to be okay with this?"

"Is that what's been bothering you?" Andi asks, squeezing my hand.

"I told you it was," Hedera says, staring at me.

"Hey, stay out of my thoughts!"

"It's kind of hard when they're so loud." She smirks at me and my cheeks heat.

I glance at my feet before meeting their eyes again. "Let's get this over with. I can't take another moment of not knowing." They beam at me and we make our way inside. When we get to the dining room, I gasp again and grab onto the wall to steady me.

Sitting around the middle table is Merr, Jillian, Brent, and his pack.

Merr sees me first and jumps up from the table, rushing over. She wraps me in a hug that feels like home. I squeeze her tight as the tears fall from my eyes.

"Oh, sweet girl. It's so nice to see you. Though, I do wish you'd had more time in Life. But you're here now and that is wonderful." She releases me from the hug, but grips my shoulders so she can take a good look at me. "I'm so happy that you and Andromeda finally got your heads out of your asses. I had placed a lot of bets on the two of you and a lot of people will owe me when they get here." She winks at me before stepping aside and letting the rest of my friends greet me with hugs and tears.

When I've had my fill of the mushy bullshit, we take our seats around the table. Before we can dig into the amazing breakfast spread before us, the front door opens and the scent of turned earth radiates through the house. I stand, wiping my hands on my shorts a moment before Gaia walks into the dining room. Everyone else is still seated, watching the interaction.

"Kira," she greets me personally and I feel like a spotlight is lit upon me causing my skin to warm. "Would you like to take a walk with me for a moment?"

I look to my friends and lovers to gauge their reactions. They all smile at me, letting me know it's okay. I walk over to Gaia and bow my head, my heart thunders in my chest. "I would be honored, my lady." I bow my head to her. Her laugh makes my cheeks heat and I glance up at her.

"There is no need for such reverence, Kira. We are all friends here." She holds out her hand for me to take, and despite my sweaty palm, I take it. Peace floods through my body at the contact as she leads me out of the orphanage. "I know you have been wondering why I have not been as forthcoming for you as I was with Andromeda. I want you to know that it is not because I do not love you as much as her. It is simply because she needed me more."

Anger courses through me at her admission. Did she not see the struggles I went through? The pain and anxiety that I would fuck up again and again?

"I see your mind racing with unanswered questions. I will explain if you're willing to listen." I nod my head and she continues. "I do not want you to think that I did not see your struggles and your pain. I did and it made me so sad for you, but I knew you would find your way. You had a fire in you that was insatiable. You wanted to prove everyone they were wrong to judge you and categorize you as the bad person. Every time I would start to come to you, you would do something that made me realize you didn't need me." She pauses as we stand in front of the fountain in the middle of the village. "Do you remember the time you stoned that boy you worked with?"

"Unfortunately," I mumble.

"That was the first time you needed me. You felt lost and untamed. But what did you do with those feelings?" At my confused look she asks, "Did you bottle them up and let them fester?"

"No, but that wasn't me, that was my parents. They put me in counseling to help quell the anxiety and anger."

She smiles at me. "It may have been your parents idea for you to go, but it was *you* that put in the work. Or how about the time they kicked you out after you stoned someone again? What did you do then?"

"I got a job and my own place. I worked my ass off to make sure I was okay."

"Exactly."

"But Andi had Merr. She had a support system. I had nothing. No one."

"You had yourself," Gaia explains. "That's all you've ever needed, Kira. You've gotten yourself through so many bad situations and you've learned and adapted and kept going. Andromeda has struggled more than she lets on for almost all of her life. Though Merridan did her best, she was still found to be lacking in Andromeda's eyes because she wasn't her mother. Andromeda would never admit it, but I know. I saw." She takes a deep breath. "Even though I never made myself known to you, you never stopped believing or praying. Your faith stayed intact through *everything*. I was right there, Kira. I watched you blossom and grow and fade and come back stronger every single time. I have never been more proud of one of my children than I am with you."

She wraps me in her arms and although her answer is not what I thought it would be, it makes my confidence in myself grow. Because at the end of the day, she's right. I'm a badass bitch who didn't need anyone but myself.

We head back to the orphanage to my waiting family, but she doesn't come inside with me. I take my seat as peace fills my chest. I look at all of my family and that peace grows, knowing that this is it.

This is the end that Hedera told me about. And I must say, she was right. It is beautiful.

The End.

Acknowledgments

I would like to give a huge thank you to my husband for always believing in me and listening to me bounce crazy ideas off of him when he has no idea what's happening.

Huge thank you to Aubs and Miranda for helping me with edits! You ladies are amazing and I appreciate you!

Thank you to Katie for being a real MVP as my only beta reader! You really saved my ass on a few of those errors and I'm forever grateful!

Last, but certainly not least, thank you to my readers. You guys make this worthwhile. I love you all and I hope you keep reading!

Other Books by Gina Hejtmanek